THE WAYS
OF GHOSTS

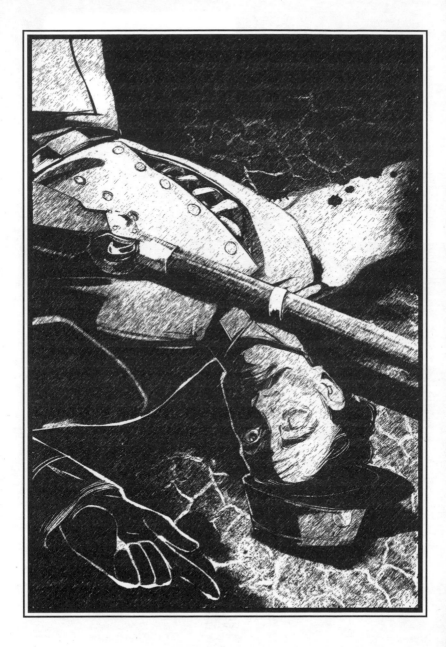

THE WAYS OF GHOSTS

and Other Dark Tales

by

AMBROSE BIERCE

Edited by

MIKE ASHLEY

This edition published 2023 by
The British Library
96 Euston Road
London NWI 2DB

Introduction, selection and notes © 2023 Mike Ashley
Volume Copyright © The British Library Board

Cataloguing in Publication Data
A catalogue record for this publication is available from the British Library

ISBN 978 0 7123 5497 4
e-ISBN 978 0 7123 6870 4

Frontispiece illustration by Sandra Gómez. Photograph on page
320 from Alexander Gardner, *Gardner's Photographic Sketch Book
of the War*, Philips & Solomons, Washington, D.C., 1865.

Cover design by Mauricio Villamayor with illustration by Sandra Gómez.
Text design and typesetting by Tetragon, London
Printed in England by CPI Group (UK) Ltd, Croydon, CRO 4YY

CONTENTS

Introduction   7
A Note from the Publisher   19

A Horseman in the Sky   21
A Tough Tussle   30
A Resumed Identity   41
One of the Missing   49
An Occurrence at Owl Creek Bridge   65
Mrs. Dennison's Head   78
A Jug of Sirup   82
An Inhabitant of Carcosa   91
A Watcher by the Dead   96
The Middle Toe of the Right Foot   111
The Boarded Window   123
The Damned Thing   129
Bodies of the Dead   141
The Secret of Macarger's Gulch   153
The Death of Halpin Frayser   163
John Bartine's Watch   184
The Eyes of the Panther   192
Staley Fleming's Hallucination   205
The Moonlit Road   209
Beyond the Wall   222

SOME HAUNTED HOUSES

The Isle of Pines   235
A Fruitless Assignment   241
The Spook House   245
The Thing at Nolan   250
At Old Man Eckert's   256
A Vine on a House   259
The Other Lodgers   264

THE WAYS OF GHOSTS

Present at a Hanging   271
A Cold Greeting   274
A Wireless Message   277
An Arrest   280

MYSTERIOUS DISAPPEARANCES

The Difficulty of Crossing a Field   285
An Unfinished Race   288
Charles Ashmore's Trail   290

Afterword: The Fate of Ambrose Bierce   295
Story Sources   315

INTRODUCTION

Dark Thoughts

There is no getting away from it—Ambrose Bierce was a miserable so-and-so. And not just when an old man. He was a misery for most of his life. Perhaps not surprising when he was the tenth of thirteen children all given a first name beginning with "A"—if you want to know who they were I've provided a list at the end of this introduction. He had no sympathy for his overworked mother and grew up as if the weight of the world was on his shoulders and a feeling that life was not what it ought to be. He would later define "birth" as "The first and direst of all disasters."

Part of Bierce's misanthropy was aggravated by his experiences in the American Civil War when he received a bullet in the head. Miraculously he survived but ever after suffered appalling headaches and dizzy spells. He had witnessed some of the worst that mankind could achieve in destroying each other and he lost all respect for authority.

There are times with his writings that you feel Bierce must have disliked everyone and every thing. That wasn't the case, but he enjoyed making it seem that way. Through his prolific journalism he could spit vitriol at whomsoever he chose and was hardly ever sued for libel. Once when the actress Lillie Langtry and the opera singer Adelina Patti visited California, where Bierce lived most of his later life, he managed to insult them both without a qualm. He called Langtry's acting "the posings of a prostitute recommended by a prince" whilst for Patti, whose singing he likened to the "squalling of a singed cat", he claimed that "Second only to the woman's fame as a singer is her fame as an adulteress."

He was equally savage to Oscar Wilde who toured San Francisco in 1882. You might think Bierce would admire Wilde's writings—though at that stage of his career Wilde had yet to write his most famous works—but Bierce utterly despised Wilde's opulence and flamboyance. He wrote, "There never was an impostor so hateful, a blockhead so stupid, a crank so variously and offensively daft."

Little wonder that early in his career Bierce was dubbed "Bitter Bierce" by his colleagues in London where he worked briefly on the magazine *Fun*—a word you would rarely associate with Bierce.

You might think that a man so offensive is not someone we should celebrate over a century later, but Bierce was regarded as one of the greatest wits and journalists of his day, and it was this mordant outlook on life that caused him to write some of the darkest, atmospheric tales of horror since Edgar Allan Poe. H. P. Lovecraft held Bierce in high esteem, rating him as "...closer to real greatness..." To appreciate Bierce's fiction, it helps to know a little about his life. I'll reserve his death for later!

Bierce was born at Horse Cave Creek in Ohio on 24 June 1842. Neither parent was rich but they made a living, the father farming and serving as occasional storekeeper. His father, Marcus Aurelius Bierce, delighted in reading and built a decent library which young Ambrose loved. Bierce did respect his father, but not his mother, and in several stories the first-person narrator goes so far as to murder one or other or both parents. Bierce suffered nightmares and there is little doubt that he found his childhood a struggle. He escaped at the earliest opportunity, leaving home at fifteen to work on a newly established abolitionist newspaper in nearby Warsaw. Unfortunately, he was accused, falsely, of theft, and left to live with his uncle, Lucius Verus Bierce. Lucius was a rowdy, larger-than-life individual, a practising lawyer and politician, two years younger than Bierce's father. Although Bierce liked him he left his uncle within a year, perhaps at his uncle's urging, to join the Kentucky Military Institute. Bierce was about to learn some discipline.

Alas Bierce was not good at discipline. He left the Institute after a year and drifted around Elkhart, Indiana, working as a labourer and a waiter. But in April 1861 the American Civil War erupted and Bierce promptly volunteered. Like his father and uncle, Bierce had abolitionist sympathies. He was enlisted into Company C of the Ninth Indiana Volunteers.

Bierce would become the only significant American writer to serve in and survive the Civil War. He served valiantly, rising to the rank of First Lieutenant. He fought in most of the major battles, notably Shiloh (April 1862) and Chickamauga (September 1863). It was at the battle of Kennesaw Mountain, Georgia, in June 1864 that he was shot in the head and hospitalized. Miraculously he survived and served again briefly until it was clear that he was too incapacitated by his head wound. He was discharged in January 1865. He worked briefly in the US Treasury identifying abandoned property, especially cotton plantations, but was disillusioned by the scale of corruption amongst Treasury agents. He signed up with Major General Hazen, under whom he had served and whom he held in high regard, to inspect western forts. He was offered a regular army commission as second lieutenant but refused. Curiously, soon afterwards he was promoted to the rank of Brevet Major by the War Office which sought to reward thousands of deserving veterans. Bierce chose not to argue as it helped his pension and allowed him time to seek work. He soon found himself in San Francisco in September 1867 working as a night watchman at the US Mint.

It did not take Bierce long to know this was not what he wanted to do, and his thoughts turned to writing. His first poem, "Basilica", was published in *The Californian*, for 21 September 1867. It was two months before another poem appeared but soon after he honed his skills as an essayist, first for *The Californian* and then the *San Francisco News Letter*. He soon became a regular columnist for the *News Letter*, with "The Town Crier".

The rest, one could say, is history. From then on, except for a brief period in 1880 working as an agent for the Black Hills Mining Company in Dakota, he was a journalist and author. He had married in December 1871, shortly after his first story "The Haunted Valley" appeared in *Overland Monthly*. It's not the most auspicious of stories and unfortunately reflects an anti-Chinese sentiment, and is not reprinted here.

In April 1872 Bierce and his wife Mollie left America for England where Bierce wrote for the magazine *Fun* under the editorship of Tom Hood. Bierce and Hood became firm friends and Bierce enjoyed the company of other writers in this close

London circle, which included George Augustus Sala and occasionally W. S. Gilbert. Unfortunately, the polluted London atmosphere was not good for Bierce's asthma and he and Mollie moved out of the city, spending time in Bath and Leamington Spa. Their first son, Day—the name being Mollie's maiden name—was born in Bristol in December 1872. Bierce was not suited to fatherhood or, for that matter, marriage. His relationship with Mollie grew progressively worse. It is surprising that they would have two more children, Leigh born in April 1874, in Leamington, and Helen in October 1875 after Mollie and the two boys had returned to California. Bierce returned separately just in time for Helen's birth.

His days in England were nevertheless amongst his most enjoyable and resulted in his first three books: *The Fiend's Delight, Nuggets and Dust* and *Cobwebs from an Empty Skull,* all under the pen name of Dod Grile. The first two reprinted material from the *News Letter* whilst the third collected items from *Fun,* an example of which, "Mrs. Dennison's Head", is included here. It was whilst in England that Bierce earned the nickname of "Bitter" Bierce. It is not clear who gave him this epithet, though it was quite possibly Hood himself. Hood died in November 1874 at the tragically young age of 39 and his passing was one of the factors that prompted Bierce to return to America. Bierce and Hood had agreed that whichever of them died first should try and contact the other. Only a few days after Hood's death Bierce felt as if Hood's spirit had rushed past him in the dark. That memory stayed with him for years and it is believed it was part of the inspiration for one of his best known stories, "The Damned Thing", included here.

Once back in San Francisco in September 1875 Bierce worked briefly again for the US Mint but was encouraged to return to writing. He became associate editor of *The Argonaut* from 1877 to 1879 for which he wrote his infamous "Prattle" column and which he continued in *Wasp* in 1881. The young William Randolph Hearst sought Bierce out to be on the staff of and a columnist for his newly acquired newspaper, *San Francisco Examiner*, and it is during these years and into the 1890s that Bierce wrote the stories for which he is best remembered, many harking back to his experiences in the Civil War. His best known War story, and one of the most reprinted of all short stories, is "An Occurrence at Owl Creek Bridge", which appeared in the *Examiner* in July 1890. His first collection of strange stories, *Tales of Soldiers and Civilians*, appeared in February 1892 and the classic volume *Can Such Things Be?* in December 1893. Bierce would revise these books for later editions with the final versions included in his *Collected Works* published between 1909 and 1912.

Hearst was only too aware of Bierce's powerful invective. In 1896 he despatched Bierce to Washington to raise public awareness in California over the unscrupulous financial chicanery of Collis P. Huntington who, over the years, had pocketed millions of government funds in his role as financier of the Central Pacific and Southern Pacific railroads. Huntington vehemently opposed a Refunding Bill intended to ensure the Central Pacific Railroad repaid over $75 million of excess funds. Huntington tried his usual tricks of bribery and corruption to forestall the Bill, but Bierce's reportage raised public opinion and Huntington was forced to admit defeat. At one point Huntington tried to bribe Bierce but with no effect and Bierce emerged as something of a hero. Although he returned briefly to California, Bierce now spent many years in Washington and New York as Hearst's correspondent, first for the *San Francisco Examiner* and then for Hearst's newly acquired magazine, *The Cosmopolitan*. He thus avoided the disaster of the earthquake in San Francisco in 1906 when the quake and the resultant fires destroyed some 80% of the city and caused at least 3,000 deaths. It deeply disturbed Bierce who wrote to old friends hoping they were safe. He feared that the conflagration had "consumed even the ghosts... of dear dead friends."

Whilst working for Hearst, Bierce continued to produce the occasional book which included *Fantastic Fables* in 1899 and arguably his best-known book, *The Devil's Dictionary*, first published as *The Cynic's Word Book*, in 1906. It shows his acerbic wit and cynical outlook on life in his definitions. For example, he defines "Love" as "A temporary insanity curable by marriage." His view of women is deplorable, defining "Woman" as "An animal usually living in the vicinity of Man and having a rudimentary susceptibility to domestication." Though men do not escape his vitriol. He defines "Man" as

> An animal so lost in rapturous contemplation of what he thinks he is as to overlook what he indubitably ought to be. His chief occupation is extermination of other animals and his own species, which, however, multiplies with such insistent rapidity as to infest the whole habitable earth and Canada.

Bierce had no love for his fellow men or women and as he aged this outlook grew worse. He had separated from Mollie early in 1889 accusing her of having an affair, even though she claimed it was no more than a friendship. A few months later their son Day, who had idolized his father, had a feud with a friend over a girl and the two shot each other. Day killed his friend and though not wounded he then killed himself. Bierce never wrote about Day's death but it may not be a coincidence that in the years immediately following the tragedy Bierce wrote some of his darkest and most evocative fiction.

More tragedy was to follow. Bierce, who had never been a good father, argued with his second son, Leigh, over his future wife and they became estranged. Leigh, who was a notorious alcoholic, caught pneumonia after a drinking bout and died in March 1901. Bierce and Mollie had never formally divorced and she filed for divorce in December 1904 but died soon after.

Bierce, now approaching seventy, was becoming tired of life. In 1909 he terminated his association with Hearst, turning his invective upon him—a perfect example of biting the hand that feeds you. He assembled his writings for the collected edition published by Walter Neale which grew into a highly unprofitable twelve volumes. Had Bierce limited it to his very best work it might have had a different reception, but instead reviewers took the opportunity to give Bierce a taste of his own medicine.

Bierce had been an inspiration to other budding writers and despite his overt rancour to all those about him, he did encourage and advise those he believed had talent. His most famous protégé was almost certainly the poet George Sterling who became a leading figure amongst San Francisco's Bohemians. They had met in 1892 at the home of Bierce's brother Albert, who then lived at Lake Temescal, near Oakland. Bierce helped nurture and encourage Sterling's talent which became established after the publication of *The Testimony of the Suns* in 1903. As thanks, Sterling and another protégé, Herman Scheffauer, arranged the publication of Bierce's volume of essays, *Shapes of Clay*. Bierce used his influence at *Cosmopolitan* to secure publication of Sterling's poem "A Wine of Wizardry" in the September 1907 issue which catapulted Sterling into national prominence.

Others who benefitted from Bierce's help and encouragement included Emma Frances Dawson, Edwin Markham, Gustav Danziger, W. C. Morrow and Clark Ashton Smith. Bierce revised and improved Danziger's translation of Richard Voss's *Der Mönch von Berchtesgaden* which appeared as *The Monk and the Hangman's Daughter*, serialized in the *Examiner* in 1891 and as a book in 1892. It did little to enhance Bierce's reputation, but Danziger, who later adopted the alias Adolphe de Castro, used his association with Bierce to inveigle his way into the lives of others more talented than he, not least H. P. Lovecraft, who revised several stories by Danziger from his 1893 collection *In the Confessional and the Following*, and placed them in the magazine *Weird Tales*. Clark Ashton Smith, who also became a major contributor to *Weird Tales* and an epistolary friend of Lovecraft's, never met Ambrose Bierce and much regretted missing the one opportunity he had of so doing. Bierce had commented kindly upon Smith's early poetry in a letter to George Sterling and in a letter published in *Town Talk* in August 1912, which proved to be one of his last pieces of writing to appear during his lifetime.

His comments might not have done much for Smith's reputation at the time but it did masses for his self-esteem.

Bierce returned to California for the last time during the summer of 1912, but the state held nothing for Bierce any more. Too many old friends had gone, and too many current friends had changed. The only new friend he made was the author Jack London.

Tired and dejected in October 1913, Bierce told his daughter and others that he was going to visit some of the old Civil War battlefields and then travel to South America via Mexico. He was believed to be in Mexico in December 1913 but reports of sightings are uncertain. By early 1914 no one knew where he was. Bierce simply disappeared. Because it is such a mystery I have attempted to pull together the known facts as an afterword at the end of this book to explore what might have happened, and how this affected his literary legacy.

The stories collected here seek to cover not only his most memorable and rewarding tales but to show the diversity of his writings in the field of the strange and unsettling. Some of the stories use language in common use at the time but now rightly regarded as wrong, and I have avoided a few stories because of the terminology. It raises the question of the extent to which Bierce held racist views and it is true that in some of his essays he does reflect the attitudes of the day which make painful reading. But this was not always the case. For instance, at the Battle of Nashville in December 1864 Bierce observed the activities of a troop of black soldiers. "Better fighting was never done," he recalled in one of his later columns, adding, "I was unable to discover that colour made any difference in the fighting of my troops..." In fact he later chastised himself for considering that black soldiers would not fight as well as they did. He was similarly sympathetic towards the Chinese community in San Francisco, where there was a violent anti-Chinese movement which Bierce regarded as caused by "...galloping Christianity of the malignant Californian type." No one could say that Bierce was not prejudiced—he most certainly was—but he wrote as he observed and was frequently supportive of threatened minorities. It is hoped that any comments in the following stories do not cause undue offence.

MIKE ASHLEY

BIERCE'S SIBLINGS

The following are listed in the order in which they were born. Only two outlived him, or three if Bierce died before 18 April 1914 when Albert died.

Abigail Bell (1823–1913) married Dwight Chappell in 1844 and had 9 children.

Amelia Josephine (1824–1897) married Benjamin Guthrie in 1848 and had 7 children.

Ann Maria (1826–1905) married William Good in 1846 and had 4 children.

Addison Byron (1828–1887) married Doretta Ferdinand in 1850(?) but divorced in 1858. They had 2 children. Addison performed in the theatre and later in a travelling circus as a strongman. He died in Durban, South Africa.

Aurelius Reely (1830–1862) married Elizabeth Holmes in 1855 and had 3 children. He worked as a carpenter and died in an accident apparently involving a circular saw.

Augustus (1832–1912) married Rebecca Pittenger in 1857. No record of any children. He worked all his life as a farmer in Ohio.

Almeda Sophia (1835–1920) married Henry Pittenger in 1853, he died in 1858; they had two children. She married William Davis in 1868 and had 1 child. She married Alexander Pittenger (her former brother-in-law) in 1878 but he died a year later. He already had 14 children by two previous marriages.

Andrew Jackson (1837–1923) married Mary Pittenger in 1889. He had served in the Civil War and retired as a farmer.

Albert Sherwood (1840–1914) married Caroline Clark in 1867 and had 3 children. He served throughout the Civil War and rendezvoused briefly with Ambrose during one of the battles. He remained a government employee. It is claimed he died of a stroke after receiving one of the last letters Ambrose wrote, as full of vitriol as ever. Bierce liked Albert's son Carlton and his wife Lora, to whom Bierce wrote one of his last letters.

Ambrose Gwinnett (1842–1914?) married Mary "Mollie" Day in 1871 and had 3 children.

Arthur Middleton (1845–1846) lived only nine months.

Adelia Wayne (May–September 1848) Aurelia's twin, lived only four months.

Aurelia Jane (1848–1850) Adelia's twin who lived for twenty-three months.

A NOTE FROM THE PUBLISHER

The original short stories reprinted in the British Library Tales of the Weird series were written and published in a period ranging across the nineteenth and twentieth centuries. There are many elements of these stories which continue to entertain modern readers, however in some cases there are also uses of language, instances of stereotyping and some attitudes expressed by narrators or characters which may not be endorsed by the publishing standards of today. We acknowledge therefore that some elements in the stories selected for reprinting may continue to make uncomfortable reading for some of our audience. With this series British Library Publishing aims to offer a new readership a chance to read some of the rare material of the British Library's collections in an affordable paperback format, to enjoy their merits and to look back into the worlds of the past two centuries as portrayed by their writers. It is not possible to separate these stories from the history of their writing and as such the following stories are presented as they were originally published with the inclusion of minor edits made for consistency of style and sense, and with pejorative terms of an extremely offensive nature partly obscured. We welcome feedback from our readers, which can be sent to the following address:

British Library Publishing
The British Library
96 Euston Road
London, NWI 2DB
United Kingdom

A HORSEMAN IN THE SKY

ne sunny afternoon in the autumn of the year 1861 a soldier lay in a clump of laurel by the side of a road in western Virginia. He lay at full length upon his stomach, his feet resting upon the toes, his head upon the left forearm. His extended right hand loosely grasped his rifle. But for the somewhat methodical disposition of his limbs and a slight rhythmic movement of the cartridge-box at the back of his belt he might have been thought to be dead. He was asleep at his post of duty. But if detected he would be dead shortly afterward, death being the just and legal penalty of his crime.

The clump of laurel in which the criminal lay was in the angle of a road which after ascending southward a steep acclivity to that point turned sharply to the west, running along the summit for perhaps one hundred yards. There it turned southward again and went zigzagging downward through the forest. At the salient of that second angle was a large flat rock, jutting out northward, overlooking the deep valley from which the road ascended. The rock capped a high cliff; a stone dropped from its outer edge would have fallen sheer downward one thousand feet to the tops of the pines. The angle where the soldier lay was on another spur of the same cliff. Had he been awake he would have commanded a view, not only of the short arm of the road and the jutting rock, but of the entire profile of the cliff below it. It might well have made him giddy to look.

The country was wooded everywhere except at the bottom of the valley to the northward, where there was a small natural meadow, through which flowed a stream scarcely visible from the valley's rim. This open ground looked hardly larger than an ordinary door-yard, but was really several acres in extent. Its green was more vivid than that of the inclosing forest. Away beyond it rose a line of giant cliffs similar to those upon which we are supposed to stand in our survey of the savage scene, and through which the road had somehow made its climb to the summit. The configuration of the valley, indeed, was such that from this point of observation it seemed entirely shut in, and one could but have wondered how the road which found a way out of it had found a way into it, and whence came and whither went the waters of the stream that parted the meadow more than a thousand feet below.

No country is so wild and difficult but men will make it a theatre of war; concealed in the forest at the bottom of that military rat-trap, in which half a hundred men in possession of the exits might have starved an army to submission, lay five regiments of Federal infantry. They had marched all the previous day and night and were resting. At nightfall they would take to the road again, climb to the place where their unfaithful sentinel now slept, and descending the other slope of the ridge fall upon a camp of the enemy at about midnight. Their hope was to surprise it, for the road led to the rear of it. In case of failure, their position would be perilous in the extreme; and fail they surely would should accident or vigilance apprise the enemy of the movement.

II

The sleeping sentinel in the clump of laurel was a young Virginian named Carter Druse. He was the son of wealthy parents, an only child, and had known such ease and cultivation and high living as wealth and taste were able to command in the mountain country of western Virginia. His home was but a few miles from where he now lay. One morning he had risen from the breakfast-table and said, quietly but gravely: "Father, a Union regiment has arrived at Grafton. I am going to join it."

The father lifted his leonine head, looked at the son a moment in silence, and replied: "Well, go, sir, and whatever may occur do what you conceive to be your duty. Virginia, to which you are a traitor, must get on without you. Should we both live to the end of the war, we will speak further of the matter. Your mother, as the physician has informed you, is in a most critical condition; at the best she cannot be with us longer than a few weeks, but that time is precious. It would be better not to disturb her."

So Carter Druse, bowing reverently to his father, who returned the salute with a stately courtesy that masked a breaking heart, left the home of his childhood to go soldiering. By conscience and courage, by deeds of devotion and daring, he soon commended himself to his fellows and his officers; and it was to these qualities and to some knowledge of the country that he owed his selection for his present perilous duty at the extreme outpost. Nevertheless, fatigue had been stronger than resolution and he had fallen asleep. What good or bad angel came in a dream to rouse him from his state of crime, who shall say? Without a movement, without a sound, in the profound silence and the languor of the late afternoon, some invisible messenger of fate touched with unsealing finger the eyes of his consciousness—whispered into the ear of his spirit the mysterious awakening word which no human lips ever have spoken, no human memory ever has recalled. He quietly raised his forehead from his arm and looked between the masking stems of the laurels, instinctively closing his right hand about the stock of his rifle.

His first feeling was a keen artistic delight. On a colossal pedestal, the cliff,—motionless at the extreme edge of the capping rock and sharply outlined against the sky,—was an equestrian statue of impressive dignity. The figure of the man sat the figure of the horse, straight and soldierly, but with the repose of a Grecian god carved in the marble which limits the suggestion of activity. The grey costume harmonized with its aerial background; the metal of accoutrement and caparison was softened and subdued by the shadow; the animal's skin had no points of high light. A carbine strikingly foreshortened lay across the pommel of the saddle, kept in place by the right hand grasping it at the "grip"; the left hand, holding the bridle rein, was invisible. In silhouette against the sky the profile of the horse was cut with the sharpness of a cameo; it looked across the heights of air to the confronting cliffs beyond. The face of the rider, turned slightly away, showed only an outline of temple and beard; he was looking downward to the bottom of the valley. Magnified by its lift against the sky and by the soldier's testifying sense of the formidableness of a near enemy the group appeared of heroic, almost colossal, size.

For an instant Druse had a strange, half-defined feeling that he had slept to the end of the war and was looking upon a noble work of art reared upon that eminence to commemorate the deeds of an heroic past of which he had been an inglorious part. The feeling was dispelled by a slight movement of the group: the horse, without moving its feet, had drawn its body slightly backward from the verge; the man remained immobile as before. Broad awake and keenly alive to the significance of the situation, Druse now brought the butt of his rifle against his cheek by cautiously pushing the barrel forward through the bushes, cocked the piece, and glancing through the sights covered a vital spot of the horseman's breast. A touch upon the trigger and all would have been well with Carter Druse. At that instant the horseman turned his head and looked in the direction of his concealed foeman—seemed to look into his very face, into his eyes, into his brave, compassionate heart.

Is it then so terrible to kill an enemy in war—an enemy who has surprised a secret vital to the safety of one's self and comrades—an enemy more formidable for his knowledge than all his army for its numbers? Carter Druse grew pale; he shook in every limb, turned faint, and saw the statuesque group before him as black figures, rising, falling, moving unsteadily in arcs of circles in a fiery sky. His hand fell away from his weapon, his head slowly dropped until his face rested on the leaves in which he lay. This courageous gentleman and hardy soldier was near swooning from intensity of emotion.

It was not for long; in another moment his face was raised from earth, his hands resumed their places on the rifle, his forefinger sought the trigger; mind, heart, and eyes were clear, conscience and reason sound. He could not hope to capture that enemy; to alarm him would but send him dashing to his camp with his fatal news. The duty of the soldier was plain: the man must be shot dead from ambush—without warning, without a moment's spiritual preparation, with never so much as an unspoken prayer, he must be sent to his account. But no—there is a hope; he may have discovered nothing—perhaps he is but admiring the sublimity of the landscape. If permitted, he may turn and ride carelessly away in the direction whence he came. Surely it will be possible to judge at the instant of his withdrawing whether he knows. It may well be that his fixity of attention—Druse turned his head and looked through the deeps of air downward, as from the surface to the bottom of a translucent sea. He saw creeping across the green meadow a sinuous line of figures of men and horses—some foolish commander was permitting the soldiers of his escort to water their beasts in the open, in plain view from a dozen summits!

Druse withdrew his eyes from the valley and fixed them again upon the group of man and horse in the sky, and again it was through the sights of his rifle. But this time his aim was at the horse. In his memory, as if they were a divine mandate, rang the words of his father at their parting: "Whatever may occur, do what you conceive to be your duty." He was calm now. His teeth were firmly but not rigidly closed; his nerves were as tranquil as a sleeping babe's—not a tremor affected any muscle of his body; his breathing, until suspended in the act of taking aim, was regular and slow. Duty had conquered; the spirit had said to the body: "Peace, be still." He fired.

III

An officer of the Federal force, who in a spirit of adventure or in quest of knowledge had left the hidden *bivouac* in the valley, and with aimless feet had made his way to the lower edge of a small open space near the foot of the cliff, was considering what he had to gain by pushing his exploration further. At a distance of a quarter-mile before him, but apparently at a stone's throw, rose from its fringe of pines the gigantic face of rock, towering to so great a height above him that it made him giddy to look up to where its edge cut a sharp, rugged line against the sky. It presented a clean, vertical profile against a background of blue sky to a point half the way down, and of distant hills, hardly less blue, thence to the tops of the trees at its base. Lifting his eyes to the dizzy altitude of its summit the officer saw an astonishing sight—a man on horseback riding down into the valley through the air!

Straight upright sat the rider, in military fashion, with a firm seat in the saddle, a strong clutch upon the rein to hold his charger from too impetuous a plunge. From his bare head his long hair streamed upward, waving like a plume. His hands were concealed in the cloud of the horse's lifted mane. The animal's body was as level as if every hoof-stroke encountered the resistant earth. Its motions were those of a wild gallop, but even as the officer looked they ceased, with all the legs thrown sharply forward as in the act of alighting from a leap. But this was a flight!

Filled with amazement and terror by this apparition of a horseman in the sky—half believing himself the chosen scribe of some new Apocalypse, the officer was overcome by the intensity of his emotions; his legs failed him and he fell. Almost at the same instant he heard a crashing sound in the trees—a sound that died without an echo—and all was still.

The officer rose to his feet, trembling. The familiar sensation of an abraded shin recalled his dazed faculties. Pulling himself together he ran rapidly obliquely away from the cliff to a point distant from its foot; thereabout he expected to find his man; and thereabout he naturally failed. In the fleeting instant of his vision his imagination had been so wrought upon by the apparent grace and ease and intention of the marvellous performance that it did not occur to him that the line of march of aerial cavalry is directly downward, and that he could find the objects of his search at the very foot of the cliff. A half-hour later he returned to camp.

This officer was a wise man; he knew better than to tell an incredible truth. He said nothing of what he had seen. But when the commander asked him if in his scout he had learned anything of advantage to the expedition he answered:

"Yes, sir; there is no road leading down into this valley from the southward."

The commander, knowing better, smiled.

IV

After firing his shot, Private Carter Druse reloaded his rifle and resumed his watch. Ten minutes had hardly passed when a Federal sergeant crept cautiously to him on hands and knees. Druse neither turned his head nor looked at him, but lay without motion or sign of recognition.

"Did you fire?" the sergeant whispered.

"Yes."

"At what?"

"A horse. It was standing on yonder rock—pretty far out. You see it is no longer there. It went over the cliff."

The man's face was white, but he showed no other sign of emotion. Having answered, he turned away his eyes and said no more. The sergeant did not understand.

"See here, Druse," he said, after a moment's silence, "it's no use making a mystery. I order you to report. Was there anybody on the horse?"

"Yes."

"Well?"

"My father."

The sergeant rose to his feet and walked away. "Good God!" he said.

A TOUGH TUSSLE

ne night in the autumn of 1861 a man sat alone in the heart of a forest in western Virginia. The region was one of the wildest on the continent—the Cheat Mountain country. There was no lack of people close at hand, however; within a mile of where the man sat was the now silent camp of a whole Federal brigade. Somewhere about—it might be still nearer—was a force of the enemy, the numbers unknown. It was this uncertainty as to its numbers and position that accounted for the man's presence in that lonely spot; he was a young officer of a Federal infantry regiment and his business there was to guard his sleeping comrades in the camp against a surprise. He was in command of a detachment of men constituting a picket-guard. These men he had stationed just at nightfall in an irregular line, determined by the nature of the ground, several hundred yards in front of where he now sat. The line ran through the forest, among the rocks and laurel thickets, the men fifteen or twenty paces apart, all in concealment and under injunction of strict silence and unremitting vigilance. In four hours, if nothing occurred, they would be relieved by a fresh detachment from the reserve now resting in care of its captain some distance away to the left and rear. Before stationing his men the young officer of whom we are writing had pointed out to his two sergeants the spot at which he would be found if it should be necessary to consult him, or if his presence at the front line should be required.

It was a quiet enough spot—the fork of an old wood-road, on the two branches of which, prolonging themselves deviously forward in the dim moonlight, the sergeants were themselves stationed, a few paces in rear of the line. If driven sharply back by a sudden onset of the enemy—and pickets are not expected to make a stand after firing—the men would come into the converging roads and naturally following them to their point of intersection could be rallied and "formed." In his small way the author of these dispositions was something of a strategist; if Napoleon had planned as intelligently at Waterloo he would have won that memorable battle and been overthrown later.

Second-Lieutenant Brainerd Byring was a brave and efficient officer, young and comparatively inexperienced as he was in the business of killing his fellow-men. He had enlisted in the very first days of the war as a private, with no military knowledge whatever, had been made first-sergeant of his company on account of his education and engaging manner, and had been lucky enough to lose his captain by a Confederate bullet; in the resulting promotions he had gained a commission. He had been in several engagements, such as they were—at Philippi, Rich Mountain, Carrick's Ford and Greenbrier—and had borne himself with such gallantry as not to attract the attention of his superior officers. The exhilaration of battle was agreeable to him, but the sight of the dead, with their clay faces, blank eyes and stiff bodies, which when not unnaturally shrunken were unnaturally swollen, had always intolerably affected him.

He felt toward them a kind of reasonless antipathy that was something more than the physical and spiritual repugnance common to us all. Doubtless this feeling was due to his unusually acute sensibilities—his keen sense of the beautiful, which these hideous things outraged. Whatever may have been the cause, he could not look upon a dead body without a loathing which had in it an element of resentment. What others have respected as the dignity of death had to him no existence—was altogether unthinkable. Death was a thing to be hated. It was not picturesque, it had no tender and solemn side—a dismal thing, hideous in all its manifestations and suggestions. Lieutenant Byring was a braver man than anybody knew, for nobody knew his horror of that which he was ever ready to incur.

Having posted his men, instructed his sergeants and retired to his station, he seated himself on a log, and with senses all alert began his vigil. For greater ease he loosened his sword-belt and taking his heavy revolver from his holster laid it on the log beside him. He felt very comfortable, though he hardly gave the fact a thought, so intently did he listen for any sound from the front which might have a menacing significance—a shout, a shot, or the footfall of one of his sergeants coming to apprise him of something worth knowing. From the vast, invisible ocean of moonlight overhead fell, here and there, a slender, broken stream that seemed to plash against the intercepting branches and trickle to earth, forming small white pools among the clumps of laurel. But these leaks were few and served only to accentuate the blackness of his environment, which his imagination found it easy to people with all manner of unfamiliar shapes, menacing, uncanny, or merely grotesque.

He to whom the portentous conspiracy of night and solitude and silence in the heart of a great forest is not an unknown experience needs not to be told what another world it all is—how even the most commonplace and familiar objects take on another character. The trees group themselves differently; they draw closer together, as if in fear. The very silence has another quality than the silence of the day. And it is full of half-heard whispers—whispers that startle—ghosts of sounds long dead. There are living sounds, too, such as are never heard under other conditions: notes of strange night-birds, the cries of small animals in sudden encounters with stealthy foes or in their dreams, a rustling in the dead leaves—it may be the leap of a wood-rat, it may be the footfall of a panther. What caused the breaking of that twig?—what the low, alarmed twittering in that bushful of birds? There are sounds without a name, forms without substance, translations in space of objects which have not been seen to move, movements wherein nothing is observed to change its place. Ah, children of the sunlight and the gaslight, how little you know of the world in which you live!

Surrounded at a little distance by armed and watchful friends, Byring felt utterly alone. Yielding himself to the solemn and mysterious spirit of the time and place, he had forgotten the nature of his connection with the visible and audible aspects and phases of the night. The forest was boundless; men and the habitations of men did not exist. The universe was one primeval mystery of darkness, without form and void, himself the sole, dumb questioner of its eternal secret. Absorbed in thoughts born of this mood, he suffered the time to slip away unnoted. Meantime the infrequent patches of white light lying amongst the tree-trunks had undergone changes of size, form and place. In one of them near by, just at the roadside, his eye fell upon an object that he had not previously observed. It was almost before his face as he sat; he could have sworn that it had not before been there. It was partly covered in shadow, but he could see that it was a human figure. Instinctively he adjusted the clasp of his sword-belt and laid hold of his pistol—again he was in a world of war, by occupation an assassin.

The figure did not move. Rising, pistol in hand, he approached. The figure lay upon its back, its upper part in shadow, but standing above it and looking down upon the face, he saw that it was a dead body. He shuddered and turned from it with a feeling of sickness and disgust, resumed his seat upon the log, and forgetting military prudence struck a match and lit a cigar. In the sudden blackness that followed the extinction of the flame he felt a sense of relief; he could no longer see the object of his aversion. Nevertheless, he kept his eyes in that direction until it appeared again with growing distinctness. It seemed to have moved a trifle nearer.

"Damn the thing!" he muttered. "What does it want?"

It did not appear to be in need of anything but a soul.

Byring turned away his eyes and began humming a tune, but he broke off in the middle of a bar and looked at the dead body. Its presence annoyed him, though he could hardly have had a quieter neighbour. He was conscious, too, of a vague, indefinable feeling that was new to him. It was not fear, but rather a sense of the supernatural—in which he did not at all believe.

"I have inherited it," he said to himself. "I suppose it will require a thousand ages—perhaps ten thousand—for humanity to outgrow this feeling. Where and when did it originate? Away back, probably, in what is called the cradle of the human race—the plains of Central Asia. What we inherit as a superstition our barbarous ancestors must have held as a reasonable conviction. Doubtless they believed themselves justified by facts whose nature we cannot even conjecture in thinking a dead body a malign thing endowed with some strange power of mischief, with perhaps a will and a purpose to exert it. Possibly they had some awful form of religion of which that was one of the chief doctrines, sedulously taught by their priesthood, as ours teach the immortality of the soul. As the Aryans moved slowly on, to and through the Caucasus passes, and spread over Europe, new conditions of life must have resulted in the formulation of new religions. The old belief in the malevolence of the dead body was lost from the creeds and even perished from tradition, but it left its heritage of terror, which is transmitted from generation to generation—is as much a part of us as are our blood and bones."

In following out his thought he had forgotten that which suggested it; but now his eye fell again upon the corpse. The shadow had now altogether uncovered it. He saw the sharp profile, the chin in the air, the whole face, ghastly white in the moonlight. The clothing was grey, the uniform of a Confederate soldier. The coat and waistcoat, unbuttoned, had fallen away on each side, exposing the white shirt. The chest seemed unnaturally prominent, but the abdomen had sunk in, leaving a sharp projection at the line of the lower ribs. The arms were extended, the left knee was thrust upward. The whole posture impressed Byring as having been studied with a view to the horrible.

"Bah!" he exclaimed; "he was an actor—he knows how to be dead."

He drew away his eyes, directing them resolutely along one of the roads leading to the front, and resumed his philosophizing where he had left off.

"It may be that our Central Asian ancestors had not the custom of burial. In that case it is easy to understand their fear of the dead, who really were a menace and an evil. They bred pestilences. Children were taught to avoid the places where they lay, and to run away if by inadvertence they came near a corpse. I think, indeed, I'd better go away from this chap."

He half rose to do so, then remembered that he had told his men in front and the officer in the rear who was to relieve him that he could at any time be found at that spot. It was a matter of pride, too. If he abandoned his post he feared they would think he feared the corpse. He was no coward and he was unwilling to incur anybody's ridicule. So he again seated himself, and to prove his courage looked boldly at the body. The right arm—the one farthest from him—was now in shadow. He could hardly see the hand which, he had before observed, lay at the root of a clump of laurel. There had been no change, a fact which gave him a certain comfort, he could not have said why. He did not at once remove his eyes; that which we do not wish to see has a strange fascination, sometimes irresistible. Of the woman who covers her eyes with her hands and looks between the fingers let it be said that the wits have dealt with her not altogether justly.

Byring suddenly became conscious of a pain in his right hand. He withdrew his eyes from his enemy and looked at it.

He was grasping the hilt of his drawn sword so tightly that it hurt him. He observed, too, that he was leaning forward in a strained attitude—crouching like a gladiator ready to spring at the throat of an antagonist. His teeth were clenched and he was breathing hard. This matter was soon set right, and as his muscles relaxed and he drew a long breath he felt keenly enough the ludicrousness of the incident. It affected him to laughter. Heavens! what sound was that? what mindless devil was uttering an unholy glee in mockery of human merriment? He sprang to his feet and looked about him, not recognizing his own laugh.

He could no longer conceal from himself the horrible fact of his cowardice; he was thoroughly frightened! He would have run from the spot, but his legs refused their office; they gave way beneath him and he sat again upon the log, violently trembling. His face was wet, his whole body bathed in a chill perspiration. He could not even cry out. Distinctly he heard behind him a stealthy tread, as of some wild animal, and dared not look over his shoulder. Had the soulless living joined forces with the soulless dead?—was it an animal? Ah, if he could but be assured of that! But by no effort of will could he now unfix his gaze from the face of the dead man.

I repeat that Lieutenant Byring was a brave and intelligent man. But what would you have? Shall a man cope, single-handed, with so monstrous an alliance as that of night and solitude and silence and the dead,—while an incalculable host of his own ancestors shriek into the ear of his spirit their coward counsel, sing their doleful death-songs in his heart, and disarm his very blood of all its iron? The odds are too great—courage was not made for so rough use as that.

One sole conviction now had the man in possession: that the body had moved. It lay nearer to the edge of its plot of light—there could be no doubt of it. It had also moved its arms, for, look, they are both in the shadow! A breath of cold air struck Byring full in the face; the boughs of trees above him stirred and moaned. A strongly defined shadow passed across the face of the dead, left it luminous, passed back upon it and left it half obscured. The horrible thing was visibly moving! At that moment a single shot rang out upon the picket-line—a lonelier and louder, though more distant, shot than ever had been heard by mortal ear! It broke the spell of that enchanted man; it slew the silence and the solitude, dispersed the hindering host from Central Asia and released his modern manhood. With a cry like that of some great bird pouncing upon its prey he sprang forward, hot-hearted for action!

Shot after shot now came from the front. There were shoutings and confusion, hoof-beats and desultory cheers. Away to the rear, in the sleeping camp, were a singing of bugles and grumble of drums. Pushing through the thickets on either side the roads came the Federal pickets, in full retreat, firing backward at random as they ran. A straggling group that had followed back one of the roads, as instructed, suddenly sprang away into the bushes as half a hundred horsemen thundered by them, striking wildly with their sabres as they passed. At headlong speed these mounted madmen shot past the spot where Byring had sat, and vanished round an angle of the road, shouting and firing their pistols. A moment later there was a roar of musketry, followed by dropping shots—they had encountered the reserve-guard in line; and back they came in dire confusion, with here and there an empty saddle and many a maddened horse, bullet-stung, snorting and plunging with pain. It was all over—"an affair of outposts."

The line was re-established with fresh men, the roll called, the stragglers were re-formed. The Federal commander, with a part of his staff, imperfectly clad, appeared upon the scene, asked a few questions, looked exceedingly wise and retired. After standing at arms for an hour the brigade in camp "swore a prayer or two" and went to bed.

Early the next morning a fatigue-party, commanded by a captain and accompanied by a surgeon, searched the ground for dead and wounded. At the fork of the road, a little to one side, they found two bodies lying close together—that of a Federal officer and that of a Confederate private. The officer had died of a sword-thrust through the heart, but not, apparently, until he had inflicted upon his enemy no fewer than five dreadful wounds. The dead officer lay on his face in a pool of blood, the weapon still in his heart. They turned him on his back and the surgeon removed it.

"Gad!" said the captain—"It is Byring!"—adding, with a glance at the other, "They had a tough tussle."

The surgeon was examining the sword. It was that of a line officer of Federal infantry—exactly like the one worn by the captain. It was, in fact, Byring's own. The only other weapon discovered was an undischarged revolver in the dead officer's belt.

The surgeon laid down the sword and approached the other body. It was frightfully gashed and stabbed, but there was no blood. He took hold of the left foot and tried to straighten the leg. In the effort the body was displaced. The dead do not wish to be moved—it protested with a faint, sickening odour. Where it had lain were a few maggots, manifesting an imbecile activity.

The surgeon looked at the captain. The captain looked at the surgeon.

A RESUMED IDENTITY

The Review as a Form of Welcome

ne summer night a man stood on a low hill overlooking a wide expanse of forest and field. By the full moon hanging low in the west he knew what he might not have known otherwise: that it was near the hour of dawn. A light mist lay along the earth, partly veiling the lower features of the landscape, but above it the taller trees showed in well-defined masses against a clear sky. Two or three farmhouses were visible through the haze, but in none of them, naturally, was a light. Nowhere, indeed, was any sign or suggestion of life except the barking of a distant dog, which, repeated with mechanical iteration, served rather to accentuate than dispel the loneliness of the scene.

The man looked curiously about him on all sides, as one who among familiar surroundings is unable to determine his exact place and part in the scheme of things. It is so, perhaps, that we shall act when, risen from the dead, we await the call to judgment.

A hundred yards away was a straight road, showing white in the moonlight. Endeavouring to orient himself, as a surveyor or navigator might say, the man moved his eyes slowly along its visible length and at a distance of a quarter-mile to the south of his station saw, dim and grey in the haze, a group of horsemen riding to the north. Behind them were men afoot, marching in column, with dimly gleaming rifles aslant above their shoulders. They moved slowly and in silence. Another group of horsemen, another regiment of infantry, another and another—all in unceasing motion toward the man's point of view, past it, and beyond. A battery of artillery followed, the cannoneers riding with folded arms on limber and caisson. And still the interminable procession came out of the obscurity to south and passed into the obscurity to north, with never a sound of voice, nor hoof, nor wheel.

The man could not rightly understand: he thought himself deaf; said so, and heard his own voice, although it had an unfamiliar quality that almost alarmed him; it disappointed his ear's expectancy in the matter of timbre and resonance. But he was not deaf, and that for the moment sufficed.

Then he remembered that there are natural phenomena to which some one has given the name "acoustic shadows." If you stand in an acoustic shadow there is one direction from which you will hear nothing. At the battle of Gaines's Mill, one of the fiercest conflicts of the Civil War, with a hundred guns in play, spectators a mile and a half away on the opposite side of the Chickahominy valley heard nothing of what they clearly saw. The bombardment of Port Royal, heard and felt at St. Augustine, a hundred and fifty miles to the south, was inaudible two miles to the north in a still atmosphere. A few days before the surrender at Appomattox a thunderous engagement between the commands of Sheridan and Pickett was unknown to the latter commander, a mile in the rear of his own line.

These instances were not known to the man of whom we write, but less striking ones of the same character had not escaped his observation. He was profoundly disquieted, but for another reason than the uncanny silence of that moonlight march.

"Good Lord!" he said to himself—and again it was as if another had spoken his thought—"if those people are what I take them to be we have lost the battle and they are moving on Nashville!"

Then came a thought of self—an apprehension—a strong sense of personal peril, such as in another we call fear. He stepped quickly into the shadow of a tree. And still the silent battalions moved slowly forward in the haze.

The chill of a sudden breeze upon the back of his neck drew his attention to the quarter whence it came, and turning to the east he saw a faint grey light along the horizon—the first sign of returning day. This increased his apprehension.

"I must get away from here," he thought, "or I shall be discovered and taken."

He moved out of the shadow, walking rapidly toward the greying east. From the safer seclusion of a clump of cedars he looked back. The entire column had passed out of sight: the straight white road lay bare and desolate in the moonlight!

Puzzled before, he was not inexpressibly astonished. So swift a passing of so slow an army!—he could not comprehend it. Minute after minute passed unnoted; he had lost his sense of time. He sought with a terrible earnestness a solution of the mystery, but sought in vain. When at last he roused himself from his abstraction the sun's rim was visible above the hills, but in the new conditions he found no other light than that of day; his understanding was involved as darkly in doubt as before.

On every side lay cultivated fields showing no sign of war and war's ravages. From the chimneys of the farmhouses thin ascensions of blue smoke signalled preparations for a day's peaceful toil. Having stilled its immemorial allocution to the moon, the watch-dog was assisting a n——o who, prefixing a team of mules to the plough, was flatting and sharping contentedly at his task. The hero of this tale stared stupidly at the pastoral picture as if he had never seen such a thing in all his life; then he put his hand to his head, passed it through his hair and, withdrawing it, attentively considered the palm—a singular thing to do. Apparently reassured by the act, he walked confidently toward the road.

II

When You Have Lost Your
Life Consult a Physician

Dr. Stilling Malson, of Murfreesboro, having visited a patient six or seven miles away, on the Nashville road, had remained with him all night. At daybreak he set out for home on horseback, as was the custom of doctors of the time and region. He had passed into the neighbourhood of Stone's River battlefield when a man approached him from the roadside and saluted in the military fashion, with a movement of the right hand to the hat-brim. But the hat was not a military hat, the man was not in uniform and had not a martial bearing. The doctor nodded civilly, half thinking that the stranger's uncommon greeting was perhaps in deference to the historic surroundings. As the stranger evidently desired speech with him he courteously reined in his horse and waited.

"Sir," said the stranger, "although a civilian, you are perhaps an enemy."

"I am a physician," was the non-committal reply.

"Thank you," said the other. "I am a lieutenant, of the staff of General Hazen." He paused a moment and looked sharply at the person whom he was addressing, then added, "Of the Federal army."

The physician merely nodded.

"Kindly tell me," continued the other, "what has happened here. Where are the armies? Which has won the battle?"

The physician regarded his questioner curiously with half-shut eyes. After a professional scrutiny, prolonged to the limit of politeness, "Pardon me," he said; "one asking information should be willing to impart it. Are you wounded?" he added, smiling.

"Not seriously—it seems."

The man removed the unmilitary hat, put his hand to his head, passed it through his hair and, withdrawing it, attentively considered the palm.

"I was struck by a bullet and have been unconscious. It must have been a light, glancing blow: I find no blood and feel no pain. I will not trouble you for treatment, but will you kindly direct me to my command—to any part of the Federal army—if you know?"

Again the doctor did not immediately reply: he was recalling much that is recorded in the books of his profession—something about lost identity and the effect of familiar scenes in restoring it. At length he looked the man in the face, smiled, and said:

"Lieutenant, you are not wearing the uniform of your rank and service."

At this the man glanced down at his civilian attire, lifted his eyes, and said with hesitation:

"That is true. I—I don't quite understand."

Still regarding him sharply but not unsympathetically, the man of science bluntly inquired:

"How old are you?"

"Twenty-three—if that has anything to do with it."

"You don't look it; I should hardly have guessed you to be just that."

The man was growing impatient. "We need not discuss that," he said; "I want to know about the army. Not two hours ago I saw a column of troops moving northward on this road. You must have met them. Be good enough to tell me the colour of their clothing, which I was unable to make out, and I'll trouble you no more."

"You are quite sure that you saw them?"

"Sure? My God, sir, I could have counted them!"

"Why, really," said the physician, with an amusing consciousness of his own resemblance to the loquacious barber of the *Arabian Nights*, "this is very interesting. I met no troops."

The man looked at him coldly, as if he had himself observed the likeness to the barber. "It is plain," he said, "that you do not care to assist me. Sir, you may go to the devil!"

He turned and strode away, very much at random, across the dewy fields, his half-penitent tormentor quietly watching him from his point of vantage in the saddle till he disappeared beyond an array of trees.

III

The Danger of Looking into a Pool of Water

After leaving the road the man slackened his pace, and now went forward, rather deviously, with a distinct feeling of fatigue. He could not account for this, though truly the interminable loquacity of that country doctor offered itself in explanation. Seating himself upon a rock, he laid one hand upon his knee, back upward, and casually looked at it. It was lean and withered. He lifted both hands to his face. It was seamed and furrowed; he could trace the lines with the tips of his fingers. How strange!—a mere bullet-stroke and a brief unconsciousness should not make one a physical wreck.

"I must have been a long time in hospital," he said aloud. "Why, what a fool I am! The battle was in December, and it is now summer!" He laughed. "No wonder that fellow thought me an escaped lunatic. He was wrong: I am only an escaped patient."

At a little distance a small plot of ground enclosed by a stone wall caught his attention. With no very definite intent he rose and went to it. In the centre was a square, solid monument of hewn stone. It was brown with age, weather-worn at the angles, spotted with moss and lichen. Between the massive blocks were strips of grass the leverage of whose roots had pushed them apart. In answer to the challenge of this ambitious structure Time had laid his destroying hand upon it, and it would soon be "one with Nineveh and Tyre." In an inscription on one side his eye caught a familiar name. Shaking with excitement, he craned his body across the wall and read:

HAZEN'S BRIGADE
to The Memory of Its Soldiers
who fell at
Stone River, Dec. 31, 1862.

The man fell back from the wall, faint and sick. Almost within an arm's length was a little depression in the earth; it had been filled by a recent rain—a pool of clear water. He crept to it to revive himself, lifted the upper part of his body on his trembling arms, thrust forward his head and saw the reflection of his face, as in a mirror. He uttered a terrible cry. His arms gave way; he fell, face downward, into the pool and yielded up the life that had spanned another life.

ONE OF THE MISSING

erome Searing, a private soldier of General Sherman's army, then confronting the enemy at and about Kennesaw Mountain, Georgia, turned his back upon a small group of officers with whom he had been talking in low tones, stepped across a light line of earthworks, and disappeared in a forest. None of the men in line behind the works had said a word to him, nor had he so much as nodded to them in passing, but all who saw understood that this brave man had been intrusted with some perilous duty. Jerome Searing, though a private, did not serve in the ranks; he was detailed for service at division headquarters, being borne upon the rolls as an orderly. "Orderly" is a word covering a multitude of duties. An orderly may be a messenger, a clerk, an officer's servant—anything. He may perform services for which no provision is made in orders and army regulations. Their nature may depend upon his aptitude, upon favour, upon accident. Private Searing, an incomparable marksman, young, hardy, intelligent and insensible to fear, was a scout. The general commanding his division was not content to obey orders blindly without knowing what was in his front, even when his command was not on detached service, but formed a fraction of the line of the army; nor was he satisfied to receive his knowledge of his *vis-à-vis* through the customary channels; he wanted to know more than he was apprised of by the corps commander and the collisions of pickets and skirmishers. Hence Jerome Searing, with his extraordinary daring, his woodcraft, his sharp eyes, and truthful tongue. On this occasion his instructions were simple: to get as near the enemy's lines as possible and learn all that he could.

In a few moments he had arrived at the picket-line, the men on duty there lying in groups of two and four behind little banks of earth scooped out of the slight depression in which they lay, their rifles protruding from the green boughs with which they had masked their small defences. The forest extended without a break toward the front, so solemn and silent that only by an effort of the imagination could it be conceived as populous with armed men, alert and vigilant—a forest formidable with possibilities of battle. Pausing a moment in one of these rifle-pits to apprise the men of his intention Searing crept stealthily forward on his hands and knees and was soon lost to view in a dense thicket of underbrush.

"That is the last of him," said one of the men; "I wish I had his rifle; those fellows will hurt some of us with it."

Searing crept on, taking advantage of every accident of ground and growth to give himself better cover. His eyes penetrated everywhere, his ears took note of every sound. He stilled his breathing, and at the cracking of a twig beneath his knee stopped his progress and hugged the earth. It was slow work, but not tedious; the danger made it exciting, but by no physical signs was the excitement manifest. His pulse was as regular, his nerves were as steady as if he were trying to trap a sparrow.

"It seems a long time," he thought, "but I cannot have come very far; I am still alive."

He smiled at his own method of estimating distance, and crept forward. A moment later he suddenly flattened himself upon the earth and lay motionless, minute after minute. Through a narrow opening in the bushes he had caught sight of a small mound of yellow clay—one of the enemy's rifle-pits. After some little time he cautiously raised his head, inch by inch, then his body upon his hands, spread out on each side of him, all the while intently regarding the hillock of clay. In another moment he was upon his feet, rifle in hand, striding rapidly forward with little attempt at concealment. He had rightly interpreted the signs, whatever they were; the enemy was gone.

To assure himself beyond a doubt before going back to report upon so important a matter, Searing pushed forward across the line of abandoned pits, running from cover to cover in the more open forest, his eyes vigilant to discover possible stragglers. He came to the edge of a plantation—one of those forlorn, deserted homesteads of the last years of the war, upgrown with brambles, ugly with broken fences and desolate with vacant buildings having blank apertures in place of doors and windows. After a keen reconnaissance from the safe seclusion of a clump of young pines Searing ran lightly across a field and through an orchard to a small structure which stood apart from the other farm buildings, on a slight elevation. This he thought would enable him to overlook a large scope of country in the direction that he supposed the enemy to have taken in withdrawing. This building, which had originally consisted of a single room elevated upon four posts about ten feet high, was now little more than a roof; the floor had fallen away, the joists and planks loosely piled on the ground below or resting on end at various angles, not wholly torn from their fastenings above. The supporting posts were themselves no longer vertical. It looked as if the whole edifice would go down at the touch of a finger.

Concealing himself in the débris of joists and flooring Searing looked across the open ground between his point of view and a spur of Kennesaw Mountain, a half-mile away. A road leading up and across this spur was crowded with troops—the rear-guard of the retiring enemy, their gun-barrels gleaming in the morning sunlight.

Searing had now learned all that he could hope to know. It was his duty to return to his own command with all possible speed and report his discovery. But the grey column of Confederates toiling up the mountain road was singularly tempting. His rifle—an ordinary "Springfield," but fitted with a globe sight and hair-trigger—would easily send its ounce and a quarter of lead hissing into their midst. That would probably not affect the duration and result of the war, but it is the business of a soldier to kill. It is also his habit if he is a good soldier. Searing cocked his rifle and "set" the trigger.

But it was decreed from the beginning of time that Private Searing was not to murder anybody that bright summer morning, nor was the Confederate retreat to be announced by him. For countless ages events had been so matching themselves together in that wondrous mosaic to some parts of which, dimly discernible, we give the name of history, that the acts which he had in will would have marred the harmony of the pattern. Some twenty-five years previously the Power charged with the execution of the work according to the design had provided against that mischance by causing the birth of a certain male child in a little village at the foot of the Carpathian Mountains, had carefully reared it, supervised its education, directed its desires into a military channel, and in due time made it an officer of artillery. By the concurrence of an infinite number of favouring influences and their preponderance over an infinite number of opposing ones, this officer of artillery had been made to commit a breach of discipline and flee from his native country to avoid punishment. He had been directed to New Orleans (instead of New York), where a recruiting officer awaited him on the wharf. He was enlisted and promoted, and things were so ordered that he now commanded a Confederate battery some two miles along the line from where Jerome Searing, the Federal scout, stood cocking his rifle. Nothing had been neglected—at every step in the progress of both these men's lives, and in the lives of their contemporaries and ancestors, and in the lives of the contemporaries of their ancestors, the right thing had been done to bring about the desired result. Had anything in all this vast concatenation been overlooked Private Searing might have fired on the retreating Confederates that morning, and would perhaps have missed. As it fell out, a Confederate captain of artillery, having nothing better to do while awaiting his turn to pull out and be off, amused himself by sighting a field-piece obliquely to his right at what he mistook for some Federal officers on the crest of a hill, and discharged it. The shot flew high of its mark.

As Jerome Searing drew back the hammer of his rifle and with his eyes upon the distant Confederates considered where he could plant his shot with the best hope of making a widow or an orphan or a childless mother,—perhaps all three, for Private

Searing, although he had repeatedly refused promotion, was not without a certain kind of ambition,—he heard a rushing sound in the air, like that made by the wings of a great bird swooping down upon its prey. More quickly than he could apprehend the gradation, it increased to a hoarse and horrible roar, as the missile that made it sprang at him out of the sky, striking with a deafening impact one of the posts supporting the confusion of timbers above him, smashing it into matchwood, and bringing down the crazy edifice with a loud clatter, in clouds of blinding dust!

When Jerome Searing recovered consciousness he did not at once understand what had occurred. It was, indeed, some time before he opened his eyes. For a while he believed that he had died and been buried, and he tried to recall some portions of the burial service. He thought that his wife was kneeling upon his grave, adding her weight to that of the earth upon his breast. The two of them, widow and earth, had crushed his coffin. Unless the children should persuade her to go home he would not much longer be able to breathe. He felt a sense of wrong. "I cannot speak to her," he thought; "the dead have no voice; and if I open my eyes I shall get them full of earth."

He opened his eyes. A great expanse of blue sky, rising from a fringe of the tops of trees. In the foreground, shutting out some of the trees, a high, dun mound, angular in outline and crossed by an intricate, pattern-less system of straight lines; the whole an immeasurable distance away—a distance so inconceivably great that it fatigued him, and he closed his eyes. The moment that he did so he was conscious of an insufferable light. A sound was in his ears like the low, rhythmic thunder of a distant sea breaking in successive waves upon the beach, and out of this noise, seeming a part of it, or possibly coming from beyond it, and intermingled with its ceaseless undertone, came the articulate words: "Jerome Searing, you are caught like a rat in a trap—in a trap, trap, trap."

Suddenly there fell a great silence, a black darkness, an infinite tranquillity, and Jerome Searing, perfectly conscious of his rathood, and well assured of the trap that he was in, remembering all and nowise alarmed, again opened his eyes to reconnoitre, to note the strength of his enemy, to plan his defence.

He was caught in a reclining posture, his back firmly supported by a solid beam. Another lay across his breast, but he had been able to shrink a little away from it so that it no longer oppressed him, though it was immovable. A brace joining it at an angle had wedged him against a pile of boards on his left, fastening the arm on that side. His legs, slightly parted and straight along the ground, were covered upward to the knees with a mass of débris which towered above his narrow horizon. His head was as rigidly fixed as in a vice; he could move his eyes, his chin—no more. Only his right arm was partly free. "You must help us out of this," he said to it. But he could not get it from under the heavy timber athwart his chest, nor move it outward more than six inches at the elbow.

Searing was not seriously injured, nor did he suffer pain. A smart rap on the head from a flying fragment of the splintered post, incurred simultaneously with the frightfully sudden shock to the nervous system, had momentarily dazed him. His term of unconsciousness, including the period of recovery, during which he had had the strange fancies, had probably not exceeded a few seconds, for the dust of the wreck had not wholly cleared away as he began an intelligent survey of the situation.

With his partly free right hand he now tried to get hold of the beam that lay across, but not quite against, his breast. In no way could he do so. He was unable to depress the shoulder so as to push the elbow beyond that edge of the timber which was nearest his knees; failing in that, he could not raise the forearm and hand to grasp the beam. The brace that made an angle with it downward and backward prevented him from doing anything in that direction, and between it and his body the space was not half so wide as the length of his forearm. Obviously he could not get his hand under the beam nor over it; the hand could not, in fact, touch it at all. Having demonstrated his inability, he desisted, and began to think whether he could reach any of the débris piled upon his legs.

In surveying the mass with a view to determining that point, his attention was arrested by what seemed to be a ring of shining metal immediately in front of his eyes. It appeared to him at first to surround some perfectly black substance, and it was somewhat more than a half-inch in diameter. It suddenly occurred to his mind that the blackness was simply shadow and that the ring was in fact the muzzle of his rifle protruding from the pile of débris. He was not long in satisfying himself that this was so—if it was a satisfaction. By closing either eye he could look a little way along the barrel—to the point where it was hidden by the rubbish that held it. He could see the one side, with the corresponding eye, at apparently the same angle as the other side with the other eye. Looking with the right eye, the weapon seemed to be directed at a point to the left of his head, and *vice versa*. He was unable to see the upper surface of the barrel, but could see the under surface of the stock at a slight angle. The piece was, in fact, aimed at the exact centre of his forehead.

In the perception of this circumstance, in the recollection that just previously to the mischance of which this uncomfortable situation was the result he had cocked the rifle and set the trigger so that a touch would discharge it, Private Searing was affected with a feeling of uneasiness. But that was as far as possible from fear; he was a brave man, somewhat familiar with the aspect of rifles from that point of view, and of cannon too. And now he recalled, with something like amusement, an incident of his experience at the storming of Missionary Ridge, where, walking up to one of the enemy's embrasures from which he had seen a heavy gun throw charge after charge of grape among the assailants he had thought for a moment that the piece had been withdrawn; he could see nothing in the opening but a brazen circle. What that was he had understood just in time to step aside as it pitched another peck of iron down that swarming slope. To face firearms is one of the commonest incidents in a soldier's life—firearms, too, with malevolent eyes blazing behind them. That is what a soldier is for. Still, Private Searing did not altogether relish the situation, and turned away his eyes.

After groping, aimless, with his right hand for a time he made an ineffectual attempt to release his left. Then he tried to disengage his head, the fixity of which was the more annoying from his ignorance of what held it. Next he tried to free his feet, but while exerting the powerful muscles of his legs for that purpose it occurred to him that a disturbance of the rubbish which held them might discharge the rifle; how it could have endured what had already befallen it he could not understand, although memory assisted him with several instances in point. One in particular he recalled, in which in a moment of mental abstraction he had clubbed his rifle and beaten out another gentleman's brains, observing afterward that the weapon which he had been diligently swinging by the muzzle was loaded, capped, and at full cock—knowledge of which circumstance would doubtless have cheered his antagonist to longer endurance. He had always smiled in recalling that blunder of his "green and salad days" as a soldier, but now he did not smile. He turned his eyes again to the muzzle of the rifle and for a moment fancied that it had moved; it seemed somewhat nearer.

Again he looked away. The tops of the distant trees beyond the bounds of the plantation interested him: he had not before observed how light and feathery they were, nor how darkly blue the sky was, even among their branches, where they somewhat paled it with their green; above him it appeared almost black. "It will be uncomfortably hot here," he thought, "as the day advances. I wonder which way I am looking."

Judging by such shadows as he could see, he decided that his face was due north; he would at least not have the sun in his eyes, and north—well, that was toward his wife and children.

"Bah!" he exclaimed aloud, "what have they to do with it?"

He closed his eyes. "As I can't get out I may as well go to sleep. The rebels are gone and some of our fellows are sure to stray out here foraging. They'll find me."

But he did not sleep. Gradually he became sensible of a pain in his forehead—a dull ache, hardly perceptible at first, but growing more and more uncomfortable. He opened his eyes and it was gone—closed them and it returned. "The devil!" he said, irrelevantly, and stared again at the sky. He heard the singing of birds, the strange metallic note of the meadow lark, suggesting the clash of vibrant blades. He fell into pleasant memories of his childhood, played again with his brother and sister, raced across the fields, shouting to alarm the sedentary larks, entered the sombre forest beyond and with timid steps followed the faint path to Ghost Rock, standing at last with audible heart-throbs before the Dead Man's Cave and seeking to penetrate its awful mystery. For the first time he observed that the opening of the haunted cavern was encircled by a ring of metal. Then all else vanished and left him gazing into the barrel of his rifle as before. But whereas before it had seemed nearer, it now seemed an inconceivable distance away, and all the more sinister for that. He cried out and, startled by something in his own voice—the note of fear—lied to himself in denial: "If I don't sing out I may stay here till I die."

He now made no further attempt to evade the menacing stare of the gun barrel. If he turned away his eyes an instant it was to look for assistance (although he could not see the ground on either side the ruin), and he permitted them to return, obedient to the imperative fascination. If he closed them it was from weariness, and instantly the poignant pain in his forehead—the prophecy and menace of the bullet—forced him to reopen them.

The tension of nerve and brain was too severe; nature came to his relief with intervals of unconsciousness. Reviving from one of these he became sensible of a sharp, smarting pain in his right hand, and when he worked his fingers together, or rubbed his palm with them, he could feel that they were wet and slippery. He could not see the hand, but he knew the sensation; it was running blood. In his delirium he had beaten it against the jagged fragments of the wreck, had clutched it full of splinters. He resolved that he would meet his fate more manly. He was a plain, common soldier, had no religion and not much philosophy; he could not die like a hero, with great and wise last words, even if there had been some one to hear them, but he could die "game," and he would. But if he could only know when to expect the shot!

Some rats which had probably inhabited the shed came sneaking and scampering about. One of them mounted the pile of débris that held the rifle; another followed and another. Searing regarded them at first with indifference, then with friendly interest; then, as the thought flashed into his bewildered mind that they might touch the trigger of his rifle, he cursed them and ordered them to go away. "It is no business of yours," he cried.

The creatures went away; they would return later, attack his face, gnaw away his nose, cut his throat—he knew that, but he hoped by that time to be dead.

Nothing could now unfix his gaze from the little ring of metal with its black interior. The pain in his forehead was fierce and incessant. He felt it gradually penetrating the brain more and more deeply, until at last its progress was arrested by the wood at the back of his head. It grew momentarily more insufferable: he began wantonly beating his lacerated hand against the splinters again to counteract that horrible ache. It seemed to throb with a slow, regular recurrence, each pulsation sharper than the preceding, and sometimes he cried out, thinking he felt the fatal bullet. No thoughts of home, of wife and children, of country, of glory. The whole record of memory was effaced. The world had passed away—not a vestige remained. Here in this confusion of timbers and boards is the sole universe. Here is immortality in time—each pain an everlasting life. The throbs tick off eternities.

Jerome Searing, the man of courage, the formidable enemy, the strong, resolute warrior, was as pale as a ghost. His jaw was fallen; his eyes protruded; he trembled in every fibre; a cold sweat bathed his entire body; he screamed with fear. He was not insane—he was terrified.

In groping about with his torn and bleeding hand he seized at last a strip of board, and, pulling, felt it give way. It lay parallel with his body, and by bending his elbow as much as the contracted space would permit, he could draw it a few inches at a time. Finally it was altogether loosened from the wreckage covering his legs; he could lift it clear of the ground its whole length. A great hope came into his mind: perhaps he could work it upward, that is to say backward, far enough to lift the end and push aside the rifle; or, if that were too tightly wedged, so place the strip of board as to deflect the bullet. With this object he passed it backward inch by inch, hardly daring to breathe lest that act somehow defeat his intent, and more than ever unable to remove his eyes from the rifle, which might perhaps now hasten to improve its waning opportunity. Something at least had been gained: in the occupation of his mind in this attempt at self-defence he was less sensible of the pain in his head and had ceased to wince. But he was still dreadfully frightened and his teeth rattled like castanets.

The strip of board ceased to move to the suasion of his hand. He tugged at it with all his strength, changed the direction of its length all he could, but it had met some extended obstruction behind him and the end in front was still too far away to clear the pile of débris and reach the muzzle of the gun. It extended, indeed, nearly as far as the trigger guard, which, uncovered by the rubbish, he could imperfectly see with his right eye. He tried to break the strip with his hand, but had no leverage. In his defeat, all his terror returned, augmented tenfold. The black aperture of the rifle appeared to threaten a sharper and more imminent death in punishment of his rebellion. The track of the bullet through his head ached with an intenser anguish. He began to tremble again.

Suddenly he became composed. His tremor subsided. He clenched his teeth and drew down his eyebrows. He had not exhausted his means of defence; a new design had shaped itself in his mind—another plan of battle. Raising the front end of the strip of board, he carefully pushed it forward through the wreckage at the side of the rifle until it pressed against the trigger guard. Then he moved the end slowly outward until he could feel that it had cleared it, then, closing his eyes, thrust it against the trigger with all his strength! There was no explosion; the rifle had been discharged as it dropped from his hand when the building fell. But it did its work.

Lieutenant Adrian Searing, in command of the picket-guard on that part of the line through which his brother Jerome had passed on his mission, sat with attentive ears in his breastwork behind the line. Not the faintest sound escaped him; the cry of a bird, the barking of a squirrel, the noise of the wind among the pines—all were anxiously noted by his overstrained sense. Suddenly, directly in front of his line, he heard a faint, confused rumble, like the clatter of a falling building translated by distance. The lieutenant mechanically looked at his watch. Six o'clock and eighteen minutes. At the same moment an officer approached him on foot from the rear and saluted.

"Lieutenant," said the officer, "the colonel directs you to move forward your line and feel the enemy if you find him. If not, continue the advance until directed to halt. There is reason to think that the enemy has retreated."

The lieutenant nodded and said nothing; the other officer retired. In a moment the men, apprised of their duty by the non-commissioned officers in low tones, had deployed from their rifle-pits and were moving forward in skirmishing order, with set teeth and beating hearts.

This line of skirmishers sweeps across the plantation toward the mountain. They pass on both sides of the wrecked building, observing nothing. At a short distance in their rear their commander comes. He casts his eyes curiously upon the ruin and sees a dead body half buried in boards and timbers. It is so covered with dust that its clothing is Confederate grey. Its face is yellowish white; the cheeks are fallen in, the temples sunken, too, with sharp ridges about them, making the forehead forbiddingly narrow; the upper lip, slightly lifted, shows the white teeth, rigidly clenched. The hair is heavy with moisture, the face as wet as the dewy grass all about. From his point of view the officer does not observe the rifle; the man was apparently killed by the fall of the building.

"Dead a week," said the officer curtly, moving on and absently pulling out his watch as if to verify his estimate of time. Six o'clock and forty minutes.

AN OCCURRENCE AT
OWL CREEK BRIDGE

I

man stood upon a railroad bridge in northern Alabama, looking down into the swift water twenty feet below. The man's hands were behind his back, the wrists bound with a cord. A rope closely encircled his neck. It was attached to a stout cross-timber above his head and the slack fell to the level of his knees. Some loose boards laid upon the sleepers supporting the metals of the railway supplied a footing for him and his executioners—two private soldiers of the Federal army, directed by a sergeant who in civil life may have been a deputy sheriff. At a short remove upon the same temporary platform was an officer in the uniform of his rank, armed. He was a captain. A sentinel at each end of the bridge stood with his rifle in the position known as "support," that is to say, vertical in front of the left shoulder, the hammer resting on the forearm thrown straight across the chest—a formal and unnatural position, enforcing an erect carriage of the body. It did not appear to be the duty of these two men to know what was occurring at the centre of the bridge; they merely blockaded the two ends of the foot planking that traversed it.

Beyond one of the sentinels nobody was in sight; the railroad ran straight away into a forest for a hundred yards, then, curving, was lost to view. Doubtless there was an outpost farther along. The other bank of the stream was open ground—a gentle acclivity topped with a stockade of vertical tree trunks, loop-holed for rifles, with a single embrasure through which protruded the muzzle of a brass cannon commanding the bridge. Midway of the slope between bridge and fort were the spectators—a single company of infantry in line, at "parade rest," the butts of the rifles on the ground, the barrels inclining slightly backward against the right shoulder, the hands crossed upon the stock. A lieutenant stood at the right of the line, the point of his sword upon the ground, his left hand resting upon his right. Excepting the group of four at the centre of the bridge, not a man moved. The company faced the bridge, staring stonily, motionless. The sentinels, facing the banks of the stream, might have been statues to adorn the bridge. The captain stood with folded arms, silent, observing the work of his subordinates, but making no sign. Death is a dignitary who when he comes announced is to be received with formal manifestations of respect, even by those most familiar with him. In the code of military etiquette silence and fixity are forms of deference.

The man who was engaged in being hanged was apparently about thirty-five years of age. He was a civilian, if one might judge from his habit, which was that of a planter. His features were good—a straight nose, firm mouth, broad forehead, from which his long, dark hair was combed straight back, falling behind his ears to the collar of his well-fitting frock-coat. He wore a moustache and pointed beard, but no whiskers; his eyes were large and dark grey, and had a kindly expression which one would hardly have expected in one whose neck was in the hemp. Evidently this was no vulgar assassin. The liberal military code makes provision for hanging many kinds of persons, and gentlemen are not excluded.

The preparations being complete, the two private soldiers stepped aside and each drew away the plank upon which he had been standing. The sergeant turned to the captain, saluted and placed himself immediately behind that officer, who in turn moved apart one pace. These movements left the condemned man and the sergeant standing on the two ends of the same plank, which spanned three of the cross-ties of the bridge. The end upon which the civilian stood almost, but not quite, reached a fourth. This plank had been held in place by the weight of the captain; it was now held by that of the sergeant. At a signal from the former the latter would step aside, the plank would tilt and the condemned man go down between two ties. The arrangement commended itself to his judgment as simple and effective. His face had not been covered nor his eyes bandaged. He looked a moment at his "unsteadfast footing," then let his gaze wander to the swirling water of the stream racing madly beneath his feet. A piece of dancing driftwood caught his attention and his eyes followed it down the current. How slowly it appeared to move! What a sluggish stream!

He closed his eyes in order to fix his last thoughts upon his wife and children. The water, touched to gold by the early sun, the brooding mists under the banks at some distance down the stream, the fort, the soldiers, the piece of drift—all had distracted him. And now he became conscious of a new disturbance. Striking through the thought of his dear ones was a sound which he could neither ignore nor understand, a sharp, distinct, metallic percussion like the stroke of a blacksmith's hammer upon the anvil; it had the same ringing quality. He wondered what it was, and whether immeasurably distant or near by—it seemed both. Its recurrence was regular, but as slow as the tolling of a death knell. He awaited each stroke with impatience and—he knew not why—apprehension. The intervals of silence grew progressively longer; the delays became maddening. With their greater infrequency the sounds increased in strength and sharpness. They hurt his ear like the thrust of a knife; he feared he would shriek. What he heard was the ticking of his watch.

He unclosed his eyes and saw again the water below him. "If I could free my hands," he thought, "I might throw off the noose and spring into the stream. By diving I could evade the bullets and, swimming vigorously, reach the bank, take to the woods and get away home. My home, thank God, is as yet outside their lines; my wife and little ones are still beyond the invader's farthest advance."

As these thoughts, which have here to be set down in words, were flashed into the doomed man's brain rather than evolved from it the captain nodded to the sergeant. The sergeant stepped aside.

II

Peyton Farquhar was a well-to-do planter, of an old and highly respected Alabama family. Being a slave owner and like other slave owners a politician he was naturally an original secessionist and ardently devoted to the Southern cause. Circumstances of an imperious nature, which it is unnecessary to relate here, had prevented him from taking service with the gallant army that had fought the disastrous campaigns ending with the fall of Corinth, and he chafed under the inglorious restraint, longing for the release of his energies, the larger life of the soldier, the opportunity for distinction. That opportunity, he felt, would come, as it comes to all in war time. Meanwhile he did what he could. No service was too humble for him to perform in aid of the South, no adventure too perilous for him to undertake if consistent with the character of a civilian who was at heart a soldier, and who in good faith and without too much qualification assented to at least a part of the frankly villainous dictum that all is fair in love and war.

One evening while Farquhar and his wife were sitting on a rustic bench near the entrance to his grounds, a grey-clad soldier rode up to the gate and asked for a drink of water. Mrs. Farquhar was only too happy to serve him with her own white hands. While she was fetching the water her husband approached the dusty horseman and inquired eagerly for news from the front.

"The Yanks are repairing the railroads," said the man, "and are getting ready for another advance. They have reached the Owl Creek bridge, put it in order and built a stockade on the north bank. The commandant has issued an order, which is posted everywhere, declaring that any civilian caught interfering with the railroad, its bridges, tunnels or trains will be summarily hanged. I saw the order."

"How far is it to the Owl Creek bridge?" Farquhar asked.

"About thirty miles."

"Is there no force on this side the creek?"

"Only a picket post half a mile out, on the railroad, and a single sentinel at this end of the bridge."

"Suppose a man—a civilian and student of hanging—should elude the picket post and perhaps get the better of the sentinel," said Farquhar, smiling, "what could he accomplish?"

The soldier reflected. "I was there a month ago," he replied. "I observed that the flood of last winter had lodged a great quantity of driftwood against the wooden pier at this end of the bridge. It is now dry and would burn like tow."

The lady had now brought the water, which the soldier drank. He thanked her ceremoniously, bowed to her husband and rode away. An hour later, after nightfall, he repassed the plantation, going northward in the direction from which he had come. He was a Federal scout.

III

As Peyton Farquhar fell straight downward through the bridge he lost consciousness and was as one already dead. From this state he was awakened—ages later, it seemed to him—by the pain of a sharp pressure upon his throat, followed by a sense of suffocation. Keen, poignant agonies seemed to shoot from his neck downward through every fibre of his body and limbs. These pains appeared to flash along well-defined lines of ramification and to beat with an inconceivably rapid periodicity. They seemed like streams of pulsating fire heating him to an intolerable temperature. As to his head, he was conscious of nothing but a feeling of fulness—of congestion. These sensations were unaccompanied by thought. The intellectual part of his nature was already effaced; he had power only to feel, and feeling was torment. He was conscious of motion. Encompassed in a luminous cloud, of which he was now merely the fiery heart, without material substance, he swung through unthinkable arcs of oscillation, like a vast pendulum. Then all at once, with terrible suddenness, the light about him shot upward with the noise of a loud plash; a frightful roaring was in his ears, and all was cold and dark. The power of thought was restored; he knew that the rope had broken and he had fallen into the stream. There was no additional strangulation; the noose about his neck was already suffocating him and kept the water from his lungs. To die of hanging at the bottom of a river!—the idea seemed to him ludicrous. He opened his eyes in the darkness and saw above him a gleam of light, but how distant, how inaccessible! He was still sinking, for the light became fainter and fainter until it was a mere glimmer. Then it began to grow and brighten, and he knew that he was rising toward the surface—knew it with reluctance, for he was now very comfortable. "To be hanged and drowned," he thought, "that is not so bad; but I do not wish to be shot. No; I will not be shot; that is not fair."

He was not conscious of an effort, but a sharp pain in his wrist apprised him that he was trying to free his hands. He gave the struggle his attention, as an idler might observe the feat of a juggler, without interest in the outcome. What splendid effort!—what magnificent, what superhuman strength! Ah, that was a fine endeavour! Bravo! The cord fell away; his arms parted and floated upward, the hands dimly seen on each side in the growing light. He watched them with a new interest as first one and then the other pounced upon the noose at his neck. They tore it away and thrust it fiercely aside, its undulations resembling those of a water-snake. "Put it back, put it back!" He thought he shouted these words to his hands, for the undoing of the noose had been succeeded by the direst pang that he had yet experienced. His neck ached horribly; his brain was on fire; his heart, which had been fluttering faintly, gave a great leap, trying to force itself out at his mouth. His whole body was racked and wrenched with an insupportable anguish! But his disobedient hands gave no heed to the command. They beat the water vigorously with quick, downward strokes, forcing him to the surface. He felt his head emerge; his eyes were blinded by the sunlight; his chest expanded convulsively, and with a supreme and crowning agony his lungs engulfed a great draught of air, which instantly he expelled in a shriek!

He was now in full possession of his physical senses. They were, indeed, preternaturally keen and alert. Something in the awful disturbance of his organic system had so exalted and refined them that they made record of things never before perceived. He felt the ripples upon his face and heard their separate sounds as they struck. He looked at the forest on the bank of the stream, saw the individual trees, the leaves and the veining of each leaf—saw the very insects upon them: the locusts, the brilliant-bodied flies, the grey spiders stretching their webs from twig to twig. He noted the prismatic colours in all the dewdrops upon a million blades of grass. The humming of the gnats that danced above the eddies of the stream, the beating of the dragon-flies' wings, the strokes of the water-spiders' legs, like oars which had lifted their boat—all these made audible music. A fish slid along beneath his eyes and he heard the rush of its body parting the water.

He had come to the surface facing down the stream; in a moment the visible world seemed to wheel slowly round, himself the pivotal point, and he saw the bridge, the fort, the soldiers upon the bridge, the captain, the sergeant, the two privates, his executioners. They were in silhouette against the blue sky. They shouted and gesticulated, pointing at him. The captain had drawn his pistol, but did not fire; the others were unarmed. Their movements were grotesque and horrible, their forms gigantic.

Suddenly he heard a sharp report and something struck the water smartly within a few inches of his head, spattering his face with spray. He heard a second report, and saw one of the sentinels with his rifle at his shoulder, a light cloud of blue smoke rising from the muzzle. The man in the water saw the eye of the man on the bridge gazing into his own through the sights of the rifle. He observed that it was a grey eye and remembered having read that grey eyes were keenest, and that all famous marksmen had them. Nevertheless, this one had missed.

A counter-swirl had caught Farquhar and turned him half round; he was again looking into the forest on the bank opposite the fort. The sound of a clear, high voice in a monotonous singsong now rang out behind him and came across the water with a distinctness that pierced and subdued all other sounds, even the beating of the ripples in his ears. Although no soldier, he had frequented camps enough to know the dread significance of that deliberate, drawling, aspirated chant; the lieutenant on shore was taking a part in the morning's work. How coldly and pitilessly—with what an even, calm intonation, presaging, and enforcing tranquillity in the men—with what accurately measured intervals fell those cruel words:

"Attention, company!... Shoulder arms!... Ready!... Aim!... Fire!"

Farquhar dived—dived as deeply as he could. The water roared in his ears like the voice of Niagara, yet he heard the dulled thunder of the volley and, rising again toward the surface, met shining bits of metal, singularly flattened, oscillating slowly downward. Some of them touched him on the face and hands, then fell away, continuing their descent. One lodged between his collar and neck; it was uncomfortably warm and he snatched it out.

As he rose to the surface, gasping for breath, he saw that he had been a long time under water; he was perceptibly farther down stream—nearer to safety. The soldiers had almost finished reloading; the metal ramrods flashed all at once in the sunshine as they were drawn from the barrels, turned in the air, and thrust into their sockets. The two sentinels fired again, independently and ineffectually.

The hunted man saw all this over his shoulder; he was now swimming vigorously with the current. His brain was as energetic as his arms and legs; he thought with the rapidity of lightning.

"The officer," he reasoned, "will not make that martinet's error a second time. It is as easy to dodge a volley as a single shot. He has probably already given the command to fire at will. God help me, I cannot dodge them all!"

An appalling plash within two yards of him was followed by a loud, rushing sound, *diminuendo*, which seemed to travel back through the air to the fort and died in an explosion which stirred the very river to its deeps! A rising sheet of water curved over him, fell down upon him, blinded him, strangled him! The cannon had taken a hand in the game. As he shook his head free from the commotion of the smitten water he heard the deflected shot humming through the air ahead, and in an instant it was cracking and smashing the branches in the forest beyond.

"They will not do that again," he thought; "the next time they will use a charge of grape. I must keep my eye upon the gun; the smoke will apprise me—the report arrives too late; it lags behind the missile. That is a good gun."

Suddenly he felt himself whirled round and round—spinning like a top. The water, the banks, the forests, the now distant bridge, fort and men—all were commingled and blurred. Objects were represented by their colours only; circular horizontal streaks of colour—that was all he saw. He had been caught in a vortex and was being whirled on with a velocity of advance and gyration that made him giddy and sick. In a few moments he was flung upon the gravel at the foot of the left bank of the stream—the southern bank—and behind a projecting point which concealed him from his enemies. The sudden arrest of his motion, the abrasion of one of his hands on the gravel, restored him, and he wept with delight. He dug his fingers into the sand, threw it over himself in handfuls and audibly blessed it. It looked like diamonds, rubies, emeralds; he could think of nothing beautiful which it did not resemble. The trees upon the bank were giant garden plants; he noted a definite order in their arrangement, inhaled the fragrance of their blooms. A strange, roseate light shone through the spaces among their trunks and the wind made in their branches the music of æolian harps. He had no wish to perfect his escape—was content to remain in that enchanting spot until retaken.

A whiz and rattle of grapeshot among the branches high above his head roused him from his dream. The baffled cannoneer had fired him a random farewell. He sprang to his feet, rushed up the sloping bank, and plunged into the forest.

All that day he travelled, laying his course by the rounding sun. The forest seemed interminable; nowhere did he discover a break in it, not even a woodman's road. He had not known that he lived in so wild a region. There was something uncanny in the revelation.

By nightfall he was fatigued, footsore, famishing. The thought of his wife and children urged him on. At last he found a road which led him in what he knew to be the right direction. It was as wide and straight as a city street, yet it seemed untravelled. No fields bordered it, no dwelling anywhere. Not so much as the barking of a dog suggested human habitation. The black bodies of the trees formed a straight wall on both sides, terminating on the horizon in a point, like a diagram in a lesson in perspective. Overhead, as he looked up through this rift in the wood, shone great golden stars looking unfamiliar and grouped in strange constellations. He was sure they were arranged in some order which had a secret and malign significance. The wood on either side was full of singular noises, among which—once, twice, and again—he distinctly heard whispers in an unknown tongue.

His neck was in pain and lifting his hand to it he found it horribly swollen. He knew that it had a circle of black where the rope had bruised it. His eyes felt congested; he could no longer close them. His tongue was swollen with thirst; he relieved its fever by thrusting it forward from between his teeth into the cold air. How softly the turf had carpeted the untravelled avenue—he could no longer feel the roadway beneath his feet!

Doubtless, despite his suffering, he had fallen asleep while walking, for now he sees another scene—perhaps he has merely recovered from a delirium. He stands at the gate of his own home. All is as he left it, and all bright and beautiful in the morning sunshine. He must have travelled the entire night. As he pushes open the gate and passes up the wide white walk, he sees a flutter of female garments; his wife, looking fresh and cool and sweet, steps down from the veranda to meet him. At the bottom of the steps she stands waiting, with a smile of ineffable joy, an attitude of matchless grace and dignity. Ah, how beautiful she is! He springs forward with extended arms. As he is about to clasp her he feels a stunning blow upon the back of the neck; a blinding white light blazes all about him with a sound like the shock of a cannon—then all is darkness and silence!

Peyton Farquhar was dead; his body, with a broken neck, swung gently from side to side beneath the timbers of the Owl Creek bridge.

MRS. DENNISON'S HEAD

hile I was employed in the Bank of Loan and Discount (said Mr. Applegarth, smiling the smile with which he always prefaced a nice old story), there was another clerk there, named Dennison—a quiet, reticent fellow, the very soul of truth, and a great favourite with us all. He always wore crape on his hat, and once when asked for whom he was in mourning he replied his wife, and seemed much affected. We all expressed our sympathy as delicately as possible, and no more was said upon the subject. Some weeks after this he seemed to have arrived at that stage of tempered grief at which it becomes a relief to give sorrow words—to speak of the departed one to sympathizing friends; for one day he voluntarily began talking of his bereavement, and of the terrible calamity by which his wife had been deprived of her head!

This sharpened our curiosity to the keenest edge; but of course we controlled it, hoping he would volunteer some further information with regard to so singular a misfortune; but when day after day went by and he did not allude to the matter, we got worked up into a fever of excitement about it. One evening after Dennison had gone, we held a kind of political meeting about it, at which all possible and impossible methods of decapitation were suggested as the ones to which Mrs. D. probably owed her extraordinary demise. I am sorry to add that we so far forgot the grave character of the event as to lay small wagers that it was done this way or that way; that it was accidental or premeditated; that she had had a hand in it herself or that it was wrought by circumstances beyond her control. All was mere conjecture, however; but from that time Dennison, as the custodian of a secret upon which we had staked our cash, was an object of more than usual interest. It wasn't entirely that, either; aside from our paltry wagers, we felt a consuming curiosity to know the truth for its own sake. Each set himself to work to elicit the dread secret in some way; and the misdirected ingenuity we developed was wonderful. All sorts of pious devices were resorted to to entice poor Dennison into clearing up the mystery. By a thousand indirect methods we sought to entrap him into divulging all. History, fiction, poesy—all were laid under contribution, and from Goliah down, through Charles I., to Sam Spigger, a local celebrity who got his head entangled in mill machinery, every one who had ever mourned the loss of a head received his due share of attention during office hours. The regularity with which we introduced, and the pertinacity with which we stuck to, this one topic came near getting us all discharged; for one day the cashier came out of his private office and intimated that if we valued our situations the subject of hanging would afford us the means of retaining them. He added that he always selected his subordinates with an eye to their conversational abilities, but variety of subject was as desirable, at times, as exhaustive treatment.

During all this discussion Dennison, albeit he had evinced from the first a singular interest in the theme, and shirked not his fair share of the conversation, never once seemed to understand that it had any reference to himself. His frank truthful nature was quite unable to detect the personal significance of the subject. It was plain that nothing short of a definite inquiry would elicit the information we were dying to obtain; and at a "caucus," one evening, we drew lots to determine who should openly propound it. The choice fell upon me.

Next morning we were at the bank somewhat earlier than usual, waiting impatiently for Dennison and the time to open the doors: they always arrived together. When Dennison stepped into the room, bowing in his engaging manner to each clerk as he passed to his own desk, I confronted him, shaking him warmly by the hand. At that moment all the others fell to writing and figuring with unusual avidity, as if thinking of anything under the sun except Dennison's wife's head.

"Oh, Dennison," I began, as carelessly as I could manage it; "speaking of decapitation reminds me of something I would like to ask you. I have intended asking it several times, but it has always slipped my memory. Of course you will pardon me if it is not a fair question."

As if by magic, the scratching of pens died away, leaving a dead silence which quite disconcerted me; but I blundered on:

"I heard the other day—that is, you said—or it was in the newspapers—or somewhere—something about your poor wife, you understand—about her losing her head. Would you mind telling me how such a distressing accident—if it was an accident—occurred?"

When I had finished, Dennison walked straight past me as if he didn't see me, went round the counter to his stool, and perched himself gravely on the top of it, facing the other clerks. Then he began speaking, calmly, and without apparent emotion:

"Gentlemen, I have long desired to speak of this thing, but you gave me no encouragement, and I naturally supposed you were indifferent. I now thank you all for the friendly interest you take in my affairs. I will satisfy your curiosity upon this point at once, if you will promise never hereafter to allude to the matter, and to ask not a single question now."

We all promised upon our sacred honour, and collected about him with the utmost eagerness. He bent his head a moment, then raised it, quietly saying:

"My poor wife's head was bitten off!"

"By what?" we all exclaimed eagerly, with suspended breath.

He gave us a look full of reproach, turned to his desk, and went at his work.

We went at ours.

A JUG OF SIRUP

his narrative begins with the death of its hero. Silas Deemer died on the 16th day of July, 1863, and two days later his remains were buried. As he had been personally known to every man, woman and well-grown child in the village, the funeral, as the local newspaper phrased it, "was largely attended." In accordance with a custom of the time and place, the coffin was opened at the graveside and the entire assembly of friends and neighbours filed past, taking a last look at the face of the dead. And then, before the eyes of all, Silas Deemer was put into the ground. Some of the eyes were a trifle dim, but in a general way it may be said that at that interment there was lack of neither observance nor observation; Silas was indubitably dead, and none could have pointed out any ritual delinquency that would have justified him in coming back from the grave. Yet if human testimony is good for anything (and certainly it once put an end to witchcraft in and about Salem) he came back.

I forgot to state that the death and burial of Silas Deemer occurred in the little village of Hillbrook, where he had lived for thirty-one years. He had been what is known in some parts of the Union (which is admittedly a free country) as a "merchant"; that is to say, he kept a retail shop for the sale of such things as are commonly sold in shops of that character. His honesty had never been questioned, so far as is known, and he was held in high esteem by all. The only thing that could be urged against him by the most censorious was a too close attention to business. It was not urged against him, though many another, who manifested it in no greater degree, was less leniently judged. The business to which Silas was devoted was mostly his own—that, possibly, may have made a difference.

At the time of Deemer's death nobody could recollect a single day, Sundays excepted, that he had not passed in his "store," since he had opened it more than a quarter-century before. His health having been perfect during all that time, he had been unable to discern any validity in whatever may or might have been urged to lure him astray from his counter and it is related that once when he was summoned to the county seat as a witness in an important law case and did not attend, the lawyer who had the hardihood to move that he be "admonished" was solemnly informed that the Court regarded the proposal with "surprise." Judicial surprise being an emotion that attorneys are not commonly ambitious to arouse, the motion was hastily withdrawn and an agreement with the other side effected as to what Mr. Deemer would have said if he had been there—the other side pushing its advantage to the extreme and making the supposititious testimony distinctly damaging to the interests of its proponents. In brief, it was the general feeling in all that region that Silas Deemer was the one immobile verity of Hillbrook, and that his translation in space would precipitate some dismal public ill or strenuous calamity.

Mrs. Deemer and two grown daughters occupied the upper rooms of the building, but Silas had never been known to sleep elsewhere than on a cot behind the counter of the store. And there, quite by accident, he was found one night, dying, and passed away just before the time for taking down the shutters. Though speechless, he appeared conscious, and it was thought by those who knew him best that if the end had unfortunately been delayed beyond the usual hour for opening the store the effect upon him would have been deplorable.

Such had been Silas Deemer—such the fixity and invariety of his life and habit, that the village humorist (who had once attended college) was moved to bestow upon him the sobriquet of "Old Ibidem," and, in the first issue of the local newspaper after the death, to explain without offence that Silas had taken "a day off." It was more than a day, but from the record it appears that well within a month Mr. Deemer made it plain that he had not the leisure to be dead.

One of Hillbrook's most respected citizens was Alvan Creede, a banker. He lived in the finest house in town, kept a carriage and was a most estimable man variously. He knew something of the advantages of travel, too, having been frequently in Boston, and once, it was thought, in New York, though he modestly disclaimed that glittering distinction. The matter is mentioned here merely as a contribution to an understanding of Mr. Creede's worth, for either way it is creditable to him—to his intelligence if he had put himself, even temporarily, into contact with metropolitan culture; to his candour if he had not.

One pleasant summer evening at about the hour of ten Mr. Creede, entering at his garden gate, passed up the gravel walk, which looked very white in the moonlight, mounted the stone steps of his fine house and pausing a moment inserted his latch-key in the door. As he pushed this open he met his wife, who was crossing the passage from the parlour to the library. She greeted him pleasantly and pulling the door further back held it for him to enter. Instead he turned and, looking about his feet in front of the threshold, uttered an exclamation of surprise.

"Why!—what the devil," he said, "has become of that jug?"

"What jug, Alvan?" his wife inquired, not very sympathetically.

"A jug of maple sirup—I brought it along from the store and set it down here to open the door. What the—"

"There, there, Alvan, please don't swear again," said the lady, interrupting. Hillbrook, by the way, is not the only place in Christendom where a vestigial polytheism forbids the taking in vain of the Evil One's name.

The jug of maple sirup which the easy ways of village life had permitted Hillbrook's foremost citizen to carry home from the store was not there.

"Are you quite sure, Alvan?"

"My dear, do you suppose a man does not know when he is carrying a jug? I bought that sirup at Deemer's as I was passing. Deemer himself drew it and lent me the jug, and I—"

The sentence remains to this day unfinished. Mr. Creede staggered into the house, entered the parlour and dropped into an armchair, trembling in every limb. He had suddenly remembered that Silas Deemer was three weeks dead.

Mrs. Creede stood by her husband, regarding him with surprise and anxiety.

"For Heaven's sake," she said, "what ails you?"

Mr. Creede's ailment having no obvious relation to the interests of the better land he did not apparently deem it necessary to expound it on that demand; he said nothing—merely stared. There were long moments of silence broken by nothing but the measured ticking of the clock, which seemed somewhat slower than usual, as if it were civilly granting them an extension of time in which to recover their wits.

"Jane, I have gone mad—that is it." He spoke thickly and hurriedly. "You should have told me; you must have observed my symptoms before they became so pronounced that I have observed them myself. I thought I was passing Deemer's store; it was open and lit up—that is what I thought; of course it is never open now. Silas Deemer stood at his desk behind the counter. My God, Jane, I saw him as distinctly as I see you. Remembering that you had said you wanted some maple sirup, I went in and bought some—that is all—I bought two quarts of maple sirup from Silas Deemer, who is dead and underground, but nevertheless drew that sirup from a cask and handed it to me in a jug. He talked with me, too, rather gravely, I remember, even more so than was his way, but not a word of what he said can I now recall. But I saw him—good Lord, I saw and talked with him—and he is dead! So I thought, but I'm mad, Jane, I'm as crazy as a beetle; and you have kept it from me."

This monologue gave the woman time to collect what faculties she had.

"Alvan," she said, "you have given no evidence of insanity, believe me. This was undoubtedly an illusion—how should it be anything else? That would be too terrible! But there is no insanity; you are working too hard at the bank. You should not have attended the meeting of directors this evening; any one could see that you were ill; I knew something would occur."

It may have seemed to him that the prophecy had lagged a bit, awaiting the event, but he said nothing of that, being concerned with his own condition. He was calm now, and could think coherently.

"Doubtless the phenomenon was subjective," he said, with a somewhat ludicrous transition to the slang of science. "Granting the possibility of spiritual apparition and even materialization, yet the apparition and materialization of a half-gallon brown clay jug—a piece of coarse, heavy pottery evolved from nothing—that is hardly thinkable."

As he finished speaking, a child ran into the room—his little daughter. She was clad in a bedgown. Hastening to her father she threw her arms about his neck, saying: "You naughty papa, you forgot to come in and kiss me. We heard you open the gate and got up and looked out. And, papa dear, Eddy says mayn't he have the little jug when it is empty?"

As the full import of that revelation imparted itself to Alvan Creede's understanding he visibly shuddered. For the child could not have heard a word of the conversation.

The estate of Silas Deemer being in the hands of an administrator who had thought it best to dispose of the "business" the store had been closed ever since the owner's death, the goods having been removed by another "merchant" who had purchased them *en bloc*. The rooms above were vacant as well, for the widow and daughters had gone to another town.

On the evening immediately after Alvan Creede's adventure (which had somehow "got out") a crowd of men, women and children thronged the sidewalk opposite the store. That the place was haunted by the spirit of the late Silas Deemer was now well known to every resident of Hillbrook, though many affected disbelief. Of these the hardiest, and in a general way the youngest, threw stones against the front of the building, the only part accessible, but carefully missed the unshuttered windows. Incredulity had not grown to malice. A few venturesome souls crossed the street and rattled the door in its frame; struck matches and held them near the window; attempted to view the black interior. Some of the spectators invited attention to their wit by shouting and groaning and challenging the ghost to a footrace.

After a considerable time had elapsed without any manifestation, and many of the crowd had gone away, all those remaining began to observe that the interior of the store was suffused with a dim, yellow light. At this all demonstrations ceased; the intrepid souls about the door and windows fell back to the opposite side of the street and were merged in the crowd; the small boys ceased throwing stones. Nobody spoke above his breath; all whispered excitedly and pointed to the now steadily growing light. How long a time had passed since the first faint glow had been observed none could have guessed, but eventually the illumination was bright enough to reveal the whole interior of the store; and there, standing at his desk behind the counter, Silas Deemer was distinctly visible!

The effect upon the crowd was marvellous. It began rapidly to melt away at both flanks, as the timid left the place. Many ran as fast as their legs would let them; others moved off with greater dignity, turning occasionally to look backward over the shoulder. At last a score or more, mostly men, remained where they were, speechless, staring, excited. The apparition inside gave them no attention; it was apparently occupied with a book of accounts.

Presently three men left the crowd on the sidewalk as if by a common impulse and crossed the street. One of them, a heavy man, was about to set his shoulder against the door when it opened, apparently without human agency, and the courageous investigators passed in. No sooner had they crossed the threshold than they were seen by the awed observers outside to be acting in the most unaccountable way. They thrust out their hands before them, pursued devious courses, came into violent collision with the counter, with boxes and barrels on the floor, and with one another. They turned awkwardly hither and thither and seemed trying to escape, but unable to retrace their steps. Their voices were heard in exclamations and curses. But in no way did the apparition of Silas Deemer manifest an interest in what was going on.

By what impulse the crowd was moved none ever recollected, but the entire mass—men, women, children, dogs—made a simultaneous and tumultuous rush for the entrance. They congested the doorway, pushing for precedence—resolving themselves at length into a line and moving up step by step. By some subtle spiritual or physical alchemy observation had been transmuted into action—the sightseers had become participants in the spectacle—the audience had usurped the stage.

To the only spectator remaining on the other side of the street—Alvan Creede, the banker—the interior of the store with its inpouring crowd continued in full illumination; all the strange things going on there were clearly visible. To those inside all was black darkness. It was as if each person as he was thrust in at the door had been stricken blind, and was maddened by the mischance. They groped with aimless imprecision, tried to force their way out against the current, pushed and elbowed, struck at random, fell and were trampled, rose and trampled in their turn. They seized one another by the garments, the hair, the beard—fought like animals, cursed, shouted, called one another opprobrious and obscene names. When, finally, Alvan Creede had seen the last person of the line pass into that awful tumult the light that had illuminated it was suddenly quenched and all was as black to him as to those within. He turned away and left the place.

In the early morning a curious crowd had gathered about "Deemer's." It was composed partly of those who had run away the night before, but now had the courage of sunshine, partly of honest folk going to their daily toil. The door of the store stood open; the place was vacant, but on the walls, the floor, the furniture, were shreds of clothing and tangles of hair. Hillbrook militant had managed somehow to pull itself out and had gone home to medicine its hurts and swear that it had been all night in bed. On the dusty desk, behind the counter, was the sales-book. The entries in it, in Deemer's handwriting, had ceased on the 16th day of July, the last of his life. There was no record of a later sale to Alvan Creede.

That is the entire story—except that men's passions having subsided and reason having resumed its immemorial sway, it was confessed in Hillbrook that, considering the harmless and honourable character of his first commercial transaction under the new conditions, Silas Deemer, deceased, might properly have been suffered to resume business at the old stand without mobbing. In that judgment the local historian from whose unpublished work these facts are compiled had the thoughtful-ness to signify his concurrence.

AN INHABITANT
OF CARCOSA

or there be divers sorts of death—some wherein the body remaineth; and in some it vanisheth quite away with the spirit. This commonly occurreth only in solitude (such is God's will) and, none seeing the end, we say the man is lost, or gone on a long journey—which indeed he hath; but sometimes it hath happened in sight of many, as abundant testimony showeth. In one kind of death the spirit also dieth, and this it hath been known to do while yet the body was in vigour for many years. Sometimes, as is veritably attested, it dieth with the body, but after a season is raised up again in that place where the body did decay.

Pondering these words of Hali (whom God rest) and questioning their full meaning, as one who, having an intimation, yet doubts if there be not something behind, other than that which he has discerned, I noted not whither I had strayed until a sudden chill wind striking my face revived in me a sense of my surroundings. I observed with astonishment that everything seemed unfamiliar. On every side of me stretched a bleak and desolate expanse of plain, covered with a tall overgrowth of sere grass, which rustled and whistled in the autumn wind with Heaven knows what mysterious and disquieting suggestion. Protruded at long intervals above it, stood strangely shaped and sombre-coloured rocks, which seemed to have an understanding with one another and to exchange looks of uncomfortable significance, as if they had reared their heads to watch the issue of some foreseen event. A few blasted trees here and there appeared as leaders in this malevolent conspiracy of silent expectation.

The day, I thought, must be far advanced, though the sun was invisible; and although sensible that the air was raw and chill my consciousness of that fact was rather mental than physical—I had no feeling of discomfort. Over all the dismal landscape a canopy of low, lead-coloured clouds hung like a visible curse. In all this there was a menace and a portent—a hint of evil, an intimation of doom. Bird, beast, or insect there was none. The wind sighed in the bare branches of the dead trees and the grey grass bent to whisper its dread secret to the earth; but no other sound nor motion broke the awful repose of that dismal place.

I observed in the herbage a number of weather-worn stones, evidently shaped with tools. They were broken, covered with moss and half sunken in the earth. Some lay prostrate, some leaned at various angles, none was vertical. They were obviously headstones of graves, though the graves themselves no longer existed as either mounds or depressions; the years had levelled all. Scattered here and there, more massive blocks showed where some pompous tomb or ambitious monument had once flung its feeble defiance at oblivion. So old seemed these relics, these vestiges of vanity and memorials of affection and piety, so battered and worn and stained—so neglected, deserted, forgotten the place, that I could not help thinking myself the discoverer of the burial-ground of a prehistoric race of men whose very name was long extinct.

Filled with these reflections, I was for some time heedless of the sequence of my own experiences, but soon I thought, "How came I hither?" A moment's reflection seemed to make this all clear and explain at the same time, though in a disquieting way, the singular character with which my fancy had invested all that I saw or heard. I was ill. I remembered now that I had been prostrated by a sudden fever, and that my family had told me that in my periods of delirium I had constantly cried out for liberty and air, and had been held in bed to prevent my escape out-of-doors. Now I had eluded the vigilance of my attendants and had wandered hither to—to where? I could not conjecture. Clearly I was at a considerable distance from the city where I dwelt—the ancient and famous city of Carcosa.

No signs of human life were anywhere visible nor audible; no rising smoke, no watch-dog's bark, no lowing of cattle, no shouts of children at play—nothing but that dismal burial-place, with its air of mystery and dread, due to my own disordered brain. Was I not becoming again delirious, there beyond human aid? Was it not indeed *all* an illusion of my madness? I called aloud the names of my wives and sons, reached out my hands in search of theirs, even as I walked among the crumbling stones and in the withered grass.

A noise behind me caused me to turn about. A wild animal—a lynx—was approaching. The thought came to me: If I break down here in the desert—if the fever return and I fail, this beast will be at my throat. I sprang toward it, shouting. It trotted tranquilly by within a hand's-breadth of me and disappeared behind a rock.

A moment later a man's head appeared to rise out of the ground a short distance away. He was ascending the farther slope of a low hill whose crest was hardly to be distinguished from the general level. His whole figure soon came into view against the background of grey cloud. He was half naked, half clad in skins. His hair was unkempt, his beard long and ragged. In one hand he carried a bow and arrow; the other held a blazing torch with a long trail of black smoke. He walked slowly and with caution, as if he feared falling into some open grave concealed by the tall grass. This strange apparition surprised but did not alarm, and taking such a course as to intercept him I met him almost face to face, accosting him with the familiar salutation, "God keep you."

He gave no heed, nor did he arrest his pace.

"Good stranger," I continued, "I am ill and lost. Direct me, I beseech you, to Carcosa."

The man broke into a barbarous chant in an unknown tongue, passing on and away.

An owl on the branch of a decayed tree hooted dismally and was answered by another in the distance. Looking upward, I saw through a sudden rift in the clouds Aldebaran and the Hyades! In all this there was a hint of night—the lynx, the man with the torch, the owl. Yet I saw—I saw even the stars in absence of the darkness. I saw, but was apparently not seen nor heard. Under what awful spell did I exist?

I seated myself at the root of a great tree, seriously to consider what it were best to go. That I was mad I could no longer doubt, yet recognized a ground of doubt in the conviction. Of fever I had no trace. I had, withal, a sense of exhilaration and vigour altogether unknown to me—a feeling of mental and physical exaltation. My senses seemed all alert; I could feel the air as a ponderous substance; I could hear the silence.

A great root of the giant tree against whose trunk I leaned as I sat held enclosed in its grasp a slab of stone, a part of which protruded into a recess formed by another root. The stone was thus partly protected from the weather, though greatly decomposed. Its edges were worn round, its corners eaten away, its surface deeply furrowed and scaled. Glittering particles of mica were visible in the earth about it—vestiges of its decomposition. This stone had apparently marked the grave out of which the tree had sprung ages ago. The tree's exacting roots had robbed the grave and made the stone a prisoner.

A sudden wind pushed some dry leaves and twigs from the uppermost face of the stone; I saw the low-relief letters of an inscription and bent to read it. God in heaven! *my* name in full!—the date of *my* birth!—the date of *my* death!

A level shaft of light illuminated the whole side of the tree as I sprang to my feet in terror. The sun was rising in the rosy east. I stood between the tree and his broad red disk—no shadow darkened the trunk!

A chorus of howling wolves saluted the dawn. I saw them sitting on their haunches, singly and in groups, on the summits of irregular mounds and tumuli filling a half of my desert prospect and extending to the horizon. And then I knew that these were ruins of the ancient and famous city of Carcosa.

Such are the facts imparted to the medium Bayrolles by the spirit Hoseib Alar Robardin.

A WATCHER BY THE DEAD

n an upper room of an unoccupied dwelling in the part of San Francisco known as North Beach lay the body of a man, under a sheet. The hour was near nine in the evening; the room was dimly lighted by a single candle. Although the weather was warm, the two windows, contrary to the custom which gives the dead plenty of air, were closed and the blinds drawn down. The furniture of the room consisted of but three pieces—an armchair, a small reading-stand supporting the candle, and a long kitchen table, supporting the body of the man. All these, as also the corpse, seemed to have been recently brought in, for an observer, had there been one, would have seen that all were free from dust, whereas everything else in the room was pretty thickly coated with it, and there were cobwebs in the angles of the walls.

Under the sheet the outlines of the body could be traced, even the features, these having that unnaturally sharp definition which seems to belong to faces of the dead, but is really characteristic of those only that have been wasted by disease. From the silence of the room one would rightly have inferred that it was not in the front of the house, facing a street. It really faced nothing but a high breast of rock, the rear of the building being set into a hill.

As a neighbouring church clock was striking nine with an indolence which seemed to imply such an indifference to the flight of time that one could hardly help wondering why it took the trouble to strike at all, the single door of the room was opened and a man entered, advancing toward the body. As he did so the door closed, apparently of its own volition; there was a grating, as of a key turned with difficulty, and the snap of the lock bolt as it shot into its socket. A sound of retiring footsteps in the passage outside ensued, and the man was to all appearance a prisoner. Advancing to the table, he stood a moment looking down at the body; then with a slight shrug of the shoulders walked over to one of the windows and hoisted the blind. The darkness outside was absolute, the panes were covered with dust, but by wiping this away he could see that the window was fortified with strong iron bars crossing it within a few inches of the glass and imbedded in the masonry on each side. He examined the other window. It was the same. He manifested no great curiosity in the matter, did not even so much as raise the sash. If he was a prisoner he was apparently a tractable one. Having completed his examination of the room, he seated himself in the armchair, took a book from his pocket, drew the stand with its candle alongside and began to read.

The man was young—not more than thirty—dark in complexion, smooth-shaven, with brown hair. His face was thin and high-nosed, with a broad forehead and a "firmness" of the chin and jaw which is said by those having it to denote resolution. The eyes were grey and steadfast, not moving except with definitive purpose. They were now for the greater part of the time fixed upon his book, but he occasionally withdrew them and turned them to the body on the table, not, apparently, from any dismal fascination which under such circumstances it might be supposed to exercise upon even a courageous person, nor with a conscious rebellion against the contrary influence which might dominate a timid one. He looked at it as if in his reading he had come upon something recalling him to a sense of his surroundings. Clearly this watcher by the dead was discharging his trust with intelligence and composure, as became him.

After reading for perhaps a half-hour he seemed to come to the end of a chapter and quietly laid away the book. He then rose and taking the reading-stand from the floor carried it into a corner of the room near one of the windows, lifted the candle from it and returned to the empty fireplace before which he had been sitting.

A moment later he walked over to the body on the table, lifted the sheet and turned it back from the head, exposing a mass of dark hair and a thin face-cloth, beneath which the features showed with even sharper definition than before. Shading his eyes by interposing his free hand between them and the candle, he stood looking at his motionless companion with a serious and tranquil regard. Satisfied with his inspection, he pulled the sheet over the face again and returning to the chair, took some matches off the candlestick, put them in the side pocket of his sack-coat and sat down. He then lifted the candle from its socket and looked at it critically, as if calculating how long it would last. It was barely two inches long; in another hour he would be in darkness. He replaced it in the candlestick and blew it out.

II

In a physician's office in Kearny Street three men sat about a table, drinking punch and smoking. It was late in the evening, almost midnight, indeed, and there had been no lack of punch. The gravest of the three, Dr. Helberson, was the host—it was in his rooms they sat. He was about thirty years of age; the others were even younger; all were physicians.

"The superstitious awe with which the living regard the dead," said Dr. Helberson, "is hereditary and incurable. One needs no more be ashamed of it than of the fact that he inherits, for example, an incapacity for mathematics, or a tendency to lie."

The others laughed. "Oughtn't a man to be ashamed to lie?" asked the youngest of the three, who was in fact a medical student not yet graduated.

"My dear Harper, I said nothing about that. The tendency to lie is one thing; lying is another."

"But do you think," said the third man, "that this superstitious feeling, this fear of the dead, reasonless as we know it to be, is universal? I am myself not conscious of it."

"Oh, but it is 'in your system' for all that," replied Helberson; "it needs only the right conditions—what Shakespeare calls the 'confederate season'—to manifest itself in some very disagreeable way that will open your eyes. Physicians and soldiers are of course more nearly free from it than others."

"Physicians and soldiers!—why don't you add hangmen and headsmen? Let us have in all the assassin classes."

"No, my dear Mancher; the juries will not let the public

executioners acquire sufficient familiarity with death to be altogether unmoved by it."

Young Harper, who had been helping himself to a fresh cigar at the sideboard, resumed his seat. "What would you consider conditions under which any man of woman born would become insupportably conscious of his share of our common weakness in this regard?" he asked, rather verbosely.

"Well, I should say that if a man were locked up all night with a corpse—alone—in a dark room—of a vacant house—with no bed covers to pull over his head—and lived through it without going altogether mad, he might justly boast himself not of woman born, nor yet, like Macduff, a product of Cæsarean section."

"I thought you never would finish piling up conditions," said Harper, "but I know a man who is neither a physician nor a soldier who will accept them all, for any stake you like to name."

"Who is he?"

"His name is Jarette—a stranger here; comes from my town in New York. I have no money to back him, but he will back himself with loads of it."

"How do you know that?"

"He would rather bet than eat. As for fear—I dare say he thinks it some cutaneous disorder, or possibly a particular kind of religious heresy."

"What does he look like?" Helberson was evidently becoming interested.

"Like Mancher, here—might be his twin brother."

"I accept the challenge," said Helberson, promptly.

"Awfully obliged to you for the compliment, I'm sure," drawled Mancher, who was growing sleepy. "Can't I get into this?"

"Not against me," Helberson said. "I don't want *your* money."

"All right," said Mancher; "I'll be the corpse."

The others laughed.

The outcome of this crazy conversation we have seen.

III

In extinguishing his meagre allowance of candle Mr. Jarette's object was to preserve it against some unforeseen need. He may have thought, too, or half thought, that the darkness would be no worse at one time than another, and if the situation became insupportable it would be better to have a means of relief, or even release. At any rate it was wise to have a little reserve of light, even if only to enable him to look at his watch.

No sooner had he blown out the candle and set it on the floor at his side than he settled himself comfortably in the armchair, leaned back and closed his eyes, hoping and expecting to sleep. In this he was disappointed; he had never in his life felt less sleepy, and in a few minutes he gave up the attempt. But what could he do? He could not go groping about in absolute darkness at the risk of bruising himself—at the risk, too, of blundering against the table and rudely disturbing the dead. We all recognize their right to lie at rest, with immunity from all that is harsh and violent. Jarette almost succeeded in making himself believe that considerations of this kind restrained him from risking the collision and fixed him to the chair.

While thinking of this matter he fancied that he heard a faint sound in the direction of the table—what kind of sound he could hardly have explained. He did not turn his head. Why should he—in the darkness? But he listened—why should he not? And listening he grew giddy and grasped the arms of the chair for support. There was a strange ringing in his ears; his head seemed bursting; his chest was oppressed by the constriction of his clothing. He wondered why it was so, and whether these were symptoms of fear. Then, with a long and strong expiration, his chest appeared to collapse, and with the great gasp with which he refilled his exhausted lungs the vertigo left him and he knew that so intently had he listened that he had held his breath almost to suffocation. The revelation was vexatious; he arose, pushed away the chair with his foot and strode to the centre of the room. But one does not stride far in darkness; he began to grope, and finding the wall followed it to an angle, turned, followed it past the two windows and there in another corner came into violent contact with the reading-stand, overturning it. It made a clatter that startled him. He was annoyed. "How the devil could I have forgotten where it was?" he muttered, and groped his way along the third wall to the fireplace. "I must put things to rights," said he, feeling the floor for the candle.

Having recovered that, he lighted it and instantly turned his eyes to the table, where, naturally, nothing had undergone any change. The reading-stand lay unobserved upon the floor: he had forgotten to "put it to rights." He looked all about the room, dispersing the deeper shadows by movements of the candle in his hand, and crossing over to the door tested it by turning and pulling the knob with all his strength. It did not yield and this seemed to afford him a certain satisfaction; indeed, he secured it more firmly by a bolt which he had not before observed. Returning to his chair, he looked at his watch; it was half-past nine. With a start of surprise he held the watch at his ear. It had not stopped. The candle was now visibly shorter. He again extinguished it, placing it on the floor at his side as before.

Mr. Jarette was not at his ease; he was distinctly dissatisfied with his surroundings, and with himself for being so. "What have I to fear?" he thought. "This is ridiculous and disgraceful; I will not be so great a fool." But courage does not come of saying, "I will be courageous," nor of recognizing its appropriateness to the occasion. The more Jarette condemned himself, the more reason he gave himself for condemnation; the greater the number of variations which he played upon the simple theme of the harmlessness of the dead, the more insupportable grew the discord of his emotions. "What!" he cried aloud in the anguish of his spirit, "what! shall I, who have not a shade of superstition in my nature—I, who have no belief in immortality—I, who know (and never more clearly than now) that the after-life is the dream of a desire—shall I lose at once my bet, my honour and my self-respect, perhaps my reason, because certain savage ancestors dwelling in caves and burrows conceived the monstrous notion that the dead walk by night?—that—" Distinctly, unmistakably, Mr. Jarette heard behind him a light, soft sound of footfalls, deliberate, regular, successively nearer!

IV

Just before daybreak the next morning Dr. Helberson and his young friend Harper were driving slowly through the streets of North Beach in the doctor's coupé.

"Have you still the confidence of youth in the courage or stolidity of your friend?" said the elder man. "Do you believe that I have lost this wager?"

"I *know* you have," replied the other, with enfeebling emphasis.

"Well, upon my soul, I hope so."

It was spoken earnestly, almost solemnly. There was a silence for a few moments.

"Harper," the doctor resumed, looking very serious in the shifting half-lights that entered the carriage as they passed the street lamps, "I don't feel altogether comfortable about this business. If your friend had not irritated me by the contemptuous manner in which he treated my doubt of his endurance—a purely physical quality—and by the cool incivility of his suggestion that the corpse be that of a physician, I should not have gone on with it. If anything should happen we are ruined, as I fear we deserve to be."

"What can happen? Even if the matter should be taking a serious turn, of which I am not at all afraid, Mancher has only to 'resurrect' himself and explain matters. With a genuine 'subject' from the dissecting-room, or one of your late patients, it might be different."

Dr. Mancher, then, had been as good as his promise; he was the "corpse."

Dr. Helberson was silent for a long time, as the carriage, at a snail's pace, crept along the same street it had travelled two or three times already. Presently he spoke: "Well, let us hope that Mancher, if he has had to rise from the dead, has been discreet about it. A mistake in that might make matters worse instead of better."

"Yes," said Harper, "Jarette would kill him. But, Doctor"—looking at his watch as the carriage passed a gas lamp—"it is nearly four o'clock at last."

A moment later the two had quitted the vehicle and were walking briskly toward the long-unoccupied house belonging to the doctor in which they had immured Mr. Jarette in accordance with the terms of the mad wager. As they neared it they met a man running. "Can you tell me," he cried, suddenly checking his speed, "where I can find a doctor?"

"What's the matter?" Helberson asked, non-committal.

"Go and see for yourself," said the man, resuming his running.

They hastened on. Arrived at the house, they saw several persons entering in haste and excitement. In some of the dwellings near by and across the way the chamber windows were thrown up, showing a protrusion of heads. All heads were asking questions, none heeding the questions of the others. A few of the windows with closed blinds were illuminated; the inmates of those rooms were dressing to come down. Exactly opposite the door of the house that they sought a street lamp threw a yellow, insufficient light upon the scene, seeming to say that it could disclose a good deal more if it wished. Harper paused at the door and laid a hand upon his companion's arm. "It is all up with us, Doctor," he said in extreme agitation, which contrasted strangely with his free-and-easy words; "the game has gone against us all. Let's not go in there; I'm for lying low."

"I'm a physician," said Dr. Helberson, calmly; "there may be need of one."

They mounted the doorsteps and were about to enter. The door was open; the street lamp opposite lighted the passage into which it opened. It was full of men. Some had ascended the stairs at the farther end, and, denied admittance above, waited for better fortune. All were talking, none listening. Suddenly, on the upper landing there was a great commotion; a man had sprung out of a door and was breaking away from those endeavouring to detain him. Down through the mass of affrighted idlers he came, pushing them aside, flattening them against the wall on one side, or compelling them to cling to the rail on the other, clutching them by the throat, striking them savagely, thrusting them back down the stairs and walking over the fallen. His clothing was in disorder, he was without a hat. His eyes, wild and restless, had in them something more terrifying than his apparently superhuman strength. His face, smooth-shaven, was bloodless, his hair frost-white.

As the crowd at the foot of the stairs, having more freedom, fell away to let him pass Harper sprang forward. "Jarette! Jarette!" he cried.

Dr. Helberson seized Harper by the collar and dragged him back. The man looked into their faces without seeming to see them and sprang through the door, down the steps, into the street, and away. A stout policeman, who had had inferior success in conquering his way down the stairway, followed a moment later and started in pursuit, all the heads in the windows—those of women and children now—screaming in guidance.

The stairway being now partly cleared, most of the crowd having rushed down to the street to observe the flight and pursuit, Dr. Helberson mounted to the landing, followed by Harper. At a door in the upper passage an officer denied them admittance. "We are physicians," said the doctor, and they passed in. The room was full of men, dimly seen, crowded about a table. The newcomers edged their way forward and looked over the shoulders of those in the front rank. Upon the table, the lower limbs covered with a sheet, lay the body of a man, brilliantly illuminated by the beam of a bull's-eye lantern held by a policeman standing at the feet. The others, excepting those near the head—the officer himself—all were in darkness. The face of the body showed yellow, repulsive, horrible! The eyes were partly open and upturned and the jaw fallen; traces of froth defiled the lips, the chin, the cheeks. A tall man, evidently a doctor, bent over the body with his hand thrust under the shirt front. He withdrew it and placed two fingers in the open mouth. "This man has been about six hours dead," said he. "It is a case for the coroner."

He drew a card from his pocket, handed it to the officer and made his way toward the door.

"Clear the room—out, all!" said the officer, sharply, and the body disappeared as if it had been snatched away, as shifting the lantern he flashed its beam of light here and there against the faces of the crowd. The effect was amazing! The men, blinded, confused, almost terrified, made a tumultuous rush for the door, pushing, crowding, and tumbling over one another as they fled, like the hosts of Night before the shafts of Apollo. Upon the struggling, trampling mass the officer poured his light without pity and without cessation. Caught in the current, Helberson and Harper were swept out of the room and cascaded down the stairs into the street.

"Good God, Doctor! did I not tell you that Jarette would kill him?" said Harper, as soon as they were clear of the crowd.

"I believe you did," replied the other, without apparent emotion.

They walked on in silence, block after block. Against the greying east the dwellings of the hill tribes showed in silhouette. The familiar milk wagon was already astir in the streets; the baker's man would soon come upon the scene; the newspaper carrier was abroad in the land.

"It strikes me, youngster," said Helberson, "that you and I have been having too much of the morning air lately. It is unwholesome; we need a change. What do you say to a tour in Europe?"

"When?"

"I'm not particular. I should suppose that four o'clock this afternoon would be early enough."

"I'll meet you at the boat," said Harper.

V

Seven years afterward these two men sat upon a bench in Madison Square, New York, in familiar conversation. Another man, who had been observing them for some time, himself unobserved, approached and, courteously lifting his hat from locks as white as frost, said: "I beg your pardon, gentlemen, but when you have killed a man by coming to life, it is best to change clothes with him, and at the first opportunity make a break for liberty."

Helberson and Harper exchanged significant glances. They were obviously amused. The former then looked the stranger kindly in the eye and replied:

"That has always been my plan. I entirely agree with you as to its advant—"

He stopped suddenly, rose and went white. He stared at the man, open-mouthed; he trembled visibly.

"Ah!" said the stranger, "I see that you are indisposed, Doctor. If you cannot treat yourself Dr. Harper can do something for you, I am sure."

"Who the devil are you?" said Harper, bluntly.

The stranger came nearer and, bending toward them, said in a whisper: "I call myself Jarette sometimes, but I don't mind telling you, for old friendship, that I am Dr. William Mancher."

The revelation brought Harper to his feet. "Mancher!" he cried; and Helberson added: "It is true, by God!"

"Yes," said the stranger, smiling vaguely, "it is true enough, no doubt."

He hesitated and seemed to be trying to recall something, then began humming a popular air. He had apparently forgotten their presence.

"Look here, Mancher," said the elder of the two, "tell us just what occurred that night—to Jarette, you know."

"Oh, yes, about Jarette," said the other. "It's odd I should have neglected to tell you—I tell it so often. You see I knew, by overhearing him talking to himself, that he was pretty badly frightened. So I couldn't resist the temptation to come to life and have a bit of fun out of him—I couldn't really. That was all right, though certainly I did not think he would take it so seriously; I did not, truly. And afterward—well, it was a tough job changing places with him, and then—damn you! you didn't let me out!"

Nothing could exceed the ferocity with which these last words were delivered. Both men stepped back in alarm.

"We?—why—why," Helberson stammered, losing his self-possession utterly, "we had nothing to do with it."

"Didn't I say you were Drs. Hell-born and Sharper?" inquired the man, laughing.

"My name is Helberson, yes; and this gentleman is Mr. Harper," replied the former, reassured by the laugh. "But we are not physicians now; we are—well, hang it, old man, we are gamblers."

And that was the truth.

"A very good profession—very good, indeed; and, by the way, I hope Sharper here paid over Jarette's money like an honest stakeholder. A very good and honourable profession," he repeated, thoughtfully, moving carelessly away; "but I stick to the old one. I am High Supreme Medical Officer of the Bloomingdale Asylum; it is my duty to cure the superintendent."

THE MIDDLE TOE OF
THE RIGHT FOOT

I

t is well known that the old Manton house is haunted.
In all the rural district near about, and even in the
town of Marshall, a mile away, not one person of
unbiased mind entertains a doubt of it; incredulity is confined
to those opinionated persons who will be called "cranks" as
soon as the useful word shall have penetrated the intellectual
demesne of the Marshall *Advance*. The evidence that the house
is haunted is of two kinds: the testimony of disinterested witnesses who have had ocular proof, and that of the house itself.
The former may be disregarded and ruled out on any of the
various grounds of objection which may be urged against it by
the ingenious; but facts within the observation of all are material and controlling.

In the first place, the Manton house has been unoccupied
by mortals for more than ten years, and with its outbuildings
is slowly falling into decay—a circumstance which in itself the
judicious will hardly venture to ignore. It stands a little way off
the loneliest reach of the Marshall and Harriston road, in an
opening which was once a farm and is still disfigured with strips
of rotting fence and half covered with brambles overrunning

a stony and sterile soil long unacquainted with the plough. The house itself is in tolerably good condition, though badly weather-stained and in dire need of attention from the glazier, the smaller male population of the region having attested in the manner of its kind its disapproval of dwelling without dwellers. It is two stories in height, nearly square, its front pierced by a single doorway flanked on each side by a window boarded up to the very top. Corresponding windows above, not protected, serve to admit light and rain to the rooms of the upper floor. Grass and weeds grow pretty rankly all about, and a few shade trees, somewhat the worse for wind, and leaning all in one direction, seem to be making a concerted effort to run away. In short, as the Marshall town humorist explained in the columns of the *Advance*, "the proposition that the Manton house is badly haunted is the only logical conclusion from the premises." The fact that in this dwelling Mr. Manton thought it expedient one night some ten years ago to rise and cut the throats of his wife and two small children, removing at once to another part of the country, has no doubt done its share in directing public attention to the fitness of the place for supernatural phenomena.

To this house, one summer evening, came four men in a wagon. Three of them promptly alighted, and the one who had been driving hitched the team to the only remaining post of what had been a fence. The fourth remained seated in the wagon. "Come," said one of his companions, approaching him, while the others moved away in the direction of the dwelling— "this is the place."

The man addressed did not move. "By God!" he said harshly, "this is a trick, and it looks to me as if you were in it."

"Perhaps I am," the other said, looking him straight in the face and speaking in a tone which had something of contempt in it. "You will remember, however, that the choice of place was with your own assent left to the other side. Of course if you are afraid of spooks—"

"I am afraid of nothing," the man interrupted with another oath, and sprang to the ground. The two then joined the others at the door, which one of them had already opened with some difficulty, caused by rust of lock and hinge. All entered. Inside it was dark, but the man who had unlocked the door produced a candle and matches and made a light. He then unlocked a door on their right as they stood in the passage. This gave them entrance to a large, square room that the candle but dimly lighted. The floor had a thick carpeting of dust, which partly muffled their footfalls. Cobwebs were in the angles of the walls and depended from the ceiling like strips of rotting lace, making undulatory movements in the disturbed air. The room had two windows in adjoining sides, but from neither could anything be seen except the rough inner surfaces of boards a few inches from the glass. There was no fireplace, no furniture; there was nothing: besides the cobwebs and the dust, the four men were the only objects there which were not a part of the structure.

Strange enough they looked in the yellow light of the candle. The one who had so reluctantly alighted was especially spectacular—he might have been called sensational. He was of middle age, heavily built, deep chested and broad shouldered. Looking at his figure, one would have said that he had a giant's strength; at his features, that he would use it like a giant. He was clean shaven, his hair rather closely cropped and grey. His low forehead was seamed with wrinkles above the eyes, and over the nose these became vertical. The heavy black brows followed the same law, saved from meeting only by an upward turn at what would otherwise have been the point of contact. Deeply sunken beneath these, glowed in the obscure light a pair of eyes of uncertain colour, but obviously enough too small. There was something forbidding in their expression, which was not bettered by the cruel mouth and wide jaw. The nose was well enough, as noses go; one does not expect much of noses. All that was sinister in the man's face seemed accentuated by an unnatural pallor—he appeared altogether bloodless.

The appearance of the other men was sufficiently commonplace: they were such persons as one meets and forgets that he met. All were younger than the man described, between whom and the eldest of the others, who stood apart, there was apparently no kindly feeling. They avoided looking at each other.

"Gentlemen," said the man holding the candle and keys, "I believe everything is right. Are you ready, Mr. Rosser?"

The man standing apart from the group bowed and smiled.

"And you, Mr. Grossmith?"

The heavy man bowed and scowled.

"You will be pleased to remove your outer clothing."

Their hats, coats, waistcoats and neckwear were soon removed and thrown outside the door, in the passage. The man with the candle now nodded, and the fourth man—he who had urged Grossmith to leave the wagon—produced from the pocket of his overcoat two long, murderous-looking bowie-knives, which he drew now from their leather scabbards.

"They are exactly alike," he said, presenting one to each of the two principals—for by this time the dullest observer would have understood the nature of this meeting. It was to be a duel to the death.

Each combatant took a knife, examined it critically near the candle and tested the strength of blade and handle across his lifted knee. Their persons were then searched in turn, each by the second of the other.

"If it is agreeable to you, Mr. Grossmith," said the man holding the light, "you will place yourself in that corner."

He indicated the angle of the room farthest from the door, whither Grossmith retired, his second parting from him with a grasp of the hand which had nothing of cordiality in it. In the angle nearest the door Mr. Rosser stationed himself, and after a whispered consultation his second left him, joining the other near the door. At that moment the candle was suddenly extinguished, leaving all in profound darkness. This may have been done by a draught from the opened door; whatever the cause, the effect was startling.

"Gentlemen," said a voice which sounded strangely unfamiliar in the altered condition affecting the relations of the senses—"gentlemen, you will not move until you hear the closing of the outer door."

A sound of trampling ensued, then the closing of the inner door; and finally the outer one closed with a concussion which shook the entire building.

A few minutes afterward a belated farmer's boy met a light wagon which was being driven furiously toward the town of Marshall. He declared that behind the two figures on the front seat stood a third, with its hands upon the bowed shoulders of the others, who appeared to struggle vainly to free themselves from its grasp. This figure, unlike the others, was clad in white, and had undoubtedly boarded the wagon as it passed the haunted house. As the lad could boast a considerable former experience with the supernatural thereabouts his word had the weight justly due to the testimony of an expert. The story (in connection with the next day's events) eventually appeared in the *Advance*, with some slight literary embellishments and a concluding intimation that the gentlemen referred to would be allowed the use of the paper's columns for their version of the night's adventure. But the privilege remained without a claimant.

II

The events that led up to this "duel in the dark" were simple enough. One evening three young men of the town of Marshall were sitting in a quiet corner of the porch of the village hotel, smoking and discussing such matters as three educated young men of a Southern village would naturally find interesting. Their names were King, Sancher and Rosser. At a little distance, within easy hearing, but taking no part in the conversation, sat a fourth. He was a stranger to the others. They merely knew that on his arrival by the stagecoach that afternoon he had written in the hotel register the name Robert Grossmith. He had not been observed to speak to anyone except the hotel clerk. He seemed, indeed, singularly fond of his own company—or, as the *personnel* of the *Advance* expressed it, "grossly addicted to evil associations." But then it should be said in justice to the stranger that the *personnel* was himself of a too convivial disposition fairly to judge one differently gifted, and had, moreover, experienced a slight rebuff in an effort at an "interview."

"I hate any kind of deformity in a woman," said King, "whether natural or—acquired. I have a theory that any physical defect has its correlative mental and moral defect."

"I infer, then," said Rosser gravely, "that a lady lacking the moral advantage of a nose would find the struggle to become Mrs. King an arduous enterprise."

"Of course you may put it that way," was the reply; "but, seriously, I once threw over a most charming girl on learning quite accidentally that she had suffered amputation of a toe. My conduct was brutal if you like, but if I had married that girl I should have been miserable for life and should have made her so."

"Whereas," said Sancher, with a light laugh, "by marrying a gentleman of more liberal views she escaped with a parted throat."

"Ah, you know to whom I refer. Yes, she married Manton, but I don't know about his liberality; I'm not sure but he cut her throat because he discovered that she lacked that excellent thing in woman, the middle toe of the right foot."

"Look at that chap!" said Rosser in a low voice, his eyes fixed upon the stranger.

"That chap" was obviously listening intently to the conversation.

"Damn his impudence!" muttered King—"what ought we to do?"

"That's an easy one," Rosser replied, rising. "Sir," he continued, addressing the stranger, "I think it would be better if you would remove your chair to the other end of the veranda. The presence of gentlemen is evidently an unfamiliar situation to you."

The man sprang to his feet and strode forward with clenched hands, his face white with rage. All were now standing. Sancher stepped between the belligerents.

"You are hasty and unjust," he said to Rosser; "this gentleman has done nothing to deserve such language."

But Rosser would not withdraw a word. By the custom of the country and the time there could be but one outcome to the quarrel.

"I demand the satisfaction due to a gentleman," said the stranger, who had become more calm. "I have not an acquaintance in this region. Perhaps you, sir," bowing to Sancher, "will be kind enough to represent me in this matter."

Sancher accepted the trust—somewhat reluctantly it must be confessed, for the man's appearance and manner were not at all to his liking. King, who during the colloquy had hardly removed his eyes from the stranger's face and had not spoken a word, consented with a nod to act for Rosser, and the upshot of it was that, the principals having retired, a meeting was arranged for the next evening. The nature of the arrangements has been already disclosed. The duel with knives in a dark room was once a commoner feature of south-western life than it is likely to be again. How thin a veneering of "chivalry" covered the essential brutality of the code under which such encounters were possible we shall see.

III

In the blaze of a midsummer noonday the old Manton house was hardly true to its traditions. It was of the earth, earthy. The sunshine caressed it warmly and affectionately, with evident disregard of its bad reputation. The grass greening all the expanse in its front seemed to grow, not rankly, but with a natural and joyous exuberance, and the weeds blossomed quite like plants. Full of charming lights and shadows and populous with pleasant-voiced birds, the neglected shade trees no longer struggled to run away, but bent reverently beneath their burden of sun and song. Even in the glassless upper windows was an expression of peace and contentment, due to the light within. Over the stony fields the visible heat danced with a lively tremor incompatible with the gravity which is an attribute of the supernatural.

Such was the aspect under which the place presented itself to Sheriff Adams and two other men who had come out from Marshall to look at it. One of these men was Mr. King, the sheriff's deputy; the other, whose name was Brewer, was a brother of the late Mrs. Manton. Under a beneficent law of the State relating to property which had been for a certain period abandoned by an owner whose residence cannot be ascertained, the sheriff was legal custodian of the Manton farm and appurtenances thereunto belonging. His present visit was in mere perfunctory compliance with some order of a court in which Mr. Brewer had an action to get possession of the property as heir to his deceased sister. By a mere coincidence, the visit was made on the day after the night that Deputy King had unlocked the house for another and very different purpose. His presence now was not of his own choosing: he had been ordered to accompany his superior, and at the moment could think of nothing more prudent than simulated alacrity in obedience to the command.

Carelessly opening the front door, which to his surprise was not locked, the sheriff was amazed to see, lying on the floor of the passage into which it opened, a confused heap of men's apparel. Examination showed it to consist of two hats, and the same number of coats, waistcoats and scarves, all in a remarkably good state of preservation, albeit somewhat defiled by the dust in which they lay. Mr. Brewer was equally astonished, but Mr. King's emotion is not on record. With a new and lively interest in his own actions the sheriff now unlatched and pushed open the door on the right, and the three entered. The room was apparently vacant—no; as their eyes became accustomed to the dimmer light something was visible in the farthest angle of the wall. It was a human figure—that of a man crouching close in the corner. Something in the attitude made the intruders halt when they had barely passed the threshold. The figure more and more clearly defined itself. The man was upon one knee, his back in the angle of the wall, his shoulders elevated to the level of his ears, his hands before his face, palms outward, the fingers spread and crooked like claws; the white face turned upward on the retracted neck had an expression of unutterable fright, the mouth half open, the eyes incredibly expanded. He was stone dead. Yet, with the exception of a bowie-knife, which had evidently fallen from his own hand, not another object was in the room.

In thick dust that covered the floor were some confused footprints near the door and along the wall through which it opened. Along one of the adjoining walls, too, past the boarded-up windows, was the trail made by the man himself in reaching his corner. Instinctively in approaching the body the three men followed that trail. The sheriff grasped one of the out-thrown arms; it was as rigid as iron, and the application of a gentle force rocked the entire body without altering the relation of its parts. Brewer, pale with excitement, gazed intently into the distorted face. "God of mercy!" he suddenly cried, "it is Manton!"

"You are right," said King, with an evident attempt at calmness: "I knew Manton. He then wore a full beard and his hair long, but this is he."

He might have added: "I recognized him when he challenged Rosser. I told Rosser and Sancher who he was before we played him this horrible trick. When Rosser left this dark room at our heels, forgetting his outer clothing in the excitement, and driving away with us in his shirt sleeves—all through the discreditable proceedings we knew whom we were dealing with, murderer and coward that he was!"

But nothing of this did Mr. King say. With his better light he was trying to penetrate the mystery of the man's death. That he had not once moved from the corner where he had been stationed; that his posture was that of neither attack nor defence; that he had dropped his weapon; that he had obviously perished of sheer horror of something that he *saw*—these were circumstances which Mr. King's disturbed intelligence could not rightly comprehend.

Groping in intellectual darkness for a clue to his maze of doubt, his gaze, directed mechanically downward in the way of one who ponders momentous matters, fell upon something which, there, in the light of day and in the presence of living companions, affected him with terror. In the dust of years that lay thick upon the floor—leading from the door by which they had entered, straight across the room to within a yard of Manton's crouching corpse—were three parallel lines of footprints—light but definite impressions of bare feet, the outer ones those of small children, the inner a woman's. From the point at which they ended they did not return; they pointed all one way. Brewer, who had observed them at the same moment, was leaning forward in an attitude of rapt attention, horribly pale.

"Look at that!" he cried, pointing with both hands at the nearest print of the woman's right foot, where she had apparently stopped and stood. "The middle toe is missing—it was Gertrude!"

Gertrude was the late Mrs. Manton, sister of Mr. Brewer.

THE BOARDED WINDOW

n 1830, only a few miles away from what is now the great city of Cincinnati, lay an immense and almost unbroken forest. The whole region was sparsely settled by people of the frontier—restless souls who no sooner had hewn fairly habitable homes out of the wilderness and attained to that degree of prosperity which today we should call indigence than impelled by some mysterious impulse of their nature they abandoned all and pushed farther westward, to encounter new perils and privations in the effort to regain the meagre comforts which they had voluntarily renounced. Many of them had already forsaken that region for the remoter settlements, but among those remaining was one who had been of those first arriving. He lived alone in a house of logs surrounded on all sides by the great forest, of whose gloom and silence he seemed a part, for no one had ever known him to smile nor speak a needless word. His simple wants were supplied by the sale or barter of skins of wild animals in the river town, for not a thing did he grow upon the land which, if needful, he might have claimed by right of undisturbed possession. There were evidences of "improvement"—a few acres of ground immediately about the house had once been cleared of its trees, the decayed stumps of which were half concealed by the new growth that had been suffered to repair the ravage wrought by the axe. Apparently the man's zeal for agriculture had burned with a failing flame, expiring in penitential ashes.

The little log house, with its chimney of sticks, its roof of warping clapboards weighted with traversing poles and its "chinking" of clay, had a single door and, directly opposite, a window. The latter, however, was boarded up—nobody could remember a time when it was not. And none knew why it was so closed; certainly not because of the occupant's dislike of light and air, for on those rare occasions when a hunter had passed that lonely spot the recluse had commonly been seen sunning himself on his doorstep if heaven had provided sunshine for his need. I fancy there are few persons living today who ever knew the secret of that window, but I am one, as you shall see.

The man's name was said to be Murlock. He was apparently seventy years old, actually about fifty. Something besides years had had a hand in his ageing. His hair and long, full beard were white, his grey, lustreless eyes sunken, his face singularly seamed with wrinkles which appeared to belong to two intersecting systems. In figure he was tall and spare, with a stoop of the shoulders—a burden bearer. I never saw him; these particulars I learned from my grandfather, from whom also I got the man's story when I was a lad. He had known him when living near by in that early day.

One day Murlock was found in his cabin, dead. It was not a time and place for coroners and newspapers, and I suppose it was agreed that he had died from natural causes or I should have been told, and should remember. I know only that with what was probably a sense of the fitness of things the body was buried near the cabin, alongside the grave of his wife, who had preceded him by so many years that local tradition had retained hardly a hint of her existence. That closes the final chapter of this true story—excepting, indeed, the circumstance that many years afterward, in company with an equally intrepid spirit, I penetrated to the place and ventured near enough to the ruined cabin to throw a stone against it, and ran away to avoid the ghost which every well-informed boy thereabout knew haunted the spot. But there is an earlier chapter—that supplied by my grandfather.

When Murlock built his cabin and began laying sturdily about with his axe to hew out a farm—the rifle, meanwhile, his means of support—he was young, strong and full of hope. In that eastern country whence he came he had married, as was the fashion, a young woman in all ways worthy of his honest devotion, who shared the dangers and privations of his lot with a willing spirit and light heart. There is no known record of her name; of her charms of mind and person tradition is silent and the doubter is at liberty to entertain his doubt; but God forbid that I should share it! Of their affection and happiness there is abundant assurance in every added day of the man's widowed life; for what but the magnetism of a blessed memory could have chained that venturesome spirit to a lot like that?

One day Murlock returned from gunning in a distant part of the forest to find his wife prostrate with fever, and delirious. There was no physician within miles, no neighbour; nor was she in a condition to be left, to summon help. So he set about the task of nursing her back to health, but at the end of the third day she fell into unconsciousness and so passed away, apparently, with never a gleam of returning reason.

From what we know of a nature like his we may venture to sketch in some of the details of the outline picture drawn by my grandfather. When convinced that she was dead, Murlock had sense enough to remember that the dead must be prepared for burial. In performance of this sacred duty he blundered now and again, did certain things incorrectly, and others which he did correctly were done over and over. His occasional failures to accomplish some simple and ordinary act filled him with astonishment, like that of a drunken man who wonders at the suspension of familiar natural laws. He was surprised, too, that he did not weep—surprised and a little ashamed; surely it is unkind not to weep for the dead. "Tomorrow," he said aloud, "I shall have to make the coffin and dig the grave; and then I shall miss her, when she is no longer in sight; but now—she is dead, of course, but it is all right—it *must* be all right, somehow. Things cannot be so bad as they seem."

He stood over the body in the fading light, adjusting the hair and putting the finishing touches to the simple toilet, doing all mechanically, with soulless care. And still through his consciousness ran an undersense of conviction that all was right—that he should have her again as before, and everything explained. He had had no experience in grief; his capacity had not been enlarged by use. His heart could not contain it all, nor his imagination rightly conceive it. He did not know he was so hard struck; *that* knowledge would come later, and never go. Grief is an artist of powers as various as the instruments upon which he plays his dirges for the dead, evoking from some the sharpest, shrillest notes, from others the low, grave chords that throb recurrent like the slow beating of a distant drum. Some natures it startles; some it stupefies. To one it comes like the stroke of an arrow, stinging all the sensibilities to a keener life; to another as the blow of a bludgeon, which in crushing benumbs. We may conceive Murlock to have been that way affected, for (and here we are upon surer ground than that of conjecture) no sooner had he finished his pious work than, sinking into a chair by the side of the table upon which the body lay, and noting how white the profile showed in the deepening gloom, he laid his arms upon the table's edge, and dropped his face into them, tearless yet and unutterably weary. At that moment came in through the open window a long, wailing sound like the cry of a lost child in the far deeps of the darkening wood! But the man did not move. Again, and nearer than before, sounded that unearthly cry upon his failing sense. Perhaps it was a wild beast; perhaps it was a dream. For Murlock was asleep.

Some hours later, as it afterward appeared, this unfaithful watcher awoke and lifting his head from his arms intently listened—he knew not why. There in the black darkness by the side of the dead, recalling all without a shock, he strained his eyes to see—he knew not what. His senses were all alert, his breath was suspended, his blood had stilled its tides as if to assist the silence. Who—what had waked him, and where was it?

Suddenly the table shook beneath his arms, and at the same moment he heard, or fancied that he heard, a light, soft step—another—sounds as of bare feet upon the floor!

He was terrified beyond the power to cry out or move. Perforce he waited—waited there in the darkness through seeming centuries of such dread as one may know, yet live to tell. He tried vainly to speak the dead woman's name, vainly to stretch forth his hand across the table to learn if she were there. His throat was powerless, his arms and hands were like lead. Then occurred something most frightful. Some heavy body seemed hurled against the table with an impetus that pushed it against his breast so sharply as nearly to overthrow him, and at the same instant he heard and felt the fall of something upon the floor with so violent a thump that the whole house was shaken by the impact. A scuffling ensued, and a confusion of sounds impossible to describe. Murlock had risen to his feet. Fear had by excess forfeited control of his faculties. He flung his hands upon the table. Nothing was there!

There is a point at which terror may turn to madness; and madness incites to action. With no definite intent, from no motive but the wayward impulse of a madman, Murlock sprang to the wall, with a little groping seized his loaded rifle, and without aim discharged it. By the flash which lit up the room with a vivid illumination, he saw an enormous panther dragging the dead woman toward the window, its teeth fixed in her throat! Then there were darkness blacker than before, and silence; and when he returned to consciousness the sun was high and the wood vocal with songs of birds.

The body lay near the window, where the beast had left it when frightened away by the flash and report of the rifle. The clothing was deranged, the long hair in disorder, the limbs lay anyhow. From the throat, dreadfully lacerated, had issued a pool of blood not yet entirely coagulated. The ribbon with which he had bound the wrists was broken; the hands were tightly clenched. Between the teeth was a fragment of the animal's ear.

THE DAMNED THING

*One Does Not Always
Eat What Is on the Table*

y the light of a tallow candle which had been placed on one end of a rough table a man was reading something written in a book. It was an old account book, greatly worn; and the writing was not, apparently, very legible, for the man sometimes held the page close to the flame of the candle to get a stronger light on it. The shadow of the book would then throw into obscurity a half of the room, darkening a number of faces and figures; for besides the reader, eight other men were present. Seven of them sat against the rough log walls, silent, motionless, and the room being small, not very far from the table. By extending an arm anyone of them could have touched the eighth man, who lay on the table, face upward, partly covered by a sheet, his arms at his sides. He was dead.

The man with the book was not reading aloud, and no one spoke; all seemed to be waiting for something to occur; the dead man only was without expectation. From the blank darkness outside came in, through the aperture that served for a window, all the ever unfamiliar noises of night in the wilderness—the long nameless note of a distant coyote; the stilly pulsing thrill of tireless insects in trees; strange cries of night birds, so different from those of the birds of day; the drone of great blundering beetles, and all that mysterious chorus of small sounds that seem always to have been but half heard when they have suddenly ceased, as if conscious of an indiscretion. But nothing of all this was noted in that company; its members were not overmuch addicted to idle interest in matters of no practical importance; that was obvious in every line of their rugged faces—obvious even in the dim light of the single candle. They were evidently men of the vicinity—farmers and woodsmen.

The person reading was a trifle different; one would have said of him that he was of the world, worldly, albeit there was that in his attire which attested a certain fellowship with the organisms of his environment. His coat would hardly have passed muster in San Francisco; his foot-gear was not of urban origin, and the hat that lay by him on the floor (he was the only one uncovered) was such that if one had considered it as an article of mere personal adornment he would have missed its meaning. In countenance the man was rather prepossessing, with just a hint of sternness; though that he may have assumed or cultivated, as appropriate to one in authority. For he was a coroner. It was by virtue of his office that he had possession of the book in which he was reading; it had been found among the dead man's effects—in his cabin, where the inquest was now taking place.

When the coroner had finished reading he put the book into his breast pocket. At that moment the door was pushed open and a young man entered. He, clearly, was not of mountain birth and breeding: he was clad as those who dwell in cities. His clothing was dusty, however, as from travel. He had, in fact, been riding hard to attend the inquest.

The coroner nodded; no one else greeted him.

"We have waited for you," said the coroner. "It is necessary to have done with this business tonight."

The young man smiled. "I am sorry to have kept you," he said. "I went away, not to evade your summons, but to post to my newspaper an account of what I suppose I am called back to relate."

The coroner smiled.

"The account that you posted to your newspaper," he said, "differs, probably, from that which you will give here under oath."

"That," replied the other, rather hotly and with a visible flush, "is as you please. I used manifold paper and have a copy of what I sent. It was not written as news, for it is incredible, but as fiction. It may go as a part of my testimony under oath."

"But you say it is incredible."

"That is nothing to you, sir, if I also swear that it is true."

The coroner was silent for a time, his eyes upon the floor. The men about the sides of the cabin talked in whispers, but seldom withdrew their gaze from the face of the corpse. Presently the coroner lifted his eyes and said: "We will resume the inquest."

The men removed their hats. The witness was sworn.

"What is your name?" the coroner asked.

"William Harker."

"Age?"

"Twenty-seven."

"You knew the deceased, Hugh Morgan?"

"Yes."

"You were with him when he died?"

"Near him."

"How did that happen—your presence, I mean?"

"I was visiting him at this place to shoot and fish. A part of my purpose, however, was to study him and his odd, solitary way of life. He seemed a good model for a character in fiction. I sometimes write stories."

"I sometimes read them."

"Thank you."

"Stories in general—not yours."

Some of the jurors laughed. Against a sombre background humour shows high lights. Soldiers in the intervals of battle laugh easily, and a jest in the death chamber conquers by surprise.

"Relate the circumstances of this man's death," said the coroner. "You may use any notes or memoranda that you please."

The witness understood. Pulling a manuscript from his breast pocket he held it near the candle and turning the leaves until he found the passage that he wanted began to read.

II

What May Happen in a Field of Wild Oats

"…The sun had hardly risen when we left the house. We were looking for quail, each with a shotgun, but we had only one dog. Morgan said that our best ground was beyond a certain ridge that he pointed out, and we crossed it by a trail through the *chaparral*. On the other side was comparatively level ground, thickly covered with wild oats. As we emerged from the *chaparral* Morgan was but a few yards in advance. Suddenly we heard, at a little distance to our right and partly in front, a noise as of some animal thrashing about in the bushes, which we could see were violently agitated.

"'We've started a deer,' I said. 'I wish we had brought a rifle.'

"Morgan, who had stopped and was intently watching the agitated *chaparral*, said nothing, but had cocked both barrels of his gun and was holding it in readiness to aim. I thought him a trifle excited, which surprised me, for he had a reputation for exceptional coolness, even in moments of sudden and imminent peril.

"'Oh, come,' I said. 'You are not going to fill up a deer with quail-shot, are you?'

"Still he did not reply; but catching a sight of his face as he turned it slightly toward me I was struck by the intensity of his look. Then I understood that we had serious business in hand, and my first conjecture was that we had 'jumped' a grizzly. I advanced to Morgan's side, cocking my piece as I moved.

"The bushes were now quiet and the sounds had ceased, but Morgan was as attentive to the place as before.

"'What is it? What the devil is it?' I asked.

"'That Damned Thing!' he replied, without turning his head. His voice was husky and unnatural. He trembled visibly.

"I was about to speak further, when I observed the wild oats near the place of the disturbance moving in the most inexplicable way. I can hardly describe it. It seemed as if stirred by a streak of wind, which not only bent it, but pressed it down—crushed it so that it did not rise; and this movement was slowly prolonging itself directly toward us.

"Nothing that I had ever seen had affected me so strangely as this unfamiliar and unaccountable phenomenon, yet I am unable to recall any sense of fear. I remember—and tell it here because, singularly enough, I recollected it then—that once in looking carelessly out of an open window I momentarily mistook a small tree close at hand for one of a group of larger trees at a little distance away. It looked the same size as the others, but being more distinctly and sharply defined in mass and detail seemed out of harmony with them. It was a mere falsification of the law of aerial perspective, but it startled, almost terrified me. We so rely upon the orderly operation of familiar natural laws that any seeming suspension of them is noted as a menace to our safety, a warning of unthinkable calamity. So now the apparently causeless movement of the herbage and the slow, undeviating approach of the line of disturbance were distinctly disquieting. My companion appeared actually frightened, and I could hardly credit my senses when I saw him suddenly throw his gun to his shoulder and fire both barrels at the agitated grain! Before the smoke of the discharge had cleared away I heard a loud savage cry—a scream like that of a wild animal—and flinging his gun upon the ground Morgan sprang away and ran swiftly from the spot. At the same instant I was thrown violently to the ground by the impact of something unseen in the smoke—some soft, heavy substance that seemed thrown against me with great force.

"Before I could get upon my feet and recover my gun, which seemed to have been struck from my hands, I heard Morgan crying out as if in mortal agony, and mingling with his cries were such hoarse, savage sounds as one hears from fighting dogs. Inexpressibly terrified, I struggled to my feet and looked in the direction of Morgan's retreat; and may Heaven in mercy spare me from another sight like that! At a distance of less than thirty yards was my friend, down upon one knee, his head thrown back at a frightful angle, hatless, his long hair in disorder and his whole body in violent movement from side to side, backward and forward. His right arm was lifted and seemed to lack the hand—at least, I could see none. The other arm was invisible. At times, as my memory now reports this extraordinary scene, I could discern but a part of his body; it was as if he had been partly blotted out—I cannot otherwise express it—then a shifting of his position would bring it all into view again.

"All this must have occurred within a few seconds, yet in that time Morgan assumed all the postures of a determined wrestler vanquished by superior weight and strength. I saw nothing but him, and him not always distinctly. During the entire incident his shouts and curses were heard, as if through an enveloping uproar of such sounds of rage and fury as I had never heard from the throat of man or brute!

"For a moment only I stood irresolute, then throwing down my gun I ran forward to my friend's assistance. I had a vague belief that he was suffering from a fit, or some form of convulsion. Before I could reach his side he was down and quiet. All sounds had ceased, but with a feeling of such terror as even these awful events had not inspired I now saw again the mysterious movement of the wild oats, prolonging itself from the trampled area about the prostrate man toward the edge of a wood. It was only when it had reached the wood that I was able to withdraw my eyes and look at my companion. He was dead."

III

A Man Though Naked May Be in Rags

The coroner rose from his seat and stood beside the dead man. Lifting an edge of the sheet he pulled it away, exposing the entire body, altogether naked and showing in the candle-light a clay-like yellow. It had, however, broad maculations of bluish black, obviously caused by extravasated blood from contusions. The chest and sides looked as if they had been beaten with a bludgeon. There were dreadful lacerations; the skin was torn in strips and shreds.

The coroner moved round to the end of the table and undid a silk handkerchief which had been passed under the chin and knotted on the top of the head. When the handkerchief was drawn away it exposed what had been the throat. Some of the jurors who had risen to get a better view repented their curiosity and turned away their faces. Witness Harker went to the open window and leaned out across the sill, faint and sick. Dropping the handkerchief upon the dead man's neck the coroner stepped to an angle of the room and from a pile of clothing produced one garment after another, each of which he held up a moment for inspection. All were torn, and stiff with blood. The jurors did not make a closer inspection. They seemed rather uninterested. They had, in truth, seen all this before; the only thing that was new to them being Harker's testimony.

"Gentlemen," the coroner said, "we have no more evidence, I think. Your duty has been already explained to you; if there is nothing you wish to ask you may go outside and consider your verdict."

The foreman rose—a tall, bearded man of sixty, coarsely clad.

"I should like to ask one question, Mr. Coroner," he said. "What asylum did this yer last witness escape from?"

"Mr. Harker," said the coroner gravely and tranquilly, "from what asylum did you last escape?"

Harker flushed crimson again, but said nothing, and the seven jurors rose and solemnly filed out of the cabin.

"If you have done insulting me, sir," said Harker, as soon as he and the officer were left alone with the dead man, "I suppose I am at liberty to go?"

"Yes."

Harker started to leave, but paused, with his hand on the door latch. The habit of his profession was strong in him—stronger than his sense of personal dignity. He turned about and said:

"The book that you have there—I recognize it as Morgan's diary. You seemed greatly interested in it; you read in it while I was testifying. May I see it? The public would like—"

"The book will cut no figure in this matter," replied the official, slipping it into his coat pocket; "all the entries in it were made before the writer's death."

As Harker passed out of the house the jury re-entered and stood about the table, on which the now covered corpse showed under the sheet with sharp definition. The foreman seated himself near the candle, produced from his breast pocket a pencil and scrap of paper and wrote rather laboriously the following verdict, which with various degrees of effort all signed:

"We, the jury, do find that the remains come to their death at the hands of a mountain lion, but some of us thinks, all the same, they had fits."

IV

An Explanation from the Tomb

In the diary of the late Hugh Morgan are certain interesting entries having, possibly, a scientific value as suggestions. At the inquest upon his body the book was not put in evidence; possibly the coroner thought it not worth while to confuse the jury. The date of the first of the entries mentioned cannot be ascertained; the upper part of the leaf is torn away; the part of the entry remaining follows:

"...would run in a half-circle, keeping his head turned always toward the centre, and again he would stand still, barking furiously. At last he ran away into the brush as fast as he could go. I thought at first that he had gone mad, but on returning to the house found no other alteration in his manner than what was obviously due to fear of punishment.

"Can a dog see with his nose? Do odours impress some cerebral centre with images of the thing that emitted them?...

"*Sept.* 2.—Looking at the stars last night as they rose above the crest of the ridge east of the house, I observed them successively disappear—from left to right. Each was eclipsed but an instant, and only a few at the same time, but along the entire length of the ridge all that were within a degree or two of the crest were blotted out. It was as if something had passed along between me and them; but I could not see it, and the stars were not thick enough to define its outline. Ugh! don't like this"...

Several weeks' entries are missing, three leaves being torn from the book.

"*Sept.* 27.—It has been about here again—I find evidences of its presence every day. I watched again all last night in the same cover, gun in hand, double-charged with buckshot. In the morning the fresh footprints were there, as before. Yet I would have sworn that I did not sleep—indeed, I hardly sleep at all. It is terrible, insupportable! If these amazing experiences are real I shall go mad; if they are fanciful I am mad already.

"*Oct.* 3.—I shall not go—it shall not drive me away. No, this is *my* house, *my* land. God hates a coward...

"*Oct.* 5.—I can stand it no longer; I have invited Harker to pass a few weeks with me—he has a level head. I can judge from his manner if he thinks me mad.

"*Oct.* 7.—I have the solution of the mystery; it came to me last night—suddenly, as by revelation. How simple—how terribly simple!

"There are sounds that we cannot hear. At either end of the scale are notes that stir no chord of that imperfect instrument, the human ear. They are too high or too grave. I have observed a flock of blackbirds occupying an entire tree-top—the tops of several trees—and all in full song. Suddenly—in a moment—at absolutely the same instant—all spring into the air and fly away. How? They could not all see one another—whole tree-tops intervened. At no point could a leader have been visible to all. There must have been a signal of warning or command, high and shrill above the din, but by me unheard. I have observed, too, the same simultaneous flight when all were silent, among not only blackbirds, but other birds—quail, for example, widely separated by bushes—even on opposite sides of a hill.

"It is known to seamen that a school of whales basking or sporting on the surface of the ocean, miles apart, with the convexity of the earth between, will sometimes dive at the same instant—all gone out of sight in a moment. The signal has been sounded—too grave for the ear of the sailor at the masthead and his comrades on the deck—who nevertheless feel its vibrations in the ship as the stones of a cathedral are stirred by the bass of the organ.

"As with sounds, so with colours. At each end of the solar spectrum the chemist can detect the presence of what are known as 'actinic' rays. They represent colours—integral colours in the composition of light—which we are unable to discern. The human eye is an imperfect instrument; its range is but a few octaves of the real 'chromatic scale.' I am not mad; here are colours that we cannot see.

"And, God help me! the Damned Thing is of such a colour!"

BODIES OF THE DEAD

That of Granny Magone

bout ten miles to the south-east of Whitesburg, Ky., in a little "cove" of the Cumberland mountains, lived for many years an old woman named Sarah (or Mary) Magone. Her house, built of logs and containing but two rooms, was a mile and a half distant from any other, in the wildest part of the "cove," entirely surrounded by forest except on one side, where a little field, or "patch," of about a half-acre served her for a vegetable garden. How she subsisted nobody exactly knew; she was reputed to be a miser with a concealed hoard; she certainly paid for what few articles she procured on her rare visits to the village store. Many of her ignorant neighbours believed her to be a witch, or thought, at least, that she possessed some kind of supernatural powers. In November, 1881, she died, and fortunately enough, the body was found while yet warm by a passing hunter, who locked the door of the cabin and conveyed the news to the nearest settlement.

Several persons living in the vicinity at once went to the cabin to prepare for her burial; others were to follow the next day with a coffin and whatever else was needful. Among those who first went was the Rev. Elias Atney, a Methodist minister of Whitesburg, who happened to be in the neighbourhood visiting a relation. He was to conduct the funeral services on the following day. Mr. Atney is, or was, well known in Whitesburg and all that country as a good and pious man of good birth and education. He was closely related to the Marshalls and several other families of distinction. It is from him that the particulars here related were learned; and the account is confirmed by the affidavits of John Hershaw, William C. Wrightman, and Catharine Doub, residents of the vicinity and eye-witnesses.

The body of "Granny" Magone had been "laid out" on a wide plank supported by two chairs at the end of the principal room, opposite the fireplace, and the persons mentioned were acting as "watchers," according to the local custom. A bright fire on the hearth lighted one end of the room brilliantly, the other dimly. The watchers sat about the fire, talking in subdued tones, when a sudden noise in the direction of the corpse caused them all to turn and look. In a black shadow near the remains, they saw two glowing eyes staring fixedly; and before they could do more than rise, uttering exclamations of alarm, a large black cat leaped upon the body and fastened its teeth into the cloth covering the face. Instantly the right hand of the dead was violently raised from the side, seized the cat, and hurled it against the wall, whence it fell to the floor, and then dashed wildly through an open window into the outer darkness, and was seen no more.

Inconceivably horrified, the watchers stood a moment speechless; but finally, with returning courage, approached the body. The face-cloth lay upon the floor; the cheek was terribly torn; the right arm hung stiffly over the side of the plank. There was not a sign of life. They chafed the forehead, the withered cheeks and neck. They carried the body to the heat of the fire and worked upon it for hours: all in vain. But the funeral was postponed until the fourth day brought unmistakable evidence of dissolution, and poor Granny was buried.

"Ah, but your eyes deceived you," said he to whom the reverend gentleman related the occurrence. "The arm was disturbed by the efforts of the cat, which, taking sudden fright, leaped blindly against the wall."

"No," he answered, "the clenched right hand, with its long nails, was full of black fur."

The Light Sleeper

John Hoskin, living in San Francisco, had a beautiful wife, to whom he was devotedly attached. In the spring of 1871 Mrs. Hoskin went East to visit her relations in Springfield, Ill., where, a week after her arrival, she suddenly died of some disease of the heart; at least the physician said so. Mr. Hoskin was at once apprised of his loss, by telegraph, and he directed that the body be sent to San Francisco. On arrival there the metallic case containing the remains was opened. The body was lying on the right side, the right hand under the cheek, the other on the breast. The posture was the perfectly natural one of a sleeping child, and in a letter to the deceased lady's father, Mr. Martin L. Whitney of Springfield, Mr. Hoskin expressed a grateful sense of the thoughtfulness that had so composed the remains as to soften the suggestion of death. To his surprise he learned from the father that nothing of the kind had been done: the body had been put in the casket in the customary way, lying on the back, with the arms extended along the sides. In the meantime the casket had been deposited in the receiving vault at Laurel Hill Cemetery, awaiting the completion of a tomb.

Greatly disquieted by this revelation, Hoskin did not at once reflect that the easy and natural posture and placid expression precluded the idea of suspended animation, subsequent revival, and eventual death by suffocation. He insisted that his wife had been murdered by medical incompetency and heedless haste. Under the influence of this feeling he wrote to Mr. Whitney again, expressing in passionate terms his horror and renewed grief. Some days afterward, someone having suggested that the casket had been opened en route, probably in the hope of plunder, and pointing out the impossibility of the change having occurred in the straitened space of the confining metal, it was resolved to reopen it.

Removal of the lid disclosed a new horror: the body now lay upon its left side. The position was cramped, and to a living person would have been uncomfortable. The face wore an expression of pain. Some costly rings on the fingers were undisturbed. Overcome by his emotions, to which was now added a sharp, if mistaken remorse, Mr. Hoskin lost his reason, dying years afterward in the asylum at Stockton.

A physician having been summoned, to assist in clearing up the mystery, viewed the body of the dead woman, pronounced life obviously extinct, and ordered the casket closed for the third and last time. "Obviously extinct," indeed: the corpse had, in fact, been embalmed at Springfield.

The Mystery of Charles Farquharson

One night in the summer of 1843 William Hayner Gordon, of Philadelphia, lay in his bed reading Goldsmith's "Traveler," by the light of a candle. It was about eleven o'clock. The room was in the third story of the house and had two windows looking out upon Chestnut Street; there was no balcony, nothing below the windows but other windows in a smooth brick wall.

Becoming drowsy, Gordon laid away his book, extinguished his candle, and composed himself to sleep. A moment later (as he afterward averred) he remembered that he had neglected to place his watch within reach, and rose in the dark to get it from the pocket of his waistcoat, which he had hung on the back of a chair on the opposite side of the room, near one of the windows. In crossing, his foot came in contact with some heavy object and he was thrown to the floor. Rising, he struck a match and lighted his candle. In the centre of the room lay the corpse of a man.

Gordon was no coward, as he afterward proved by his gallant death upon the enemy's parapet at Chapultepee, but this strange apparition of a human corpse where but a moment before, as he believed, there had been nothing, was too much for his nerves, and he cried aloud. Henri Granier, who occupied an adjoining room, but had not retired, came instantly to Gordon's door and attempted to enter. The door being bolted, and Gordon too greatly agitated to open it, Granier burst it in.

Gordon was taken into custody and an inquest held, but what has been related was all that could be ascertained. The most diligent efforts on the part of the police and the press failed to identify the dead. Physicians testifying at the inquest agreed that death had occurred but a few hours before the discovery, but none was able to divine the cause; all the organs of the body were in an apparently healthy condition; there were no traces of either violence or poison.

Eight or ten months later Gordon received a letter from Charles Ritcher in Bombay, relating the death in that city of Charles Farquharson, whom both Gordon and Ritcher had known when all were boys. Enclosed in the letter was a daguerreotype of the deceased, found among his effects. As nearly as the living can look like the dead it was an exact likeness of the mysterious body found in Gordon's bedroom, and it was with a strange feeling that Gordon observed that the death, making allowance for the difference of time, was said to have occurred on the very night of the adventure. He wrote for further particulars, with especial reference to what disposition had been made of Farquharson's body.

"You know he turned Parsee," wrote Ritcher in reply; "so his naked remains were exposed on the grating of the Tower of Silence, as those of all good Parsees are. I saw the buzzards fighting for them and gorging themselves helpless on his fragments."

On some pretence Gordon and his friends obtained authority to open the dead man's grave. The coffin had evidently not been disturbed. They unscrewed the lid. The shroud was a trifle mouldy. There was no body nor any vestige of one.

Dead and "Gone"

On the morning of the 14th day of August, 1872, George L. Reid, a young man of twenty-one years, living at Xenia, O., fell while walking across the dining room on his father's house. The family consisted of his father, mother, two sisters, and a cousin, a boy of fifteen. All were present at the breakfast table. George entered the room, but instead of taking his accustomed seat near the door by which he had entered, passed it and went obliquely toward one of the windows—with what purpose no one knows. He had passed the table but a few steps when he fell heavily to the floor and did not again breathe. The body was carried into a bedroom and, after vain efforts at resuscitation by the stricken family, left lying on the bed with composed limbs and covered face.

In the meantime the boy had been hastily dispatched for a physician, who arrived some twenty minutes after the death. He afterward remembered as an uncommon circumstance that when he arrived the weeping relations—father, mother, and two sisters—were all in the room out of which the bedroom door opened, and that the door was closed. There was no other door to the bedroom. This door was at once opened by the father of the deceased, and as the physician passed through it he observed the dead man's clothing lying in a heap on the floor. He saw, too, the outlines of the body under the sheet that had been thrown over it; and the profile was plainly discernible under the face-cloth, clear-cut and sharp, as profiles of the dead seem always to be. He approached and lifted the cloth. There was nothing there. He pulled away the sheet. Nothing.

The family had followed him into the room. At this astonishing discovery——if so it may be called——they looked at one another, at the physician, at the bed, in speechless amazement, forgetting to weep. A moment later the three ladies required the physician's care. The father's condition was but little better; he stood in a stupor, muttering inarticulately and staring like an idiot.

Having restored the ladies to a sense of their surroundings, the physician went to the window——the only one the room had, opening upon a garden. It was locked on the inside with the usual fastening attached to the bottom bar of the upper sash and engaging with the lower.

No inquest was held——there was nothing to hold it on; but the physician and many others who were curious as to this occurrence made the most searching investigation into all the circumstances; all without result. George Reid was dead and "gone," and that is all that is known to this day.

A Cold Night

The first day's battle at Stone River had been fought, resulting in disaster to the Federal army, which had been driven from its original ground at every point except its extreme left. The weary troops at this point lay behind a railway embankment to which they had retired, and which had served them during the last hours of the fight as a breastwork to repel repeated charges of the enemy. Behind the line the ground was open and rocky. Great boulders lay about everywhere, and among them lay many of the Federal dead, where they had been carried out of the way. Before the embankment the dead of both armies lay more thickly, but they had not been disturbed.

Among the dead in the boulders lay one whom nobody seemed to know—a Federal sergeant, shot directly in the centre of the forehead. One of our surgeons, from idle curiosity, or possibly with a view to the amusement of a group of officers during a lull in the engagement (we needed something to divert our minds), had pushed his probe clean through the head. The body lay on its back, its chin in the air, and with straightened limbs, as rigid as steel; frost on its white face and in its beard and hair. Some Christian soul had covered it with a blanket, but when the night became pretty sharp a companion of the writer removed this, and we lay beneath it ourselves.

With the exception of our pickets, who had been posted well out in front of the embankment, every man lay silent. Conversation was forbidden; to have made a fire, or even struck a match to light a pipe would have been a grave offence. Stamping horses, moaning wounded—everything that made a noise had been sent to the rear; the silence was absolute. Those whom the chill prevented from sleeping nevertheless reclined as they shivered, or sat with their hands on their arms, suffering but making no sign. Everyone had lost friends, and all expected death on the morrow. These matters are mentioned to show the improbability of anyone going about during these solemn hours to commit a ghastly practical joke.

When the dawn broke the sky was still clear. "We shall have a warm day," the writer's companion whispered as we rose in the grey light; "let's give back the poor devil his blanket."

The sergeant's body lay in the same place, two yards away. But not in the same attitude. It was upon its right side. The knees were drawn up nearly to the breast, both hands thrust to the wrist between the buttons of the jacket, the collar of which was turned up, concealing the ears. The shoulders were elevated, the head was retracted, the chin rested on the collar bone. The posture was that of one suffering from intense cold. But for what had been previously observed—but for the ghastly evidence of the bullet-hole—one might have thought the man had died of cold.

A Creature of Habit

At Hawley's Bar, a mining camp near Virginia City, Mont., a gambler named Henry Graham, but commonly known as "Gray Hank," met a miner named Dreyfuss one day, with whom he had had a dispute the previous night about a game of cards, and asked him into a barroom to have a drink. The unfortunate miner, taking this as an overture of peace, gladly accepted. They stood at the counter, and while Dreyfuss was in the act of drinking Graham shot him dead. This was in 1865. Within an hour after the murder Graham was in the hands of the vigilantes, and that evening at sunset, after a fair, if informal, trial, he was hanged to the limb of a tree which grew upon a little eminence within sight of the whole camp. The original intention had been to "string him up," as is customary in such affairs; and with a view to that operation the long rope had been thrown over the limb, while a dozen pairs of hands were ready to hoist away. For some reason this plan was abandoned; the free end of the rope was made fast to a bush and the victim compelled to stand on the back of a horse, which at the cut of a whip sprang from under him, leaving him swinging. When steadied, his feet were about eighteen inches from the earth.

The body remained suspended for exactly half an hour, the greater part of the crowd remaining about it: then the "judge" ordered it taken down. The rope was untied from the bush, and two men stood by to lower away. The moment the feet came squarely upon the ground the men engaged in lowering, thinking doubtless that those standing about the body had hold of it to support it, let go the rope. The body at once ran quickly forward toward the main part of the crowd, the rope paying out as it went. The head rolled from side to side, the eyes and tongue protruding, the face ghastly purple, the lips covered with bloody froth. With cries of horror the crowd ran hither and thither, stumbling, falling over one another, cursing. In and out among them—over the fallen, coming into collision with others, the horrible dead man "pranced," his feet lifted so high at each step that his knees struck his breast, his tongue swinging like that of a panting dog, the foam flying in flakes from his swollen lips. The deepening twilight added its terror to the scene; and men fled from the spot, not daring to look behind.

Straight into this confusion from the outskirts of the crowd walked with rapid steps the tall figure of a man whom all who saw instantly recognized as a master spirit. This was Dr. Arnold Spier, who with two other physicians had pronounced the man dead and had been returning to the camp. He moved as directly toward the dead man as the now somewhat less rapid and erratic movements of the latter would permit, and seized him in his arms. Encouraged by this, a score of men sprang shouting to the free end of the rope, which had not been drawn entirely over the limb, and laid hold of it, intending to make a finish of their work. They ran with it toward the bush to which it had been fastened, but there was no resistance; the physician had cut it from the murderer's neck. In a moment the body was lying on its back, with composed limbs and face upturned to the kindling stars, in the motionless rigidity appropriate to death. The hanging had been done well enough—the neck was broken.

"The dead are creatures of habit," said Dr. Spier. "A corpse which when on its feet will walk and run will lie still when placed on its back."

THE SECRET OF
MACARGER'S GULCH

orthwestwardly from Indian Hill, about nine miles as
the crow flies, is Macarger's Gulch. It is not much of
a gulch—a mere depression between two wooded
ridges of inconsiderable height. From its mouth up to its head—
for gulches, like rivers, have an anatomy of their own—the distance does not exceed two miles, and the width at bottom is at
only one place more than a dozen yards; for most of the distance
on either side of the little brook which drains it in winter, and
goes dry in the early spring, there is no level ground at all; the
steep slopes of the hills covered with an almost impenetrable
growth of manzanita and chamisal, are parted by nothing but the
width of the watercourse. No one but an occasional enterprising
hunter of the vicinity ever goes into Macarger's Gulch, and five
miles away it is unknown, even by name. Within that distance in
any direction are far more conspicuous topographical features
without names, and one might try in vain to ascertain by local
inquiry the origin of the name of this one.

About midway between the head and the mouth of
Macarger's Gulch, the hill on the right as you ascend is cloven
by another gulch, a short dry one, and at the junction of the two
is a level space of two or three acres, and there a few years ago
stood an old board house containing one small room. How the
component parts of the house, few and simple as they were, had

been assembled at that almost inaccessible point is a problem in the solution of which there would be greater satisfaction than advantage. Possibly the creek bed is a reformed road. It is certain that the gulch was at one time pretty thoroughly prospected by miners, who must have had some means of getting in with at least pack animals carrying tools and supplies; their profits, apparently, were not such as would have justified any considerable outlay to connect Macarger's Gulch with any centre of civilization enjoying the distinction of a sawmill. The house, however, was there, most of it. It lacked a door and a window frame, and the chimney of mud and stones had fallen into an unlovely heap, overgrown with rank weeds. Such humble furniture as there may once have been and much of the lower weatherboarding, had served as fuel in the camp fires of hunters; as had also, probably, the kerbing of an old well, which at the time I write of existed in the form of a rather wide but not very deep depression near by.

One afternoon in the summer of 1874, I passed up Macarger's Gulch from the narrow valley into which it opens, by following the dry bed of the brook. I was quail-shooting and had made a bag of about a dozen birds by the time I had reached the house described, of whose existence I was until then unaware. After rather carelessly inspecting the ruin I resumed my sport, and having fairly good success prolonged it until near sunset, when it occurred to me that I was a long way from any human habitation—too far to reach one by nightfall. But in my game bag was food, and the old house would afford shelter, if shelter were needed on a warm and dewless night in the foothills of the Sierra Nevada, where one may sleep in comfort on the pine needles, without covering. I am fond of solitude and love the night, so my resolution to "camp out" was soon taken, and by the time that it was dark I had made my bed of boughs and grasses in a corner of the room and was roasting a quail at a fire that I had kindled on the hearth. The smoke escaped out of the ruined chimney, the light illuminated the room with a kindly glow, and as I ate my simple meal of plain bird and drank the remains of a bottle of red wine which had served me all the afternoon in place of the water, which the region did not supply, I experienced a sense of comfort which better fare and accommodations do not always give.

Nevertheless, there was something lacking. I had a sense of comfort, but not of security. I detected myself staring more frequently at the open doorway and blank window than I could find warrant for doing. Outside these apertures all was black, and I was unable to repress a certain feeling of apprehension as my fancy pictured the outer world and filled it with unfriendly entities, natural and supernatural—chief among which, in their respective classes, were the grizzly bear, which I knew was occasionally still seen in that region, and the ghost, which I had reason to think was not. Unfortunately, our feelings do not always respect the law of probabilities, and to me that evening, the possible and the impossible were equally disquieting.

Every one who has had experience in the matter must have observed that one confronts the actual and imaginary perils of the night with far less apprehension in the open air than in a house with an open doorway. I felt this now as I lay on my leafy couch in a corner of the room next to the chimney and permitted my fire to die out. So strong became my sense of the presence of something malign and menacing in the place, that I found myself almost unable to withdraw my eyes from the opening, as in the deepening darkness it became more and more indistinct. And when the last little flame flickered and went out I grasped the shotgun which I had laid at my side and actually turned the muzzle in the direction of the now invisible entrance, my thumb on one of the hammers, ready to cock the piece, my breath suspended, my muscles rigid and tense. But later I laid down the weapon with a sense of shame and mortification. What did I fear, and why?—I, to whom the night had been

> a more familiar face
> Than that of man—

I, in whom that element of hereditary superstition from which none of us is altogether free had given to solitude and darkness and silence only a more alluring interest and charm! I was unable to comprehend my folly, and losing in the conjecture the thing conjectured of, I fell asleep. And then I dreamed.

I was in a great city in a foreign land—a city whose people were of my own race, with minor differences of speech and costume; yet precisely what these were I could not say; my sense of them was indistinct. The city was dominated by a great castle upon an overlooking height whose name I knew, but could not speak. I walked through many streets, some broad and straight with high, modern buildings, some narrow, gloomy, and tortuous, between the gables of quaint old houses whose overhanging stories, elaborately ornamented with carvings in wood and stone, almost met above my head.

I sought some one whom I had never seen, yet knew that I should recognize when found. My quest was not aimless and fortuitous; it had a definite method. I turned from one street into another without hesitation and threaded a maze of intricate passages, devoid of the fear of losing my way.

Presently I stopped before a low door in a plain stone house which might have been the dwelling of an artisan of the better sort, and without announcing myself, entered. The room, rather sparely furnished, and lighted by a single window with small diamond-shaped panes, had but two occupants: a man and a woman. They took no notice of my intrusion, a circumstance which, in the manner of dreams, appeared entirely natural. They were not conversing; they sat apart, unoccupied and sullen.

The woman was young and rather stout, with fine large eyes and a certain grave beauty; my memory of her expression is exceedingly vivid, but in dreams one does not observe the details of faces. About her shoulders was a plaid shawl. The man was older, dark, with an evil face made more forbidding by a long scar extending from near the left temple diagonally downward into the black moustache; though in my dreams it seemed rather to haunt the face as a thing apart—I can express it no otherwise—than to belong to it. The moment that I found the man and woman I knew them to be husband and wife.

What followed, I remember indistinctly; all was confused and inconsistent—made so, I think, by gleams of consciousness. It was as if two pictures, the scene of my dream, and my actual surroundings, had been blended, one overlying the other, until the former, gradually fading, disappeared, and I was broad awake in the deserted cabin, entirely and tranquilly conscious of my situation.

My foolish fear was gone, and opening my eyes I saw that my fire, not altogether burned out, had revived by the falling of a stick and was again lighting the room. I had probably slept only a few minutes, but my commonplace dream had somehow so strongly impressed me that I was no longer drowsy; and after a little while I rose, pushed the embers of my fire together, and lighting my pipe proceeded in a rather ludicrously methodical way to meditate upon my vision.

It would have puzzled me then to say in what respect it was worth attention. In the first moment of serious thought that I gave to the matter I recognized the city of my dream as Edinburgh, where I had never been; so if the dream was a memory it was a memory of pictures and description. The recognition somehow deeply impressed me; it was as if something in my mind insisted rebelliously against will and reason on the importance of all this. And that faculty, whatever it was, asserted also a control of my speech. "Surely," I said aloud, quite involuntarily, "the MacGregors must have come here from Edinburgh."

At the moment, neither the substance of this remark nor the fact of my making it, surprised me in the least; it seemed entirely natural that I should know the name of my dreamfolk and something of their history. But the absurdity of it all soon dawned upon me: I laughed aloud, knocked the ashes from my pipe and again stretched myself upon my bed of boughs and grass, where I lay staring absently into my failing fire, with no further thought of either my dream or my surroundings. Suddenly the single remaining flame crouched for a moment, then, springing upward, lifted itself clear of its embers and expired in air. The darkness was absolute.

At that instant—almost, it seemed, before the gleam of the blaze had faded from my eyes—there was a dull, dead sound, as of some heavy body falling upon the floor, which shook beneath me as I lay. I sprang to a sitting posture and groped at my side for my gun; my notion was that some wild beast had leaped in through the open window. While the flimsy structure was still shaking from the impact I heard the sound of blows, the scuffling of feet upon the floor, and then—it seemed to come from almost within reach of my hand, the sharp shrieking of a woman in mortal agony. So horrible a cry I had never heard nor conceived; it utterly unnerved me; I was conscious for a moment of nothing but my own terror! Fortunately my hand now found the weapon of which it was in search, and the familiar touch somewhat restored me. I leaped to my feet, straining my eyes to pierce the darkness. The violent sounds had ceased, but more terrible than these, I heard, at what seemed long intervals, the faint intermittent gasping of some living, dying thing!

As my eyes grew accustomed to the dim light of the coals in the fireplace, I saw first the shapes of the door and window looking blacker than the black of the walls. Next, the distinction between wall and floor became discernible, and at last I was sensible to the form and full expanse of the floor from end to end and side to side. Nothing was visible and the silence was unbroken.

With a hand that shook a little, the other still grasping my gun, I restored my fire and made a critical examination of the place. There was nowhere any sign that the cabin had been entered. My own tracks were visible in the dust covering the floor, but there were no others. I relit my pipe, provided fresh fuel by ripping a thin board or two from the inside of the house—I did not care to go into the darkness out of doors—and passed the rest of the night smoking and thinking, and feeding my fire; not for added years of life would I have permitted that little flame to expire again.

Some years afterward I met in Sacramento a man named Morgan, to whom I had a note of introduction from a friend in San Francisco. Dining with him one evening at his home I observed various "trophies" upon the wall, indicating that he was fond of shooting. It turned out that he was, and in relating some of his feats he mentioned having been in the region of my adventure.

"Mr. Morgan," I asked abruptly, "do you know a place up there called Macarger's Gulch?"

"I have good reason to," he replied; "it was I who gave to the newspapers, last year, the accounts of the finding of the skeleton there."

I had not heard of it; the accounts had been published, it appeared, while I was absent in the East.

"By the way," said Morgan, "the name of the gulch is a corruption; it should have been called 'MacGregor's.' My dear," he added, speaking to his wife, "Mr. Elderson has upset his wine."

That was hardly accurate—I had simply dropped it, glass and all.

"There was an old shanty once in the gulch," Morgan resumed when the ruin wrought by my awkwardness had been repaired, "but just previously to my visit it had been blown down, or rather blown away, for its *débris* was scattered all about, the very floor being parted, plank from plank. Between two of the sleepers still in position I and my companion observed the remnant of a plaid shawl, and examining it found that it was wrapped about the shoulders of the body of a woman; of course but little remained besides the bones, partly covered with fragments of clothing, and brown dry skin. But we will spare Mrs. Morgan," he added with a smile. The lady had indeed exhibited signs of disgust rather than sympathy.

"It is necessary to say, however," he went on, "that the skull was fractured in several places, as by blows of some blunt instrument; and that instrument itself—a pick-handle, still stained with blood—lay under the boards near by."

Mr. Morgan turned to his wife. "Pardon me, my dear," he said with affected solemnity, "for mentioning these disagreeable particulars, the natural though regrettable incidents of a conjugal quarrel—resulting, doubtless, from the luckless wife's insubordination."

"I ought to be able to overlook it," the lady replied with composure; "you have so many times asked me to in those very words."

I thought he seemed rather glad to go on with his story.

"From these and other circumstances," he said, "the coroner's jury found that the deceased, Janet MacGregor, came to her death from blows inflicted by some person to the jury unknown; but it was added that the evidence pointed strongly to her husband, Thomas MacGregor, as the guilty person. But Thomas MacGregor has never been found nor heard of. It was learned that the couple came from Edinburgh, but not—my dear, do you not observe that Mr. Elderson's bone-plate has water in it?"

I had deposited a chicken bone in my finger bowl.

"In a little cupboard I found a photograph of MacGregor, but it did not lead to his capture."

"Will you let me see it?" I said.

The picture showed a dark man with an evil face made more forbidding by a long scar extending from near the temple diagonally downward into the black moustache.

"By the way, Mr. Elderson," said my affable host, "may I know why you asked about 'Macarger's Gulch'?"

"I lost a mule near there once," I replied, "and the mischance has—has quite—upset me."

"My dear," said Mr. Morgan, with the mechanical intonation of an interpreter translating, "the loss of Mr. Elderson's mule has peppered his coffee."

THE DEATH OF
HALPIN FRAYSER

I

For by death is wrought greater change than hath been shown. Whereas in general the spirit that removed cometh back upon occasion, and is sometimes seen of those in flesh (appearing in the form of the body it bore) yet it hath happened that the veritable body without the spirit hath walked. And it is attested of those encountering who have lived to speak thereon that a lich so raised up hath no natural affection, nor remembrance thereof, but only hate. Also, it is known that some spirits which in life were benign become by death evil altogether. —HALL.

ne dark night in midsummer a man waking from a dreamless sleep in a forest lifted his head from the earth, and staring a few moments into the blackness, said: "Catharine Larue." He said nothing more; no reason was known to him why he should have said so much.

The man was Halpin Frayser. He lived in St. Helena, but where he lives now is uncertain, for he is dead. One who practises sleeping in the woods with nothing under him but the dry leaves and the damp earth, and nothing over him but the branches from which the leaves have fallen and the sky from which the earth has fallen, cannot hope for great longevity, and Frayser had already attained the age of thirty-two. There are persons in this world, millions of persons, and far and away the best persons, who regard that as a very advanced age. They are the children. To those who view the voyage of life from the port of departure the bark that has accomplished any considerable distance appears already in close approach to the farther shore. However, it is not certain that Halpin Frayser came to his death by exposure.

He had been all day in the hills west of the Napa Valley, looking for doves and such small game as was in season. Late in the afternoon it had come on to be cloudy, and he had lost his bearings; and although he had only to go always downhill— everywhere the way to safety when one is lost—the absence of trails had so impeded him that he was overtaken by night while still in the forest. Unable in the darkness to penetrate the thickets of manzanita and other undergrowth, utterly bewildered and overcome with fatigue, he had lain down near the root of a large madroño and fallen into a dreamless sleep. It was hours later, in the very middle of the night, that one of God's mysterious messengers, gliding ahead of the incalculable host of his companions sweeping westward with the dawn line, pronounced the awakening word in the ear of the sleeper, who sat upright and spoke, he knew not why, a name, he knew not whose.

Halpin Frayser was not much of a philosopher, nor a scientist. The circumstance that, waking from a deep sleep at night in the midst of a forest, he had spoken aloud a name that he had not in memory and hardly had in mind did not arouse an enlightened curiosity to investigate the phenomenon. He thought it odd, and with a little perfunctory shiver, as if in deference to a seasonal presumption that the night was chill, he lay down again and went to sleep. But his sleep was no longer dreamless.

He thought he was walking along a dusty road that showed white in the gathering darkness of a summer night. Whence and whither it led, and why he travelled it, he did not know, though all seemed simple and natural, as is the way in dreams; for in the Land Beyond the Bed surprises cease from troubling and the judgment is at rest. Soon he came to a parting of the ways; leading from the highway was a road less travelled, having the appearance, indeed, of having been long abandoned, because, he thought, it led to something evil; yet he turned into it without hesitation, impelled by some imperious necessity.

As he pressed forward he became conscious that his way was haunted by invisible existences whom he could not definitely figure to his mind. From among the trees on either side he caught broken and incoherent whispers in a strange tongue which yet he partly understood. They seemed to him fragmentary utterances of a monstrous conspiracy against his body and soul.

It was now long after nightfall, yet the interminable forest through which he journeyed was lit with a wan glimmer having no point of diffusion, for in its mysterious lumination nothing cast a shadow. A shallow pool in the guttered depression of an old wheel rut, as from a recent rain, met his eye with a crimson gleam. He stooped and plunged his hand into it. It stained his fingers; it was blood! Blood, he then observed, was about him everywhere. The weeds growing rankly by the roadside showed it in blots and splashes on their big, broad leaves. Patches of dry dust between the wheel-ways were pitted and spattered as with a red rain. Defiling the trunks of the trees were broad maculations of crimson, and blood dripped like dew from their foliage.

All this he observed with a terror which seemed not incompatible with the fulfilment of a natural expectation. It seemed to him that it was all in expiation of some crime which, though conscious of his guilt, he could not rightly remember. To the menaces and mysteries of his surroundings the consciousness was an added horror. Vainly he sought, by tracing life backward in memory, to reproduce the moment of his sin; scenes and incidents came crowding tumultuously into his mind, one picture effacing another, or commingling with it in confusion and obscurity, but nowhere could he catch a glimpse of what he sought. The failure augmented his terror; he felt as one who has murdered in the dark, not knowing whom nor why. So frightful was the situation—the mysterious light burned with so silent and awful a menace; the noxious plants, the trees that by common consent are invested with a melancholy or baleful character, so openly in his sight conspired against his peace; from overhead and all about came so audible and startling whispers and the sighs of creatures so obviously not of earth—that he could endure it no longer, and with a great effort to break some malign spell that bound his faculties to silence and inaction, he shouted with the full strength of his lungs! His voice, broken, it seemed, into an infinite multitude of unfamiliar sounds, went babbling and stammering away into the distant reaches of the forest, died into silence, and all was as before. But he had made a beginning at resistance and was encouraged. He said:

"I will not submit unheard. There may be powers that are not malignant travelling this accursed road. I shall leave them a

record and an appeal. I shall relate my wrongs, the persecutions
that I endure—I, a helpless mortal, a penitent, an unoffending
poet!" Halpin Frayser was a poet only as he was a penitent: in
his dream.

Taking from his clothing a small red-leather pocketbook, one
half of which was leaved for memoranda, he discovered that he
was without a pencil. He broke a twig from a bush, dipped it
into a pool of blood and wrote rapidly. He had hardly touched
the paper with the point of his twig when a low, wild peal of
laughter broke out at a measureless distance away, and growing
ever louder, seemed approaching ever nearer; a soulless, heart-
less, and unjoyous laugh, like that of the loon, solitary by the
lakeside at midnight; a laugh which culminated in an unearthly
shout close at hand, then died away by slow gradations, as if the
accursed being that uttered it had withdrawn over the verge of
the world whence it had come. But the man felt that this was
not so—that it was near by and had not moved.

A strange sensation began slowly to take possession of his
body and his mind. He could not have said which, if any, of his
senses was affected; he felt it rather as a consciousness—a mysterious mental assurance of some overpowering presence—some
supernatural malevolence different in kind from the invisible
existences that swarmed about him, and superior to them in
power. He knew that it had uttered that hideous laugh. And
now it seemed to be approaching him; from what direction he
did not know—dared not conjecture. All his former fears were
forgotten or merged in the gigantic terror that now held him in
thrall. Apart from that, he had but one thought: to complete his
written appeal to the benign powers who, traversing the haunted

wood, might some time rescue him if he should be denied the blessing of annihilation. He wrote with terrible rapidity, the twig in his fingers rilling blood without renewal; but in the middle of a sentence his hands denied their service to his will, his arms fell to his sides, the book to the earth; and powerless to move or cry out, he found himself staring into the sharply drawn face and blank, dead eyes of his own mother, standing white and silent in the garments of the grave!

II

In his youth Halpin Frayser had lived with his parents in Nashville, Tennessee. The Fraysers were well-to-do, having a good position in such society as had survived the wreck wrought by civil war. Their children had the social and educational opportunities of their time and place, and had responded to good associations and instruction with agreeable manners and cultivated minds. Halpin being the youngest and not over robust was perhaps a trifle "spoiled." He had the double disadvantage of a mother's assiduity and a father's neglect. Frayser *père* was what no Southern man of means is not—a politician. His country, or rather his section and State, made demands upon his time and attention so exacting that to those of his family he was compelled to turn an ear partly deafened by the thunder of the political captains and the shouting, his own included.

Young Halpin was of a dreamy, indolent and rather romantic turn, somewhat more addicted to literature than law, the profession to which he was bred. Among those of his relations who professed the modern faith of heredity it was well understood that in him the character of the late Myron Bayne, a maternal great-grandfather, had revisited the glimpses of the moon—by which orb Bayne had in his lifetime been sufficiently affected to be a poet of no small Colonial distinction. If not specially observed, it was observable that while a Frayser who was not the proud possessor of a sumptuous copy of the ancestral "poetical works" (printed at the family expense, and long ago withdrawn from an inhospitable market) was a rare Frayser indeed, there was an illogical indisposition to honour the great deceased in the person of his spiritual successor. Halpin was pretty generally deprecated as an intellectual black sheep who was likely at any moment to disgrace the flock by bleating in metre. The Tennessee Fraysers were a practical folk—not practical in the popular sense of devotion to sordid pursuits, but having a robust contempt for any qualities unfitting a man for the wholesome vocation of politics.

In justice to young Halpin it should be said that while in him were pretty faithfully reproduced most of the mental and moral characteristics ascribed by history and family tradition to the famous Colonial bard, his succession to the gift and faculty divine was purely inferential. Not only had he never been known to court the Muse, but in truth he could not have written correctly a line of verse to save himself from the Killer of the Wise. Still, there was no knowing when the dormant faculty might wake and smite the lyre.

In the meantime the young man was rather a loose fish, anyhow. Between him and his mother was the most perfect sympathy, for secretly the lady was herself a devout disciple of the late and great Myron Bayne, though with the tact so generally and justly admired in her sex (despite the hardy calumniators who insist that it is essentially the same thing as cunning) she had always taken care to conceal her weakness from all eyes but those of him who shared it. Their common guilt in respect of that was an added tie between them. If in Halpin's youth his mother had "spoiled" him he had assuredly done his part toward being spoiled. As he grew to such manhood as is attainable by a Southerner who does not care which way elections go, the attachment between him and his beautiful mother—whom from early childhood he had called Katy—became yearly stronger and more tender. In these two romantic natures was manifest in a signal way that neglected phenomenon, the dominance of the sexual element in all the relations of life, strengthening, softening, and beautifying even those of consanguinity. The two were nearly inseparable, and by strangers observing their manners were not infrequently mistaken for lovers.

Entering his mother's boudoir one day Halpin Frayser kissed her upon the forehead, toyed for a moment with a lock of her dark hair which had escaped from its confining pins, and said, with an obvious effort at calmness:

"Would you greatly mind, Katy, if I were called away to California for a few weeks?"

It was hardly needful for Katy to answer with her lips a question to which her tell-tale cheeks had made instant reply. Evidently she would greatly mind; and the tears, too, sprang into her large brown eyes as corroborative testimony.

"Ah, my son," she said, looking up into his face with infinite tenderness, "I should have known that this was coming. Did I not lie awake a half of the night weeping because, during the other half, Grandfather Bayne had come to me in a dream, and standing by his portrait—young, too, and handsome as that—pointed to yours on the same wall? And when I looked it seemed that I could not see the features; you had been painted with a face cloth, such as we put upon the dead. Your father has laughed at me, but you and I, dear, know that such things are not for nothing. And I saw below the edge of the cloth the marks of hands on your throat—forgive me, but we have not been used to keep such things from each other. Perhaps you have another interpretation. Perhaps it does not mean that you will go to California. Or maybe you will take me with you?"

It must be confessed that this ingenious interpretation of the dream in the light of newly discovered evidence did not wholly commend itself to the son's more logical mind; he had, for the moment at least, a conviction that it foreshadowed a more simple and immediate, if less tragic, disaster than a visit to the Pacific Coast. It was Halpin Frayser's impression that he was to be garroted on his native heath.

"Are there not medicinal springs in California?" Mrs. Frayser resumed before he had time to give her the true reading of the dream—"places where one recovers from rheumatism and neuralgia? Look—my fingers feel so stiff; and I am almost sure they have been giving me great pain while I slept."

She held out her hands for his inspection. What diagnosis of her case the young man may have thought it best to conceal with a smile the historian is unable to state, but for himself he feels bound to say that fingers looking less stiff, and showing fewer evidences of even insensible pain, have seldom been submitted for medical inspection by even the fairest patient desiring a prescription of unfamiliar scenes.

The outcome of it was that of these two odd persons having equally odd notions of duty, the one went to California, as the interest of his client required, and the other remained at home in compliance with a wish that her husband was scarcely conscious of entertaining.

While in San Francisco Halpin Frayser was walking one dark night along the water-front of the city, when, with a suddenness that surprised and disconcerted him, he became a sailor. He was in fact "shanghaied" aboard a gallant, gallant ship, and sailed for a far countree. Nor did his misfortunes end with the voyage; for the ship was cast ashore on an island of the South Pacific, and it was six years afterward when the survivors were taken off by a venturesome trading schooner and brought back to San Francisco.

Though poor in purse, Frayser was no less proud in spirit than he had been in the years that seemed ages and ages ago. He would accept no assistance from strangers, and it was while living with a fellow survivor near the town of St. Helena, awaiting news and remittances from home, that he had gone gunning and dreaming.

III

The apparition confronting the dreamer in the haunted wood— the thing so like, yet so unlike, his mother—was horrible! It stirred no love nor longing in his heart; it came unattended with pleasant memories of a golden past—inspired no sentiment of any kind; all the finer emotions were swallowed up in fear. He tried to turn and run from before it, but his legs were as lead; he was unable to lift his feet from the ground. His arms hung helpless at his sides; of his eyes only he retained control, and these he dared not remove from the lustreless orbs of the apparition, which he knew was not a soul without a body, but that most dreadful of all existences infesting that haunted wood—a body without a soul! In its blank stare was neither love, nor pity, nor intelligence—nothing to which to address an appeal for mercy. "An appeal will not lie," he thought, with an absurd reversion to professional slang, making the situation more horrible, as the fire of a cigar might light up a tomb.

For a time, which seemed so long that the world grew grey with age and sin, and the haunted forest, having fulfilled its purpose in this monstrous culmination of its terrors, vanished out of his consciousness with all its sights and sounds, the apparition stood within a pace, regarding him with the mindless malevolence of a wild brute; then thrust its hands forward and sprang upon him with appalling ferocity! The act released his physical energies without unfettering his will; his mind was still spellbound, but his powerful body and agile limbs, endowed with a blind, insensate life of their own, resisted stoutly and well. For an instant he seemed to see this unnatural contest between a dead intelligence and a breathing mechanism only as a spectator—such fancies are in dreams; then he regained his identity almost as if by a leap forward into his body, and the straining automaton had a directing will as alert and fierce as that of its hideous antagonist.

But what mortal can cope with a creature of his dream? The imagination creating the enemy is already vanquished; the combat's result is the combat's cause. Despite his struggles—despite his strength and activity, which seemed wasted in a void, he felt the cold fingers close upon his throat. Borne backward to the earth, he saw above him the dead and drawn face within a hand's-breadth of his own, and then all was black. A sound as of the beating of distant drums—a murmur of swarming voices, a sharp, far cry signing all to silence, and Halpin Frayser dreamed that he was dead.

IV

A warm, clear night had been followed by a morning of drenching fog. At about the middle of the afternoon of the preceding day a little whiff of light vapour—a mere thickening of the atmosphere, the ghost of a cloud—had been observed clinging to the western side of Mount St. Helena, away up along the barren altitudes near the summit. It was so thin, so diaphanous, so like a fancy made visible, that one would have said: "Look quickly! in a moment it will be gone."

In a moment it was visibly larger and denser. While with one edge it clung to the mountain, with the other it reached farther and farther out into the air above the lower slopes. At the same time it extended itself to north and south, joining small patches of mist that appeared to come out of the mountain-side on exactly the same level, with an intelligent design to be absorbed. And so it grew and grew until the summit was shut out of view from the valley, and over the valley itself was an ever-extending canopy, opaque and grey. At Calistoga, which lies near the head of the valley and the foot of the mountain, there were a starless night and a sunless morning. The fog, sinking into the valley, had reached southward, swallowing up ranch after ranch, until it had blotted out the town of St. Helena, nine miles away. The dust in the road was laid; trees were adrip with moisture; birds sat silent in their coverts; the morning light was wan and ghastly, with neither colour nor fire.

Two men left the town of St. Helena at the first glimmer of dawn, and walked along the road northward up the valley toward Calistoga. They carried guns on their shoulders, yet no one having knowledge of such matters could have mistaken them for hunters of bird or beast. They were a deputy sheriff from Napa and a detective from San Francisco—Holker and Jaralson, respectively. Their business was man-hunting.

"How far is it?" inquired Holker, as they strode along, their feet stirring white the dust beneath the damp surface of the road.

"The White Church? Only a half mile farther," the other answered. "By the way," he added, "it is neither white nor a church; it is an abandoned schoolhouse, grey with age and neglect. Religious services were once held in it—when it was white, and there is a graveyard that would delight a poet. Can you guess why I sent for you, and told you to come armed?"

"Oh, I never have bothered you about things of that kind. I've always found you communicative when the time came. But if I may hazard a guess, you want me to help you arrest one of the corpses in the graveyard."

"You remember Branscom?" said Jaralson, treating his companion's wit with the inattention that it deserved.

"The chap who cut his wife's throat? I ought; I wasted a week's work on him and had my expenses for my trouble. There is a reward of five hundred dollars, but none of us ever got a sight of him. You don't mean to say—"

"Yes, I do. He has been under the noses of you fellows all the time. He comes by night to the old graveyard at the White Church."

"The devil! That's where they buried his wife."

"Well, you fellows might have had sense enough to suspect that he would return to her grave some time?"

"The very last place that anyone would have expected him to return to."

"But you had exhausted all the other places. Learning your failure at them, I 'laid for him' there."

"And you found him?"

"Damn it! he found *me*. The rascal got the drop on me— regularly held me up and made me travel. It's God's mercy that he didn't go through me. Oh, he's a good one, and I fancy the half of that reward is enough for me if you're needy."

Holker laughed good-humouredly, and explained that his creditors were never more importunate.

"I wanted merely to show you the ground, and arrange a plan with you," the detective explained. "I thought it as well for us to be armed, even in daylight."

"The man must be insane," said the deputy sheriff. "The reward is for his capture and conviction. If he's mad he won't be convicted."

Mr. Holker was so profoundly affected by that possible failure of justice that he involuntarily stopped in the middle of the road, then resumed his walk with abated zeal.

"Well, he looks it," assented Jaralson. "I'm bound to admit that a more unshaven, unshorn, unkempt, and uneverything wretch I never saw outside the ancient and honourable order of tramps. But I've gone in for him, and can't make up my mind to let go. There's glory in it for us, anyhow. Not another soul knows that he is this side of the Mountains of the Moon."

"All right," Holker said; "we will go and view the ground," and he added, in the words of a once favourite inscription for tombstones: "'where you must shortly lie'—I mean if old Branscom ever gets tired of you and your impertinent intrusion. By the way, I heard the other day that 'Branscom' was not his real name."

"What is?"

"I can't recall it. I had lost all interest in the wretch, and it did not fix itself in my memory—something like Pardee. The woman whose throat he had the bad taste to cut was a widow when he met her. She had come to California to look up some relatives—there are persons who will do that sometimes. But you know all that."

"Naturally."

"But not knowing the right name, by what happy inspiration did you find the right grave? The man who told me what the name was said it had been cut on the headboard."

"I don't know the right grave." Jaralson was apparently a trifle reluctant to admit his ignorance of so important a point of his plan. "I have been watching about the place generally.

A part of our work this morning will be to identify that grave. Here is the White Church."

For a long distance the road had been bordered by fields on both sides, but now on the left there was a forest of oaks, madroños, and gigantic spruces whose lower parts only could be seen, dim and ghostly in the fog. The undergrowth was, in places, thick, but nowhere impenetrable. For some moments Holker saw nothing of the building, but as they turned into the woods it revealed itself in faint grey outline through the fog, looking huge and far away. A few steps more, and it was within an arm's length, distinct, dark with moisture, and insignificant in size. It had the usual country-schoolhouse form—belonged to the packing-box order of architecture; had an underpinning of stones, a moss-grown roof, and blank window spaces, whence both glass and sash had long departed. It was ruined, but not a ruin—a typical Californian substitute for what are known to guide-bookers abroad as "monuments of the past." With scarcely a glance at this uninteresting structure Jaralson moved on into the dripping undergrowth beyond.

"I will show you where he held me up," he said. "This is the graveyard."

Here and there among the bushes were small enclosures containing graves, sometimes no more than one. They were recognized as graves by the discoloured stones or rotting boards at head and foot, leaning at all angles, some prostrate; by the ruined picket fences surrounding them; or, infrequently, by the mound itself showing its gravel through the fallen leaves. In many instances nothing marked the spot where lay the vestiges of some poor mortal—who, leaving "a large circle of sorrowing friends," had been left by them in turn—except a depression in the earth, more lasting than that in the spirits of the mourners. The paths, if any paths had been, were long obliterated; trees of a considerable size had been permitted to grow up from the graves and thrust aside with root or branch the enclosing fences. Over all was that air of abandonment and decay which seems nowhere so fit and significant as in a village of the forgotten dead.

As the two men, Jaralson leading, pushed their way through the growth of young trees, that enterprising man suddenly stopped and brought up his shotgun to the height of his breast, uttered a low note of warning, and stood motionless, his eyes fixed upon something ahead. As well as he could, obstructed by brush, his companion, though seeing nothing, imitated the posture and so stood, prepared for what might ensue. A moment later Jaralson moved cautiously forward, the other following.

Under the branches of an enormous spruce lay the dead body of a man. Standing silent above it they noted such particulars as first strike the attention—the face, the attitude, the clothing; whatever most promptly and plainly answers the unspoken question of a sympathetic curiosity.

The body lay upon its back, the legs wide apart. One arm was thrust upward, the other outward; but the latter was bent acutely, and the hand was near the throat. Both hands were tightly clenched. The whole attitude was that of desperate but ineffectual resistance to—what?

Near by lay a shotgun and a game bag through the meshes of which was seen the plumage of shot birds. All about were evidences of a furious struggle; small sprouts of poison-oak were bent and denuded of leaf and bark; dead and rotting leaves had been pushed into heaps and ridges on both sides of the legs by the action of other feet than theirs; alongside the hips were unmistakable impressions of human knees.

The nature of the struggle was made clear by a glance at the dead man's throat and face. While breast and hands were white, those were purple—almost black. The shoulders lay upon a low mound, and the head was turned back at an angle otherwise impossible, the expanded eyes staring blankly backward in a direction opposite to that of the feet. From the froth filling the open mouth the tongue protruded, black and swollen. The throat showed horrible contusions; not mere finger-marks, but bruises and lacerations wrought by two strong hands that must have buried themselves in the yielding flesh, maintaining their terrible grasp until long after death. Breast, throat, face, were wet; the clothing was saturated; drops of water, condensed from the fog, studded the hair and moustache.

All this the two men observed without speaking—almost at a glance. Then Holker said:

"Poor devil! he had a rough deal."

Jaralson was making a vigilant circumspection of the forest, his shotgun held in both hands and at full cock, his finger upon the trigger.

"The work of a maniac," he said, without withdrawing his eyes from the enclosing wood. "It was done by Branscom—Pardee."

Something half hidden by the disturbed leaves on the earth caught Holker's attention. It was a red-leather pocketbook. He picked it up and opened it. It contained leaves of white paper for memoranda, and upon the first leaf was the name "Halpin

Frayser." Written in red on several succeeding leaves—scrawled as if in haste and barely legible—were the following lines, which Holker read aloud, while his companion continued scanning the dim grey confines of their narrow world and hearing matter of apprehension in the drip of water from every burdened branch:

"Enthralled by some mysterious spell, I stood
In the lit gloom of an enchanted wood.
The cypress there and myrtle twined their boughs,
Significant, in baleful brotherhood.

"The brooding willow whispered to the yew;
Beneath, the deadly nightshade and the rue,
With immortelles self-woven into strange
Funereal shapes, and horrid nettles grew.

"No song of bird nor any drone of bees,
Nor light leaf lifted by the wholesome breeze:
The air was stagnant all, and Silence was
A living thing that breathed among the trees.

"Conspiring spirits whispered in the gloom,
Half-heard, the stilly secrets of the tomb.
With blood the trees were all adrip; the leaves
Shone in the witch-light with a ruddy bloom.

"I cried aloud!—the spell, unbroken still,
Rested upon my spirit and my will.

Unsouled, unhearted, hopeless and forlorn,
I strove with monstrous presages of ill!

"At last the viewless—"

Holker ceased reading; there was no more to read. The manuscript broke off in the middle of a line.

"That sounds like Bayne," said Jaralson, who was something of a scholar in his way. He had abated his vigilance and stood looking down at the body.

"Who's Bayne?" Holker asked rather incuriously.

"Myron Bayne, a chap who flourished in the early years of the nation—more than a century ago. Wrote mighty dismal stuff; I have his collected works. That poem is not among them, but it must have been omitted by mistake."

"It is cold," said Holker; "let us leave here; we must have up the coroner from Napa."

Jaralson said nothing, but made a movement in compliance. Passing the end of the slight elevation of earth upon which the dead man's head and shoulders lay, his foot struck some hard substance under the rotting forest leaves, and he took the trouble to kick it into view. It was a fallen headboard, and painted on it were the hardly decipherable words, "Catharine Larue."

"Larue, Larue!" exclaimed Holker, with sudden animation. "Why, that is the real name of Branscom—not Pardee. And— bless my soul! how it all comes to me—the murdered woman's name had been Frayser!"

"There is some rascally mystery here," said Detective Jaralson. "I hate anything of that kind."

There came to them out of the fog—seemingly from a great distance—the sound of a laugh, a low, deliberate, soulless laugh which had no more of joy than that of a hyena night-prowling in the desert; a laugh that rose by slow gradation, louder and louder, clearer, more distinct and terrible, until it seemed barely outside the narrow circle of their vision; a laugh so unnatural, so unhuman, so devilish, that it filled those hardy man-hunters with a sense of dread unspeakable! They did not move their weapons nor think of them; the menace of that horrible sound was not of the kind to be met with arms. As it had grown out of silence, so now it died away; from a culminating shout which had seemed almost in their ears, it drew itself away into the distance, until its failing notes, joyless and mechanical to the last, sank to silence at a measureless remove.

JOHN BARTINE'S WATCH

A Story by a Physician

"he exact time? Good God! my friend, why do you insist? One would think—but what does it matter; it is easily bedtime—isn't that near enough? But, here, if you must set your watch, take mine and see for yourself."

With that he detached his watch—a tremendously heavy, old-fashioned one—from the chain, and handed it to me; then turned away, and walking across the room to a shelf of books, began an examination of their backs. His agitation and evident distress surprised me; they appeared reasonless. Having set my watch by his I stepped over to where he stood and said, "Thank you."

As he took his timepiece and reattached it to the guard I observed that his hands were unsteady. With a tact upon which I greatly prided myself, I sauntered carelessly to the sideboard and took some brandy and water; then, begging his pardon for my thoughtlessness, asked him to have some and went back to my seat by the fire, leaving him to help himself, as was our custom. He did so and presently joined me at the hearth, as tranquil as ever.

This odd little incident occurred in my apartment, where John Bartine was passing an evening. We had dined together at the club, had come home in a cab and—in short, everything had been done in the most prosaic way; and why John Bartine should break in upon the natural and established order of things to make himself spectacular with a display of emotion, apparently for his own entertainment, I could nowise understand. The more I thought of it, while his brilliant conversational gifts were commending themselves to my inattention, the more curious I grew, and of course had no difficulty in persuading myself that my curiosity was friendly solicitude. That is the disguise that curiosity usually assumes to evade resentment. So I ruined one of the finest sentences of his disregarded monologue by cutting it short without ceremony.

"John Bartine," I said, "you must try to forgive me if I am wrong, but with the light that I have at present I cannot concede your right to go all to pieces when asked the time o' night. I cannot admit that it is proper to experience a mysterious reluctance to look your own watch in the face and to cherish in my presence, without explanation, painful emotions which are denied to me, and which are none of my business."

To this ridiculous speech Bartine made no immediate reply, but sat looking gravely into the fire. Fearing that I had offended I was about to apologize and beg him to think no more about the matter, when looking me calmly in the eyes he said:

"My dear fellow, the levity of your manner does not at all disguise the hideous impudence of your demand; but happily I had already decided to tell you what you wish to know, and no manifestation of your unworthiness to hear it shall alter my decision. Be good enough to give me your attention and you shall hear all about the matter.

"This watch," he said, "had been in my family for three generations before it fell to me. Its original owner, for whom it was made, was my great-grandfather, Bramwell Olcott Bartine, a wealthy planter of Colonial Virginia, and as staunch a Tory as ever lay awake nights contriving new kinds of maledictions for the head of Mr. Washington, and new methods of aiding and abetting good King George. One day this worthy gentleman had the deep misfortune to perform for his cause a service of capital importance which was not recognized as legitimate by those who suffered its disadvantages. It does not matter what it was, but among its minor consequences was my excellent ancestor's arrest one night in his own house by a party of Mr. Washington's rebels. He was permitted to say farewell to his weeping family, and was then marched away into the darkness which swallowed him up for ever. Not the slenderest clue to his fate was ever found. After the war the most diligent inquiry and the offer of large rewards failed to turn up any of his captors or any fact concerning his disappearance. He had disappeared, and that was all."

Something in Bartine's manner that was not in his words—I hardly knew what it was—prompted me to ask:

"What is your view of the matter—of the justice of it?"

"My view of it," he flamed out, bringing his clenched hand down upon the table as if he had been in a public-house dicing with blackguards—"my view of it is that it was a characteristically dastardly assassination by that damned traitor, Washington, and his ragamuffin rebels!"

For some minutes nothing was said: Bartine was recovering his temper, and I waited. Then I said:

"Was that all?"

"No—there was something else. A few weeks after my great-grandfather's arrest his watch was found lying on the porch at the front door of his dwelling. It was wrapped in a sheet of letter paper bearing the name of Rupert Bartine, his only son, my grandfather. I am wearing that watch."

Bartine paused. His usually restless black eyes were staring fixedly into the grate, a point of red light in each, reflected from the glowing coals. He seemed to have forgotten me. A sudden threshing of the branches of a tree outside one of the windows, and almost at the same instant a rattle of rain against the glass, recalled him to a sense of his surroundings. A storm had risen, heralded by a single gust of wind, and in a few moments the steady plash of the water on the pavement was distinctly heard. I hardly know why I relate this incident; it seemed somehow to have a certain significance and relevancy which I am unable now to discern. It at least added an element of seriousness, almost solemnity. Bartine resumed:

"I have a singular feeling toward this watch—a kind of affection for it; I like to have it about me, though partly from its weight, and partly for a reason I shall now explain, I seldom carry it. The reason is this: Every evening when I have it with me I feel an unaccountable desire to open and consult it, even if I can think of no reason for wishing to know the time. But if I yield to it, the moment my eyes rest upon the dial I am filled with a mysterious apprehension—a sense of imminent calamity. And this is the more insupportable the nearer it is to eleven o'clock—by this watch, no matter what the actual hour may be. After the hands have registered eleven the desire to look is gone; I am entirely indifferent. Then I can consult the thing as often as I like, with no more emotion than you feel in looking at your own. Naturally I have trained myself not to look at that watch in the evening before eleven; nothing could induce me. Your insistence this evening upset me a trifle. I felt very much as I suppose an opium-eater might feel if his yearning for his special and particular kind of hell were reinforced by opportunity and advice.

"Now that is my story, and I have told it in the interest of your trumpery science; but if on any evening hereafter you observe me wearing this damnable watch, and you have the thoughtfulness to ask me the hour, I shall beg leave to put you to the inconvenience of being knocked down."

His humour did not amuse me. I could see that in relating his delusion he was again somewhat disturbed. His concluding smile was positively ghastly, and his eyes had resumed something more than their old restlessness; they shifted hither and thither about the room with apparent aimlessness and I fancied had taken on a wild expression, such as is sometimes observed in cases of dementia. Perhaps this was my own imagination, but at any rate I was now persuaded that my friend was afflicted with a most singular and interesting monomania. Without, I trust, any abatement of my affectionate solicitude for him as a friend, I began to regard him as a patient, rich in possibilities of profitable study. Why not? Had he not described his delusion in the interest of science? Ah, poor fellow, he was doing more for science than he knew: not only his story but himself was in evidence. I should cure him if I could, of course, but first I should make a little experiment in psychology—nay, the experiment itself might be a step in his restoration.

"That is very frank and friendly of you, Bartine," I said cordially, "and I'm rather proud of your confidence. It is all very odd, certainly. Do you mind showing me the watch?"

He detached it from his waistcoat, chain and all, and passed it to me without a word. The case was of gold, very thick and strong, and singularly engraved. After closely examining the dial and observing that it was nearly twelve o'clock, I opened it at the back and was interested to observe an inner case of ivory, upon which was painted a miniature portrait in that exquisite and delicate manner which was in vogue during the eighteenth century.

"Why, bless my soul!" I exclaimed, feeling a sharp artistic delight—"how under the sun did you get that done? I thought miniature painting on ivory was a lost art."

"That," he replied, gravely smiling, "is not I; it is my excellent great-grandfather, the late Bramwell Olcott Bartine, Esquire, of Virginia. He was younger then than later—about my age, in fact. It is said to resemble me; do you think so?"

"Resemble you? I should say so! Barring the costume, which I supposed you to have assumed out of compliment to the art—or for *vraisemblance*, so to say—and the no moustache, that portrait is you in every feature, line, and expression."

No more was said at that time. Bartine took a book from the table and began reading. I heard outside the incessant plash of the rain in the street. There were occasional hurried footfalls on the sidewalks; and once a slower, heavier tread seemed to cease at my door—a policeman, I thought, seeking shelter in the doorway. The boughs of the trees tapped significantly on the window panes, as if asking for admittance. I remember it all through these years and years of a wiser, graver life.

Seeing myself unobserved, I took the old-fashioned key that dangled from the chain and quickly turned back the hands of the watch a full hour; then, closing the case, I handed Bartine his property and saw him replace it on his person.

"I think you said," I began, with assumed carelessness, "that after eleven the sight of the dial no longer affects you. As it is now nearly twelve"—looking at my own timepiece—"perhaps, if you don't resent my pursuit of proof, you will look at it now."

He smiled good-humouredly, pulled out the watch again, opened it, and instantly sprang to his feet with a cry that Heaven has not had the mercy to permit me to forget! His eyes, their blackness strikingly intensified by the pallor of his face, were fixed upon the watch, which he clutched in both hands. For some time he remained in that attitude without uttering another sound; then, in a voice that I should not have recognized as his, he said;

"Damn you! it is two minutes to eleven!"

I was not unprepared for some such outbreak, and without rising replied, calmly enough:

"I beg your pardon; I must have misread your watch in setting my own by it."

He shut the case with a sharp snap and put the watch in his pocket. He looked at me and made an attempt to smile, but his lower lip quivered and he seemed unable to close his mouth. His hands, also, were shaking, and he thrust them, clenched, into the pockets of his sack-coat. The courageous spirit was manifestly endeavouring to subdue the coward body. The effort was too great; he began to sway from side to side, as from vertigo, and before I could spring from my chair to support him his knees gave way and he pitched awkwardly forward and fell upon his face. I sprang to assist him to rise; but when John Bartine rises we shall all rise.

The *post-mortem* examination disclosed nothing; every organ was normal and sound. But when the body had been prepared for burial a faint dark circle was seen to have developed around the neck; at least I was so assured by several persons who said they saw it, but of my own knowledge I cannot say if that was true.

Nor can I set limitations to the law of heredity. I do not know that in the spiritual world a sentiment or emotion may not survive the heart that held it, and seek expression in a kindred life, ages removed. Surely, if I were to guess at the fate of Bramwell Olcott Bartine, I should guess that he was hanged at eleven o'clock in the evening, and that he had been allowed several hours in which to prepare for the change.

As to John Bartine, my friend, my patient for five minutes, and—Heaven forgive me!—my victim for eternity, there is no more to say. He is buried, and his watch with him—I saw to that. May God rest his soul in Paradise, and the soul of his Virginian ancestor, if, indeed, they are two souls.

THE EYES OF THE PANTHER

One Does Not Always Marry When Insane

man and a woman—nature had done the grouping— sat on a rustic seat, in the late afternoon. The man was middle-aged, slender, swarthy, with the expression of a poet and the complexion of a pirate—a man at whom one would look again. The woman was young, blonde, graceful, with something in her figure and movements suggesting the word "lithe." She was habited in a grey gown with odd brown markings in the texture. She may have been beautiful; one could not readily say, for her eyes denied attention to all else. They were grey-green, long and narrow, with an expression defying analysis. One could only know that they were disquieting. Cleopatra may have had such eyes.

The man and the woman talked.

"Yes," said the woman, "I love you, God knows! But marry you, no. I cannot, will not."

"Irene, you have said that many times, yet always have denied me a reason. I've a right to know, to understand, to feel and prove my fortitude if I have it. Give me a reason."

"For loving you?"

The woman was smiling through her tears and her pallor. That did not stir any sense of humour in the man.

"No; there is no reason for that. A reason for not marrying me. I've a right to know. I must know. I will know!"

He had risen and was standing before her with clenched hands, on his face a frown—it might have been called a scowl. He looked as if he might attempt to learn by strangling her. She smiled no more—merely sat looking up into his face with a fixed, set regard that was utterly without emotion or sentiment. Yet it had something in it that tamed his resentment and made him shiver.

"You are determined to have my reason?" she asked in a tone that was entirely mechanical—a tone that might have been her look made audible.

"If you please—if I'm not asking too much."

Apparently this lord of creation was yielding some part of his dominion over his co-creature.

"Very well, you shall know: I am insane."

The man started, then looked incredulous and was conscious that he ought to be amused. But, again, the sense of humour failed him in his need and despite his disbelief he was profoundly disturbed by that which he did not believe. Between our convictions and our feelings there is no good understanding.

"That is what the physicians would say," the woman continued—"if they knew. I might myself prefer to call it a case of 'possession.' Sit down and hear what I have to say."

The man silently resumed his seat beside her on the rustic bench by the wayside. Over-against them on the eastern side of the valley the hills were already sunset-flushed and the stillness all about was of that peculiar quality that foretells the twilight. Something of its mysterious and significant solemnity had imparted itself to the man's mood. In the spiritual, as in the material world, are signs and presages of night. Rarely meeting her look, and whenever he did so conscious of the indefinable dread with which, despite their feline beauty, her eyes always affected him, Jenner Brading listened in silence to the story told by Irene Marlowe. In deference to the reader's possible prejudice against the artless method of an unpractised historian the author ventures to substitute his own version for hers.

II

A Room May Be Too Narrow for Three, Though One Is Outside

In a little log house containing a single room sparely and rudely furnished, crouching on the floor against one of the walls, was a woman, clasping to her breast a child. Outside, a dense unbroken forest extended for many miles in every direction. This was at night and the room was black dark: no human eye could have discerned the woman and the child. Yet they were observed, narrowly, vigilantly, with never even a momentary slackening of attention; and that is the pivotal fact upon which this narrative turns.

Charles Marlowe was of the class, now extinct in this country, of woodmen pioneers—men who found their most acceptable surroundings in sylvan solitudes that stretched along the eastern slope of the Mississippi Valley, from the Great Lakes to the Gulf of Mexico. For more than a hundred years these men pushed ever westward, generation after generation, with rifle and axe, reclaiming from Nature and her savage children here and there an isolated acreage for the plough, no sooner reclaimed than surrendered to their less venturesome but more thrifty successors. At last they burst through the edge of the forest into the open country and vanished as if they had fallen over a cliff. The woodman pioneer is no more; the pioneer of the plains—he whose easy task it was to subdue for occupancy two-thirds of the country in a single generation—is another and inferior creation. With Charles Marlowe in the wilderness, sharing the dangers, hardships and privations of that strange, unprofitable life, were his wife and child, to whom, in the manner of his class, in which the domestic virtues were a religion, he was passionately attached. The woman was still young enough to be comely, new enough to the awful isolation of her lot to be cheerful. By withholding the large capacity for happiness which the simple satisfactions of the forest life could not have filled, Heaven had dealt honourably with her. In her light household tasks, her child, her husband and her few foolish books, she found abundant provision for her needs.

One morning in midsummer Marlowe took down his rifle from the wooden hooks on the wall and signified his intention of getting game.

"We've meat enough," said the wife; "please don't go out today. I dreamed last night, O, such a dreadful thing! I cannot recollect it, but I'm almost sure that it will come to pass if you go out."

It is painful to confess that Marlowe received this solemn statement with less of gravity than was due to the mysterious nature of the calamity foreshadowed. In truth, he laughed.

"Try to remember," he said. "Maybe you dreamed that Baby had lost the power of speech."

The conjecture was obviously suggested by the fact that Baby, clinging to the fringe of his hunting-coat with all her ten pudgy thumbs was at that moment uttering her sense of the situation in a series of exultant goo-goos inspired by sight of her father's raccoon-skin cap.

The woman yielded: lacking the gift of humour she could not hold out against his kindly badinage. So, with a kiss for the mother and a kiss for the child, he left the house and closed the door upon his happiness forever.

At nightfall he had not returned. The woman prepared supper and waited. Then she put Baby to bed and sang softly to her until she slept. By this time the fire on the hearth, at which she had cooked supper, had burned out and the room was lighted by a single candle. This she afterward placed in the open window as a sign and welcome to the hunter if he should approach from that side. She had thoughtfully closed and barred the door against such wild animals as might prefer it to an open window—of the habits of beasts of prey in entering a house uninvited she was not advised, though with true female prevision she may have considered the possibility of their entrance by way of the chimney. As the night wore on she became not less anxious, but more drowsy, and at last rested her arms upon the bed by the child and her head upon the arms. The candle in the window burned down to the socket, sputtered and flared a moment and went out unobserved; for the woman slept and dreamed.

In her dreams she sat beside the cradle of a second child. The first one was dead. The father was dead. The home in the forest was lost and the dwelling in which she lived was unfamiliar. There were heavy oaken doors, always closed, and outside the windows, fastened into the thick stone walls, were iron bars, obviously (so she thought) a provision against Indians. All this she noted with an infinite self-pity, but without surprise—an emotion unknown in dreams. The child in the cradle was invisible under its coverlet which something impelled her to remove. She did so, disclosing the face of a wild animal! In the shock of this dreadful revelation the dreamer awoke, trembling in the darkness of her cabin in the wood.

As a sense of her actual surroundings came slowly back to her she felt for the child that was not a dream, and assured herself by its breathing that all was well with it; nor could she forbear to pass a hand lightly across its face. Then, moved by some impulse for which she probably could not have accounted, she rose and took the sleeping babe in her arms, holding it close against her breast. The head of the child's cot was against the wall to which the woman now turned her back as she stood. Lifting her eyes she saw two bright objects starring the darkness with a reddish-green glow. She took them to be two coals on the hearth, but with her returning sense of direction came the disquieting consciousness that they were not in that quarter of the room, moreover were too high, being nearly at the level of the eyes—of her own eyes. For these were the eyes of a panther.

The beast was at the open window directly opposite and not five paces away. Nothing but those terrible eyes was visible, but in the dreadful tumult of her feelings as the situation disclosed itself to her understanding she somehow knew that the animal was standing on its hinder feet, supporting itself with its paws on the window-ledge. That signified a malign interest—not the mere gratification of an indolent curiosity. The consciousness of the attitude was an added horror, accentuating the menace of those awful eyes, in whose steadfast fire her strength and courage were alike consumed. Under their silent questioning she shuddered and turned sick. Her knees failed her, and by degrees, instinctively striving to avoid a sudden movement that might bring the beast upon her, she sank to the floor, crouched against the wall and tried to shield the babe with her trembling body without withdrawing her gaze from the luminous orbs that were killing her. No thought of her husband came to her in her agony—no hope nor suggestion of rescue or escape. Her capacity for thought and feeling had narrowed to the dimensions of a single emotion—fear of the animal's spring, of the impact of its body, the buffeting of its great arms, the feel of its teeth in her throat, the mangling of her babe. Motionless now and in absolute silence, she awaited her doom, the moments growing to hours, to years, to ages; and still those devilish eyes maintained their watch.

Returning to his cabin late at night with a deer on his shoulders Charles Marlowe tried the door. It did not yield. He knocked; there was no answer. He laid down his deer and went round to the window. As he turned the angle of the building he fancied he heard a sound as of stealthy footfalls and a rustling in the undergrowth of the forest, but they were too slight for certainty, even to his practised ear. Approaching the window, and to his surprise finding it open, he threw his leg over the sill and entered. All was darkness and silence. He groped his way to the fireplace, struck a match and lit a candle. Then he looked about. Cowering on the floor against a wall was his wife, clasping his child. As he sprang toward her she rose and broke into laughter, long, loud, and mechanical, devoid of gladness and devoid of sense—the laughter that is not out of keeping with the clanking of a chain. Hardly knowing what he did he extended his arms. She laid the babe in them. It was dead—pressed to death in its mother's embrace.

III

The Theory of the Defence

That is what occurred during a night in a forest, but not all of it did Irene Marlowe relate to Jenner Brading; not all of it was known to her. When she had concluded the sun was below the horizon and the long summer twilight had begun to deepen in the hollows of the land. For some moments Brading was silent, expecting the narrative to be carried forward to some definite connection with the conversation introducing it; but the narrator was as silent as he, her face averted, her hands clasping and unclasping themselves as they lay in her lap, with a singular suggestion of an activity independent of her will.

"It is a sad, a terrible story," said Brading at last, "but I do not understand. You call Charles Marlowe father; that I know. That he is old before his time, broken by some great sorrow, I have seen, or thought I saw. But, pardon me, you said that you—that you—"

"That I am insane," said the girl, without a movement of head or body.

"But, Irene, you say—please, dear, do not look away from me—you say that the child was dead, not demented."

"Yes, that one—I am the second. I was born three months after that night, my mother being mercifully permitted to lay down her life in giving me mine."

Brading was again silent; he was a trifle dazed and could not at once think of the right thing to say. Her face was still turned away. In his embarrassment he reached impulsively toward the hands that lay closing and unclosing in her lap, but something—he could not have said what—restrained him. He then remembered, vaguely, that he had never altogether cared to take her hand.

"Is it likely," she resumed, "that a person born under such circumstances is like others—is what you call sane?"

Brading did not reply; he was preoccupied with a new thought that was taking shape in his mind—what a scientist would have called an hypothesis; a detective, a theory. It might throw an added light, albeit a lurid one, upon such doubt of her sanity as her own assertion had not dispelled.

The country was still new and, outside the villages, sparsely populated. The professional hunter was still a familiar figure, and among his trophies were heads and pelts of the larger kinds of game. Tales variously credible of nocturnal meetings with savage animals in lonely roads were sometimes current, passed through the customary stages of growth and decay, and were forgotten. A recent addition to these popular apocrypha, originating, apparently, by spontaneous generation in several households, was of a panther which had frightened some of their members by looking in at windows by night. The yarn had caused its little ripple of excitement—had even attained to the distinction of a place in the local newspaper; but Brading had given it no attention. Its likeness to the story to which he had just listened now impressed him as perhaps more than accidental. Was it not possible that the one story had suggested the other—that finding congenial conditions in a morbid mind and a fertile fancy, it had grown to the tragic tale that he had heard?

Brading recalled certain circumstances of the girl's history and disposition, of which, with love's incuriosity, he had hitherto been heedless—such as her solitary life with her father, at whose house no one, apparently, was an acceptable visitor and her strange fear of the night, by which those who knew her best accounted for her never being seen after dark. Surely in such a mind imagination once kindled might burn with a lawless flame, penetrating and enveloping the entire structure. That she was mad, though the conviction gave him the acutest pain, he could no longer doubt; she had only mistaken an effect of her mental disorder for its cause, bringing into imaginary relation with her own personality the vagaries of the local myth-makers. With some vague intention of testing his new "theory," and no very definite notion of how to set about it he said, gravely, but with hesitation:

"Irene, dear, tell me—I beg you will not take offence, but tell me—"

"I have told you," she interrupted, speaking with a passionate earnestness that he had not known her to show—"I have already told you that we cannot marry; is anything else worth saying?"

Before he could stop her she had sprung from her seat and without another word or look was gliding away among the trees toward her father's house. Brading had risen to detain her; he stood watching her in silence until she had vanished in the gloom. Suddenly he started as if he had been shot; his face took on an expression of amazement and alarm: in one of the black shadows into which she had disappeared he had caught a quick, brief glimpse of shining eyes! For an instant he was dazed and irresolute; then he dashed into the wood after her, shouting: "Irene, Irene, look out! The panther! The panther!"

In a moment he had passed through the fringe of forest into open ground and saw the girl's grey skirt vanishing into her father's door. No panther was visible.

IV

An Appeal to the Conscience of God

Jenner Brading, attorney-at-law, lived in a cottage at the edge of the town. Directly behind the dwelling was the forest. Being a bachelor, and therefore, by the Draconian moral code of the time and place denied the services of the only species of domestic servant known thereabout, the "hired girl," he boarded at the village hotel, where also was his office. The woodside cottage was merely a lodging maintained—at no great cost, to be sure—as an evidence of prosperity and respectability. It would hardly do for one to whom the local newspaper had pointed with pride as "the foremost jurist of his time" to be "homeless," albeit he may sometimes have suspected that the words "home" and "house" were not strictly synonymous. Indeed, his consciousness of the disparity and his will to harmonize it were matters of logical inference, for it was generally reported that soon after the cottage was built its owner had made a futile venture in the direction of marriage—had, in truth, gone so far as to be rejected by the beautiful but eccentric daughter of Old Man Marlowe, the recluse. This was publicly believed because he had told it himself and she had not—a reversal of the usual order of things which could hardly fail to carry conviction.

Brading's bedroom was at the rear of the house, with a single window facing the forest. One night he was awakened by a noise at that window; he could hardly have said what it was like. With a little thrill of the nerves he sat up in bed and laid hold of the revolver which, with a forethought most commendable in one addicted to the habit of sleeping on the ground floor with an open window, he had put under his pillow. The room was in absolute darkness, but being unterrified he knew where to direct his eyes, and there he held them, awaiting in silence what further might occur. He could now dimly discern the aperture—a square of lighter black. Presently there appeared at its lower edge two gleaming eyes that burned with a malignant lustre inexpressibly terrible! Brading's heart gave a great jump, then seemed to stand still. A chill passed along his spine and through his hair; he felt the blood forsake his cheeks. He could not have cried out—not to save his life; but being a man of courage he would not, to save his life, have done so if he had been able. Some trepidation his coward body might feel, but his spirit was of sterner stuff. Slowly the shining eyes rose with a steady motion that seemed an approach, and slowly rose Brading's right hand, holding the pistol. He fired!

Blinded by the flash and stunned by the report, Brading nevertheless heard, or fancied that he heard, the wild, high scream of the panther, so human in sound, so devilish in suggestion. Leaping from the bed he hastily clothed himself and, pistol in hand, sprang from the door, meeting two or three men who came running up from the road. A brief explanation was followed by a cautious search of the house. The grass was wet with dew; beneath the window it had been trodden and partly levelled for a wide space, from which a devious trail, visible in the light of a lantern, led away into the bushes. One of the men stumbled and fell upon his hands, which as he rose and rubbed them together were slippery. On examination they were seen to be red with blood.

An encounter, unarmed, with a wounded panther was not agreeable to their taste; all but Brading turned back. He, with lantern and pistol, pushed courageously forward into the wood. Passing through a difficult undergrowth he came into a small opening, and there his courage had its reward, for there he found the body of his victim. But it was no panther. What it was is told, even to this day, upon a weather-worn headstone in the village churchyard, and for many years was attested daily at the graveside by the bent figure and sorrow-seamed face of Old Man Marlowe, to whose soul, and to the soul of his strange, unhappy child, peace. Peace and reparation.

STALEY FLEMING'S
HALLUCINATION

f two men who were talking one was a physician.

"I sent for you, Doctor," said the other, "but I don't think you can do me any good. Maybe you can recommend a specialist in psychopathy. I fancy I'm a bit loony."

"You look all right," the physician said.

"You shall judge—I have hallucinations. I wake every night and see in my room, intently watching me, a big black Newfoundland dog with a white forefoot."

"You say you wake; are you sure about that? 'Hallucinations' are sometimes only dreams."

"Oh, I wake all right. Sometimes I lie still a long time, looking at the dog as earnestly as the dog looks at me—I always leave the light going. When I can't endure it any longer I sit up in bed—and nothing is there!"

"'M, 'm—what is the beast's expression?"

"It seems to me sinister. Of course I know that, except in art, an animal's face in repose has always the same expression. But this is not a real animal. Newfoundland dogs are pretty mild looking, you know; what's the matter with this one?"

"Really, my diagnosis would have no value: I am not going to treat the dog."

The physician laughed at his own pleasantry, but narrowly watched his patient from the corner of his eye. Presently he said: "Fleming, your description of the beast fits the dog of the late Atwell Barton."

Fleming half rose from his chair, sat again and made a visible attempt at indifference. "I remember Barton," he said; "I believe he was—it was reported that—wasn't there something suspicious in his death?"

Looking squarely now into the eyes of his patient, the physician said: "Three years ago the body of your old enemy, Atwell Barton, was found in the woods near his house and yours. He had been stabbed to death. There have been no arrests; there was no clue. Some of us had 'theories.' I had one. Have you?"

"I? Why, bless your soul, what could I know about it? You remember that I left for Europe almost immediately afterward—a considerable time afterward. In the few weeks since my return you could not expect me to construct a 'theory.' In fact, I have not given the matter a thought. What about his dog?"

"It was first to find the body. It died of starvation on his grave."

We do not know the inexorable law underlying coincidences. Staley Fleming did not, or he would perhaps not have sprung to his feet as the night wind brought in through the open window the long wailing howl of a distant dog. He strode several times across the room in the steadfast gaze of the physician; then, abruptly confronting him, almost shouted: "What has all this to do with my trouble, Dr. Halderman? You forget why you were sent for."

Rising, the physician laid his hand upon his patient's arm and said, gently: "Pardon me. I cannot diagnose your disorder offhand—tomorrow, perhaps. Please go to bed, leaving your door unlocked; I will pass the night here with your books. Can you call me without rising?"

"Yes, there is an electric bell."

"Good. If anything disturbs you push the button without sitting up. Good night."

Comfortably installed in an armchair the man of medicine stared into the glowing coals and thought deeply and long, but apparently to little purpose, for he frequently rose and opening a door leading to the staircase, listened intently; then resumed his seat. Presently, however, he fell asleep, and when he woke it was past midnight. He stirred the failing fire, lifted a book from the table at his side and looked at the title. It was Denneker's "Meditations." He opened it at random and began to read:

"Forasmuch as it is ordained of God that all flesh hath spirit and thereby taketh on spiritual powers, so, also, the spirit hath powers of the flesh, even when it is gone out of the flesh and liveth as a thing apart, as many a violence performed by wraith and lemure sheweth. And there be who say that man is not single in this, but the beasts have the like evil inducement, and—"

The reading was interrupted by a shaking of the house, as by the fall of a heavy object. The reader flung down the book, rushed from the room and mounted the stairs to Fleming's bed-chamber. He tried the door, but contrary to his instructions it was locked. He set his shoulder against it with such force that it gave way. On the floor near the disordered bed, in his night-clothes, lay Fleming, gasping away his life.

The physician raised the dying man's head from the floor and observed a wound in the throat. "I should have thought of this," he said, believing it suicide.

When the man was dead an examination disclosed the unmistakable marks of an animal's fangs deeply sunken into the jugular vein.

But there was no animal.

THE MOONLIT ROAD

I

Statement of Joel Hetman, Jr.

am the most unfortunate of men. Rich, respected, fairly well educated and of sound health—with many other advantages usually valued by those having them and coveted by those who have them not—I sometimes think that I should be less unhappy if they had been denied me, for then the contrast between my outer and my inner life would not be continually demanding a painful attention. In the stress of privation and the need of effort I might sometimes forget the sombre secret ever baffling the conjecture that it compels.

I am the only child of Joel and Julia Hetman. The one was a well-to-do country gentleman, the other a beautiful and accomplished woman to whom he was passionately attached with what I now know to have been a jealous and exacting devotion. The family home was a few miles from Nashville, Tennessee, a large, irregularly built dwelling of no particular order of architecture, a little way off the road, in a park of trees and shrubbery.

At the time of which I write I was nineteen years old, a student at Yale. One day I received a telegram from my father of such urgency that in compliance with its unexplained demand

I left at once for home. At the railway station in Nashville a distant relative awaited me to apprise me of the reason for my recall: my mother had been barbarously murdered—why and by whom none could conjecture, but the circumstances were these:

My father had gone to Nashville, intending to return the next afternoon. Something prevented his accomplishing the business in hand, so he returned on the same night, arriving just before the dawn. In his testimony before the coroner he explained that having no latchkey and not caring to disturb the sleeping servants, he had, with no clearly defined intention, gone round to the rear of the house. As he turned an angle of the building, he heard a sound as of a door gently closed, and saw in the darkness, indistinctly, the figure of a man, which instantly disappeared among the trees of the lawn. A hasty pursuit and brief search of the grounds in the belief that the trespasser was some one secretly visiting a servant proving fruitless, he entered at the unlocked door and mounted the stairs to my mother's chamber. Its door was open, and stepping into black darkness he fell headlong over some heavy object on the floor. I may spare myself the details; it was my poor mother, dead of strangulation by human hands!

Nothing had been taken from the house, the servants had heard no sound, and excepting those terrible finger-marks upon the dead woman's throat—dear God! that I might forget them!—no trace of the assassin was ever found.

I gave up my studies and remained with my father, who, naturally, was greatly changed. Always of a sedate, taciturn disposition, he now fell into so deep a dejection that nothing could hold his attention, yet anything—a footfall, the sudden closing of a door—aroused in him a fitful interest; one might have called it an apprehension. At any small surprise of the senses he would start visibly and sometimes turn pale, then relapse into a melancholy apathy deeper than before. I suppose he was what is called a "nervous wreck." As to me, I was younger then than now—there is much in that. Youth is Gilead, in which is balm for every wound. Ah, that I might again dwell in that enchanted land! Unacquainted with grief, I knew not how to appraise my bereavement; I could not rightly estimate the strength of the stroke.

One night, a few months after the dreadful event, my father and I walked home from the city. The full moon was about three hours above the eastern horizon; the entire countryside had the solemn stillness of a summer night; our footfalls and the ceaseless song of the katydids were the only sound aloof. Black shadows of bordering trees lay athwart the road, which, in the short reaches between, gleamed a ghostly white. As we approached the gate to our dwelling, whose front was in shadow, and in which no light shone, my father suddenly stopped and clutched my arm, saying, hardly above his breath:

"God! God! what is that?"

"I hear nothing," I replied.

"But see—see!" he said, pointing along the road, directly ahead.

I said: "Nothing is there. Come, father, let us go in—you are ill."

He had released my arm and was standing rigid and motionless in the centre of the illuminated roadway, staring like one bereft of sense. His face in the moonlight showed a pallor and fixity inexpressibly distressing. I pulled gently at his sleeve, but he had forgotten my existence. Presently he began to retire backward, step by step, never for an instant removing his eyes from what he saw, or thought he saw. I turned half round to follow, but stood irresolute. I do not recall any feeling of fear, unless a sudden chill was its physical manifestation. It seemed as if an icy wind had touched my face and enfolded my body from head to foot; I could feel the stir of it in my hair.

At that moment my attention was drawn to a light that suddenly streamed from an upper window of the house: one of the servants, awakened by what mysterious premonition of evil who can say, and in obedience to an impulse that she was never able to name, had lit a lamp. When I turned to look for my father he was gone, and in all the years that have passed no whisper of his fate has come across the borderland of conjecture from the realm of the unknown.

II

Statement of Caspar Grattan

Today I am said to live; tomorrow, here in this room, will lie a senseless shape of clay that all too long was I. If anyone lift the cloth from the face of that unpleasant thing it will be in gratification of a mere morbid curiosity. Some, doubtless, will go further and inquire, "Who was he?" In this writing I supply the only answer that I am able to make—Caspar Grattan. Surely, that should be enough. The name has served my small need for more than twenty years of a life of unknown length. True, I gave it to myself, but lacking another I had the right. In this world one must have a name; it prevents confusion, even when it does not establish identity. Some, though, are known by numbers, which also seem inadequate distinctions.

One day, for illustration, I was passing along a street of a city, far from here, when I met two men in uniform, one of whom, half pausing and looking curiously into my face, said to his companion, "That man looks like 767." Something in the number seemed familiar and horrible. Moved by an uncontrollable impulse, I sprang into a side street and ran until I fell exhausted in a country lane.

I have never forgotten that number, and always it comes to memory attended by gibbering obscenity, peals of joyless laughter, the clang of iron doors. So I say a name, even if self-bestowed, is better than a number. In the register of the potter's field I shall soon have both. What wealth!

Of him who shall find this paper I must beg a little consideration. It is not the history of my life; the knowledge to write that is denied me. This is only a record of broken and apparently unrelated memories, some of them as distinct and sequent as brilliant beads upon a thread, others remote and strange, having the character of crimson dreams with interspaces blank and black—witch-fires glowing still and red in a great desolation.

Standing upon the shore of eternity, I turn for a last look landward over the course by which I came. There are twenty years of footprints fairly distinct, the impressions of bleeding feet. They lead through poverty and pain, devious and unsure, as of one staggering beneath a burden—

Remote, unfriended, melancholy, slow.

Ah, the poet's prophecy of Me—how admirable, how dreadfully admirable!

Backward beyond the beginning of this *via dolorosa*—this epic of suffering with episodes of sin—I see nothing clearly; it comes out of a cloud. I know that it spans only twenty years, yet I am an old man.

One does not remember one's birth—one has to be told. But with me it was different; life came to me full-handed and dowered me with all my faculties and powers. Of a previous existence I know no more than others, for all have stammering intimations that may be memories and may be dreams. I know only that my first consciousness was of maturity in body and mind—a consciousness accepted without surprise or conjecture. I merely found myself walking in a forest, half-clad, footsore, unutterably weary and hungry. Seeing a farmhouse, I approached and asked for food, which was given me by one who inquired my name. I did not know, yet knew that all had names. Greatly embarrassed, I retreated, and night coming on, lay down in the forest and slept.

The next day I entered a large town which I shall not name. Nor shall I recount further incidents of the life that is now to end—a life of wandering, always and everywhere haunted by an overmastering sense of crime in punishment of wrong and of terror in punishment of crime. Let me see if I can reduce it to narrative.

I seem once to have lived near a great city, a prosperous planter, married to a woman whom I loved and distrusted. We had, it sometimes seems, one child, a youth of brilliant parts and promise. He is at all times a vague figure, never clearly drawn, frequently altogether out of the picture.

One luckless evening it occurred to me to test my wife's fidelity in a vulgar, commonplace way familiar to everyone who has acquaintance with the literature of fact and fiction. I went to the city, telling my wife that I should be absent until the following afternoon. But I returned before daybreak and went to the rear of the house, purposing to enter by a door with which I had secretly so tampered that it would seem to lock, yet not actually fasten. As I approached it, I heard it gently open and close, and saw a man steal away into the darkness. With murder in my heart, I sprang after him, but he had vanished without even the bad luck of identification. Sometimes now I cannot even persuade myself that it was a human being.

Crazed with jealousy and rage, blind and bestial with all the elemental passions of insulted manhood, I entered the house and sprang up the stairs to the door of my wife's chamber. It was closed, but having tampered with its lock also, I easily entered and despite the black darkness soon stood by the side of her bed. My groping hands told me that although disarranged it was unoccupied.

"She is below," I thought, "and terrified by my entrance has evaded me in the darkness of the hall."

With the purpose of seeking her I turned to leave the room, but took a wrong direction—the right one! My foot struck her, cowering in a corner of the room. Instantly my hands were at her throat, stifling a shriek, my knees were upon her struggling body; and there in the darkness, without a word of accusation or reproach, I strangled her till she died!

There ends the dream. I have related it in the past tense, but the present would be the fitter form, for again and again the sombre tragedy reenacts itself in my consciousness—over and over I lay the plan, I suffer the confirmation, I redress the wrong. Then all is blank; and afterward the rains beat against the grimy window-panes, or the snows fall upon my scant attire, the wheels rattle in the squalid streets where my life lies in poverty and mean employment. If there is ever sunshine I do not recall it; if there are birds they do not sing.

There is another dream, another vision of the night. I stand among the shadows in a moonlit road. I am aware of another presence, but whose I cannot rightly determine. In the shadow of a great dwelling I catch the gleam of white garments; then the figure of a woman confronts me in the road—my murdered wife! There is death in the face; there are marks upon the throat. The eyes are fixed on mine with an infinite gravity which is not reproach, nor hate, nor menace, nor anything less terrible than recognition. Before this awful apparition I retreat in terror—a terror that is upon me as I write. I can no longer rightly shape the words. See! they—

Now I am calm, but truly there is no more to tell: the incident ends where it began—in darkness and in doubt.

Yes, I am again in control of myself: "the captain of my soul."

But that is not respite; it is another stage and phase of expiation. My penance, constant in degree, is mutable in kind: one of its variants is tranquillity. After all, it is only a life-sentence. "To Hell for life"—that is a foolish penalty: the culprit chooses the duration of his punishment. Today my term expires.

To each and all, the peace that was not mine.

III

Statement of the Late Julia Hetman, Through the Medium Bayrolles

I had retired early and fallen almost immediately into a peaceful sleep, from which I awoke with that indefinable sense of peril which is, I think, a common experience in that other, earlier life. Of its unmeaning character, too, I was entirely persuaded, yet that did not banish it. My husband, Joel Hetman, was away from home; the servants slept in another part of the house. But these were familiar conditions; they had never before distressed me. Nevertheless, the strange terror grew so insupportable that conquering my reluctance to move I sat up and lit the lamp at my bedside. Contrary to my expectation this gave me no relief; the light seemed rather an added danger, for I reflected that it would shine out under the door, disclosing my presence to whatever evil thing might lurk outside. You that are still in the flesh, subject to horrors of the imagination, think what a monstrous fear that must be which seeks in darkness security from malevolent existences of the night.

That is to spring to close quarters with an unseen enemy—the strategy of despair!

Extinguishing the lamp I pulled the bed-clothing about my head and lay trembling and silent, unable to shriek, forgetful to pray. In this pitiable state I must have lain for what you call hours—with us there are no hours, there is no time.

At last it came—a soft, irregular sound of footfalls on the stairs! They were slow, hesitant, uncertain, as of something that did not see its way; to my disordered reason all the more terrifying for that, as the approach of some blind and mindless malevolence to which is no appeal. I even thought that I must have left the hall lamp burning and the groping of this creature proved it a monster of the night. This was foolish and inconsistent with my previous dread of the light, but what would you have? Fear has no brains; it is an idiot. The dismal witness that it bears and the cowardly counsel that it whispers are unrelated. We know this well, we who have passed into the Realm of Terror, who skulk in eternal dusk among the scenes of our former lives, invisible even to ourselves and one another, yet hiding forlorn in lonely places; yearning for speech with our loved ones, yet dumb, and as fearful of them as they of us. Sometimes the disability is removed, the law suspended: by the deathless power of love or hate we break the spell—we are seen by those whom we would warn, console, or punish. What form we seem to them to bear we know not; we know only that we terrify even those whom we most wish to comfort, and from whom we most crave tenderness and sympathy.

Forgive, I pray you, this inconsequent digression by what was once a woman. You who consult us in this imperfect way—you do not understand. You ask foolish questions about things unknown and things forbidden. Much that we know and could impart in our speech is meaningless in yours. We must communicate with you through a stammering intelligence in that small fraction of our language that you yourselves can speak. You think that we are of another world. No, we have knowledge of no world but yours, though for us it holds no sunlight, no warmth, no music, no laughter, no song of birds, nor any companionship. O God! what a thing it is to be a ghost, cowering and shivering in an altered world, a prey to apprehension and despair!

No, I did not die of fright: the Thing turned and went away. I heard it go down the stairs, hurriedly, I thought, as if itself in sudden fear. Then I rose to call for help. Hardly had my shaking hand found the door-knob when—merciful heaven!—I heard it returning. Its footfalls as it remounted the stairs were rapid, heavy and loud; they shook the house. I fled to an angle of the wall and crouched upon the floor. I tried to pray. I tried to call the name of my dear husband. Then I heard the door thrown open. There was an interval of unconsciousness, and when I revived I felt a strangling clutch upon my throat—felt my arms feebly beating against something that bore me backward—felt my tongue thrusting itself from between my teeth! And then I passed into this life.

No, I have no knowledge of what it was. The sum of what we knew at death is the measure of what we know afterward of all that went before. Of this existence we know many things, but no new light falls upon any page of that; in memory is written all of it that we can read. Here are no heights of truth overlooking the confused landscape of that dubitable domain. We still dwell in the Valley of the Shadow, lurk in its desolate places, peering from brambles and thickets at its mad, malign inhabitants. How should we have new knowledge of that fading past?

What I am about to relate happened on a night. We know when it is night, for then you retire to your houses and we can venture from our places of concealment to move unafraid about our old homes, to look in at the windows, even to enter and gaze upon your faces as you sleep. I had lingered long near the dwelling where I had been so cruelly changed to what I am, as we do while any that we love or hate remain. Vainly I had sought some method of manifestation, some way to make my continued existence and my great love and poignant pity understood by my husband and son. Always if they slept they would wake, or if in my desperation I dared approach them when they were awake, would turn toward me the terrible eyes of the living, frightening me by the glances that I sought from the purpose that I held.

On this night I had searched for them without success, fearing to find them; they were nowhere in the house, nor about the moonlit lawn. For, although the sun is lost to us forever, the moon, full-orbed or slender, remains to us. Sometimes it shines by night, sometimes by day, but always it rises and sets, as in that other life.

I left the lawn and moved in the white light and silence along the road, aimless and sorrowing. Suddenly I heard the voice of my poor husband in exclamations of astonishment, with that of my son in reassurance and dissuasion; and there by the shadow of a group of trees they stood—near, so near! Their faces were toward me, the eyes of the elder man fixed upon mine. He saw me—at last, at last, he saw me! In the consciousness of that, my terror fled as a cruel dream. The death-spell was broken: Love had conquered Law! Mad with exultation I shouted—I *must* have shouted, "He sees, he sees: he will understand!" Then, controlling myself, I moved forward, smiling and consciously beautiful, to offer myself to his arms, to comfort him with endearments, and, with my son's hand in mine, to speak words that should restore the broken bonds between the living and the dead.

Alas! alas! his face went white with fear, his eyes were as those of a hunted animal. He backed away from me, as I advanced, and at last turned and fled into the wood—whither, it is not given to me to know.

To my poor boy, left doubly desolate, I have never been able to impart a sense of my presence. Soon he, too, must pass to this Life Invisible and be lost to me forever.

BEYOND THE WALL

any years ago, on my way from Hong-Kong to New York, I passed a week in San Francisco. A long time had gone by since I had been in that city, during which my ventures in the Orient had prospered beyond my hope; I was rich and could afford to revisit my own country to renew my friendship with such of the companions of my youth as still lived and remembered me with the old affection. Chief of these, I hoped, was Mohun Dampier, an old schoolmate with whom I had held a desultory correspondence which had long ceased, as is the way of correspondence between men. You may have observed that the indisposition to write a merely social letter is in the ratio of the square of the distance between you and your correspondent. It is a law.

I remembered Dampier as a handsome, strong young fellow of scholarly tastes, with an aversion to work and a marked indifference to many of the things that the world cares for, including wealth, of which, however, he had inherited enough to put him beyond the reach of want. In his family, one of the oldest and most aristocratic in the country, it was, I think, a matter of pride that no member of it had ever been in trade nor politics, nor suffered any kind of distinction. Mohun was a trifle sentimental, and had in him a singular element of superstition, which led him to the study of all manner of occult subjects, although his sane mental health safeguarded him against fantastic and perilous faiths. He made daring incursions into the realm of the unreal without renouncing his residence in the partly surveyed and charted region of what we are pleased to call certitude.

The night of my visit to him was stormy. The Californian winter was on, and the incessant rain plashed in the deserted streets, or, lifted by irregular gusts of wind, was hurled against the houses with incredible fury. With no small difficulty my cabman found the right place, away out toward the ocean beach, in a sparsely populated suburb. The dwelling, a rather ugly one, apparently, stood in the centre of its grounds, which as nearly as I could make out in the gloom were destitute of either flowers or grass. Three or four trees, writhing and moaning in the torment of the tempest, appeared to be trying to escape from their dismal environment and take the chance of finding a better one out at sea. The house was a two-story brick structure with a tower, a story higher, at one corner. In a window of that was the only visible light. Something in the appearance of the place made me shudder, a performance that may have been assisted by a rill of rain-water down my back as I scuttled to cover in the doorway.

In answer to my note apprising him of my wish to call, Dampier had written, "Don't ring—open the door and come up." I did so. The staircase was dimly lighted by a single gas-jet at the top of the second flight. I managed to reach the landing without disaster and entered by an open door into the lighted square room of the tower. Dampier came forward in gown and slippers to receive me, giving me the greeting that I wished, and if I had held a thought that it might more fitly have been accorded me at the front door the first look at him dispelled any sense of his inhospitality.

He was not the same. Hardly past middle age, he had gone grey and had acquired a pronounced stoop. His figure was thin and angular, his face deeply lined, his complexion dead-white, without a touch of colour. His eyes, unnaturally large, glowed with a fire that was almost uncanny.

He seated me, proffered a cigar, and with grave and obvious sincerity assured me of the pleasure that it gave him to meet me. Some unimportant conversation followed, but all the while I was dominated by a melancholy sense of the great change in him. This he must have perceived, for he suddenly said with a bright enough smile, "You are disappointed in me—*non sum qualis eram*."

I hardly knew what to reply, but managed to say: "Why, really, I don't know: your Latin is about the same."

He brightened again. "No," he said, "being a dead language, it grows in appropriateness. But please have the patience to wait: where I am going there is perhaps a better tongue. Will you care to have a message in it?"

The smile faded as he spoke, and as he concluded he was looking into my eyes with a gravity that distressed me. Yet I would not surrender myself to his mood, nor permit him to see how deeply his prescience of death affected me.

"I fancy that it will be long," I said, "before human speech will cease to serve our need; and then the need, with its possibilities of service, will have passed."

He made no reply, and I too was silent, for the talk had taken a dispiriting turn, yet I knew not how to give it a more agreeable character. Suddenly, in a pause of the storm, when the dead silence was almost startling by contrast with the previous uproar, I heard a gentle tapping, which appeared to come from the wall behind my chair. The sound was such as might have been made by a human hand, not as upon a door by one asking admittance, but rather, I thought, as an agreed signal, an assurance of some one's presence in an adjoining room; most of us, I fancy, have had more experience of such communications than we should care to relate. I glanced at Dampier. If possibly there was something of amusement in the look he did not observe it. He appeared to have forgotten my presence, and was staring at the wall behind me with an expression in his eyes that I am unable to name, although my memory of it is as vivid today as was my sense of it then. The situation was embarrassing; I rose to take my leave. At this he seemed to recover himself.

"Please be seated," he said; "it is nothing—no one is there."

But the tapping was repeated, and with the same gentle, slow insistence as before.

"Pardon me," I said, "it is late. May I call tomorrow?"

He smiled—a little mechanically, I thought. "It is very delicate of you," said he, "but quite needless. Really, this is the only room in the tower, and no one is there. At least—" He left the sentence incomplete, rose, and threw up a window, the only opening in the wall from which the sound seemed to come. "See."

Not clearly knowing what else to do I followed him to the window and looked out. A street-lamp some little distance away gave enough light through the murk of the rain that was again falling in torrents to make it entirely plain that "no one was there." In truth there was nothing but the sheer blank wall of the tower.

Dampier closed the window and signing me to my seat resumed his own.

The incident was not in itself particularly mysterious; any one of a dozen explanations was possible (though none has occurred to me), yet it impressed me strangely, the more, perhaps, from my friend's effort to reassure me, which seemed to dignify it with a certain significance and importance. He had proved that no one was there, but in that fact lay all the interest; and he proffered no explanation. His silence was irritating and made me resentful.

"My good friend," I said, somewhat ironically, I fear, "I am not disposed to question your right to harbour as many spooks as you find agreeable to your taste and consistent with your notions of companionship; that is no business of mine. But being just a plain man of affairs, mostly of this world, I find spooks needless to my peace and comfort. I am going to my hotel, where my fellow-guests are still in the flesh."

It was not a very civil speech, but he manifested no feeling about it. "Kindly remain," he said. "I am grateful for your presence here. What you have heard tonight I believe myself to have heard twice before. Now I *know* it was no illusion. That is much to me—more than you know. Have a fresh cigar and a good stock of patience while I tell you the story."

The rain was now falling more steadily, with a low, monotonous susurration, interrupted at long intervals by the sudden slashing of the boughs of the trees as the wind rose and failed. The night was well advanced, but both sympathy and curiosity held me a willing listener to my friend's monologue, which I did not interrupt by a single word from beginning to end.

"Ten years ago," he said, "I occupied a ground-floor apartment in one of a row of houses, all alike, away at the other end of the town, on what we call Rincon Hill. This had been the best quarter of San Francisco, but had fallen into neglect and decay, partly because the primitive character of its domestic architecture no longer suited the maturing tastes of our wealthy citizens, partly because certain public improvements had made a wreck of it. The row of dwellings in one of which I lived stood a little way back from the street, each having a miniature garden, separated from its neighbours by low iron fences and bisected with mathematical precision by a box-bordered gravel walk from gate to door.

"One morning as I was leaving my lodging I observed a young girl entering the adjoining garden on the left. It was a warm day in June, and she was lightly gowned in white. From her shoulders hung a broad straw hat profusely decorated with flowers and wonderfully beribboned in the fashion of the time. My attention was not long held by the exquisite simplicity of her costume, for no one could look at her face and think of anything earthly. Do not fear; I shall not profane it by description; it was beautiful exceedingly. All that I had ever seen or dreamed of loveliness was in that matchless living picture by the hand of the Divine Artist. So deeply did it move me that, without a thought of the impropriety of the act, I unconsciously bared my head, as a devout Catholic or well-bred Protestant uncovers before an image of the Blessed Virgin. The maiden showed no displeasure; she merely turned her glorious dark eyes upon me with a look that made me catch my breath, and without other recognition of my act passed into the house. For a moment I stood motionless, hat in hand, painfully conscious of my rudeness, yet so dominated by the emotion inspired by that vision of incomparable beauty that my penitence was less poignant than it should have been. Then I went my way, leaving my heart behind. In the natural course of things I should probably have remained away until nightfall, but by the middle of the afternoon I was back in the little garden, affecting an interest in the few foolish flowers that I had never before observed. My hope was vain; she did not appear.

"To a night of unrest succeeded a day of expectation and disappointment, but on the day after, as I wandered aimlessly about the neighbourhood, I met her. Of course I did not repeat my folly of uncovering, nor venture by even so much as too long a look to manifest an interest in her; yet my heart was beating audibly. I trembled and consciously coloured as she turned her big black eyes upon me with a look of obvious recognition entirely devoid of boldness or coquetry.

"I will not weary you with particulars; many times afterward I met the maiden, yet never either addressed her or sought to fix her attention. Nor did I take any action toward making her acquaintance. Perhaps my forbearance, requiring so supreme an effort of self-denial, will not be entirely clear to you. That I was heels over head in love is true, but who can overcome his habit of thought, or reconstruct his character?

"I was what some foolish persons are pleased to call, and others, more foolish, are pleased to be called—an aristocrat; and despite her beauty, her charms and grace, the girl was not of my class. I had learned her name—which it is needless to speak—and something of her family. She was an orphan, a dependent niece of the impossible elderly fat woman in whose lodging-house she lived. My income was small and I lacked the talent for marrying; it is perhaps a gift. An alliance with that family would condemn me to its manner of life, part me from my books and studies, and in a social sense reduce me to the ranks. It is easy to deprecate such considerations as these and I have not retained myself for the defence. Let judgment be entered against me, but in strict justice all my ancestors for generations should be made co-defendants and I be permitted, to plead in mitigation of punishment the imperious mandate of heredity. To a *mésalliance* of that kind every globule of my ancestral blood spoke in opposition. In brief, my tastes, habits, instinct, with whatever of reason my love had left me—all fought against it. Moreover, I was an irreclaimable sentimentalist, and found a subtle charm in an impersonal and spiritual relation which acquaintance might vulgarize and marriage would certainly dispel. No woman, I argued, is what this lovely creature seems. Love is a delicious dream; why should I bring about my own awakening?

"The course dictated by all this sense and sentiment was obvious. Honour, pride, prudence, preservation of my ideals— all commanded me to go away, but for that I was too weak. The utmost that I could do by a mighty effort of will was to cease meeting the girl, and that I did. I even avoided the chance encounters of the garden, leaving my lodging only when I knew that she had gone to her music lessons, and returning after nightfall. Yet all the while I was as one in a trance, indulging the most fascinating fancies and ordering my entire intellectual life in accordance with my dream. Ah, my friend, as one whose actions have a traceable relation to reason, you cannot know the fool's paradise in which I lived.

"One evening the devil put it into my head to be an unspeakable idiot. By apparently careless and purposeless questioning I learned from my gossipy landlady that the young woman's bedroom adjoined my own, a party-wall between. Yielding to a sudden and coarse impulse I gently rapped on the wall. There was no response, naturally, but I was in no mood to accept a rebuke. A madness was upon me and I repeated the folly, the offence, but again ineffectually, and I had the decency to desist.

"An hour later, while absorbed in some of my infernal studies, I heard, or thought I heard, my signal answered. Flinging down my books I sprang to the wall and as steadily as my beating heart would permit gave three slow taps upon it. This time the response was distinct, unmistakable: one, two, three—an exact repetition of my signal. That was all I could elicit, but it was enough—too much.

"The next evening, and for many evenings afterward, that folly went on, I always having 'the last word.' During the whole period I was deliriously happy, but with the perversity of my nature I persevered in my resolution not to see her. Then, as I should have expected, I got no further answers. 'She is disgusted,' I said to myself, 'with what she thinks my timidity in making no more definite advances'; and I resolved to seek her and make her acquaintance and—what? I did not know, nor do I now know, what might have come of it. I know only that I passed days and days trying to meet her, and all in vain; she was invisible as well as inaudible. I haunted the streets where we had met, but she did not come. From my window I watched the garden in front of her house, but she passed neither in nor out. I fell into the deepest dejection, believing that she had gone away, yet took no steps to resolve my doubt by inquiry of my landlady, to whom, indeed, I had taken an unconquerable aversion from her having once spoken of the girl with less of reverence than I thought befitting.

"There came a fateful night. Worn out with emotion, irresolution and despondency, I had retired early and fallen into such sleep as was still possible to me. In the middle of the night something—some malign power bent upon the wrecking of my peace for ever—caused me to open my eyes and sit up, wide awake and listening intently for I knew not what. Then I thought I heard a faint tapping on the wall—the mere ghost of the familiar signal. In a few moments it was repeated: one, two, three—no louder than before, but addressing a sense alert and strained to receive it. I was about to reply when the Adversary of Peace again intervened in my affairs with a rascally suggestion of retaliation. She had long and cruelly ignored me; now I would ignore her. Incredible fatuity—may God forgive it! All the rest of the night I lay awake, fortifying my obstinacy with shameless justifications and—listening.

"Late the next morning, as I was leaving the house, I met my landlady, entering.

"'Good morning, Mr. Dampier,' she said. 'Have you heard the news?'

"I replied in words that I had heard no news; in manner, that I did not care to hear any. The manner escaped her observation.

"'About the sick young lady next door,' she babbled on. 'What! you did not know? Why, she has been ill for weeks. And now—'

"I almost sprang upon her. 'And now,' I cried, 'now what?'"

"'She is dead.'"

"That is not the whole story. In the middle of the night, as I learned later, the patient, awakening from a long stupor after a week of delirium, had asked—it was her last utterance—that her bed be moved to the opposite side of the room. Those in attendance had thought the request a vagary of her delirium, but had complied. And there the poor passing soul had exerted its failing will to restore a broken connection—a golden thread of sentiment between its innocence and a monstrous baseness owning a blind, brutal allegiance to the Law of Self.

"What reparation could I make? Are there masses that can be said for the repose of souls that are abroad such nights as this—spirits 'blown about by the viewless winds'—coming in the storm and darkness with signs and portents, hints of memory and presages of doom?

"This is the third visitation. On the first occasion I was too sceptical to do more than verify by natural methods the character of the incident; on the second, I responded to the signal after it had been several times repeated, but without result. Tonight's recurrence completes the 'fatal triad' expounded by Parapelius Necromantius. There is no more to tell."

When Dampier had finished his story I could think of nothing relevant that I cared to say, and to question him would have been a hideous impertinence. I rose and bade him good night in a way to convey to him a sense of my sympathy, which he silently acknowledged by a pressure of the hand. That night, alone with his sorrow and remorse, he passed into the Unknown.

SOME
HAUNTED
HOUSES

THE ISLE OF PINES

or many years there lived near the town of Gallipolis, Ohio, an old man named Herman Deluse. Very little was known of his history, for he would neither speak of it himself nor suffer others. It was a common belief among his neighbours that he had been a pirate—if upon any better evidence than his collection of boarding pikes, cutlasses, and ancient flintlock pistols, no one knew. He lived entirely alone in a small house of four rooms, falling rapidly into decay and never repaired further than was required by the weather. It stood on a slight elevation in the midst of a large, stony field overgrown with brambles, and cultivated in patches and only in the most primitive way. It was his only visible property, but could hardly have yielded him a living, simple and few as were his wants. He seemed always to have ready money, and paid cash for all his purchases at the village stores roundabout, seldom buying more than two or three times at the same place until after the lapse of a considerable time. He got no commendation, however, for this equitable distribution of his patronage; people were disposed to regard it as an ineffectual attempt to conceal his possession of so much money. That he had great hoards of ill-gotten gold buried somewhere about his tumble-down dwelling was not reasonably to be doubted by any honest soul conversant with the facts of local tradition and gifted with a sense of the fitness of things.

On the 9th of November, 1867, the old man died; at least his dead body was discovered on the 10th, and physicians testified that death had occurred about twenty-four hours previously— precisely how, they were unable to say; for the *post-mortem* examination showed every organ to be absolutely healthy, with no indication of disorder or violence. According to them, death must have taken place about noonday, yet the body was found in bed. The verdict of the coroner's jury was that he "came to his death by a visitation of God." The body was buried and the public administrator took charge of the estate.

A rigorous search disclosed nothing more than was already known about the dead man, and much patient excavation here and there about the premises by thoughtful and thrifty neighbours went unrewarded. The administrator locked up the house against the time when the property, real and personal, should be sold by law with a view to defraying, partly, the expenses of the sale.

The night of November 20 was boisterous. A furious gale stormed across the country, scourging it with desolating drifts of sleet. Great trees were torn from the earth and hurled across the roads. So wild a night had never been known in all that region, but toward morning the storm had blown itself out of breath and day dawned bright and clear. At about eight o'clock that morning the Rev. Henry Galbraith, a well-known and highly esteemed Lutheran minister, arrived on foot at his house, a mile and a half from the Deluse place. Mr. Galbraith had been for a month in Cincinnati. He had come up the river in a steamboat, and landing at Gallipolis the previous evening had immediately obtained a horse and buggy and set out for home. The violence of the storm had delayed him over night, and in the morning the fallen trees had compelled him to abandon his conveyance and continue his journey afoot.

"But where did you pass the night?" inquired his wife, after he had briefly related his adventure.

"With old Deluse at the 'Isle of Pines,'"* was the laughing reply; "and a glum enough time I had of it. He made no objection to my remaining, but not a word could I get out of him."

Fortunately for the interests of truth there was present at this conversation Mr. Robert Mosely Maren, a lawyer and *littérateur* of Columbus, the same who wrote the delightful "Mellowcraft Papers." Noting, but apparently not sharing, the astonishment caused by Mr. Galbraith's answer this ready-witted person checked by a gesture the exclamations that would naturally have followed, and tranquilly inquired: "How came you to go in there?"

This is Mr. Maren's version of Mr. Galbraith's reply:

"I saw a light moving about the house, and being nearly blinded by the sleet, and half frozen besides, drove in at the gate and put up my horse in the old rail stable, where it is now. I then rapped at the door, and getting no invitation went in without one. The room was dark, but having matches I found a candle and lit it. I tried to enter the adjoining room, but the door was fast, and although I heard the old man's heavy footsteps in there he made no response to my calls. There was no fire on the hearth, so I made one and laying [*sic*] down before it with my overcoat under my head, prepared myself for sleep. Pretty

---

* The Isle of Pines was once a famous rendezvous of pirates.

soon the door that I had tried silently opened and the old man came in, carrying a candle. I spoke to him pleasantly, apologizing for my intrusion, but he took no notice of me. He seemed to be searching for something, though his eyes were unmoved in their sockets. I wonder if he ever walks in his sleep. He took a circuit a part of the way round the room, and went out the same way he had come in. Twice more before I slept he came back into the room, acting precisely the same way, and departing as at first. In the intervals I heard him tramping all over the house, his footsteps distinctly audible in the pauses of the storm. When I woke in the morning he had already gone out."

Mr. Maren attempted some further questioning, but was unable longer to restrain the family's tongues; the story of Deluse's death and burial came out, greatly to the good minister's astonishment.

"The explanation of your adventure is very simple," said Mr. Maren. "I don't believe old Deluse walks in his sleep—not in his present one; but you evidently dream in yours."

And to this view of the matter Mr. Galbraith was compelled reluctantly to assent.

Nevertheless, a late hour of the next night found these two gentlemen, accompanied by a son of the minister, in the road in front of the old Deluse house. There was a light inside; it appeared now at one window and now at another. The three men advanced to the door. Just as they reached it there came from the interior a confusion of the most appalling sounds—the clash of weapons, steel against steel, sharp explosions as of fire-arms, shrieks of women, groans and the curses of men in combat! The investigators stood a moment, irresolute, frightened. Then

Mr. Galbraith tried the door. It was fast. But the minister was a man of courage, a man, moreover, of Herculean strength. He retired a pace or two and rushed against the door, striking it with his right shoulder and bursting it from the frame with a loud crash. In a moment the three were inside. Darkness and silence! The only sound was the beating of their hearts.

Mr. Maren had provided himself with matches and a candle. With some difficulty, begotten of his excitement, he made a light, and they proceeded to explore the place, passing from room to room. Everything was in orderly arrangement, as it had been left by the sheriff; nothing had been disturbed. A light coating of dust was everywhere. A back door was partly open, as if by neglect, and their first thought was that the authors of the awful revelry might have escaped. The door was opened, and the light of the candle shone through upon the ground. The expiring effort of the previous night's storm had been a light fall of snow; there were no footprints; the white surface was unbroken. They closed the door and entered the last room of the four that the house contained—that farthest from the road, in an angle of the building. Here the candle in Mr. Maren's hand was suddenly extinguished as by a draught of air. Almost immediately followed the sound of a heavy fall. When the candle had been hastily relighted young Mr. Galbraith was seen prostrate on the floor at a little distance from the others. He was dead. In one hand the body grasped a heavy sack of coins, which later examination showed to be all of old Spanish mintage. Directly over the body as it lay, a board had been torn from its fastenings in the wall, and from the cavity so disclosed it was evident that the bag had been taken.

Another inquest was held: another *post-mortem* examination failed to reveal a probable cause of death. Another verdict of "the visitation of God" left all at liberty to form their own conclusions. Mr. Maren contended that the young man died of excitement.

A FRUITLESS ASSIGNMENT

enry Saylor, who was killed in Covington, in a quarrel with Antonio Finch, was a reporter on the Cincinnati *Commercial*. In the year 1859 a vacant dwelling in Vine Street, in Cincinnati, became the centre of a local excitement because of the strange sights and sounds said to be observed in it nightly. According to the testimony of many reputable residents of the vicinity these were inconsistent with any other hypothesis than that the house was haunted. Figures with something singularly unfamiliar about them were seen by crowds on the sidewalk to pass in and out. No one could say just where they appeared upon the open lawn on their way to the front door by which they entered, nor at exactly what point they vanished as they came out; or, rather, while each spectator was positive enough about these matters, no two agreed. They were all similarly at variance in their descriptions of the figures themselves. Some of the bolder of the curious throng ventured on several evenings to stand upon the doorsteps to intercept them, or failing in this, get a nearer look at them. These courageous men, it was said, were unable to force the door by their united strength, and always were hurled from the steps by some invisible agency and severely injured; the door immediately afterward opening, apparently of its own volition, to admit or free some ghostly guest. The dwelling was known as the Roscoe house, a family of that name having lived there for some years, and then, one by

241

one, disappeared, the last to leave being an old woman. Stories of foul play and successive murders had always been rife, but never were authenticated.

One day during the prevalence of the excitement Saylor presented himself at the office of the *Commercial* for orders. He received a note from the city editor which read as follows: "Go and pass the night alone in the haunted house in Vine Street and if anything occurs worth while make two columns." Saylor obeyed his superior; he could not afford to lose his position on the paper.

Apprising the police of his intention, he effected an entrance through a rear window before dark, walked through the deserted rooms, bare of furniture, dusty and desolate, and seating himself at last in the parlour on an old sofa which he had dragged in from another room watched the deepening of the gloom as night came on. Before it was altogether dark the curious crowd had collected in the street, silent, as a rule, and expectant, with here and there a scoffer uttering his incredulity and courage with scornful remarks or ribald cries. None knew of the anxious watcher inside. He feared to make a light; the uncurtained windows would have betrayed his presence, subjecting him to insult, possibly to injury. Moreover, he was too conscientious to do anything to enfeeble his impressions and unwilling to alter any of the customary conditions under which the manifestations were said to occur.

It was now dark outside, but light from the street faintly illuminated the part of the room that he was in. He had set open every door in the whole interior, above and below, but all the outer ones were locked and bolted. Sudden exclamations from the crowd caused him to spring to the window and look out. He saw the figure of a man moving rapidly across the lawn toward the building—saw it ascend the steps; then a projection of the wall concealed it. There was a noise as of the opening and closing of the hall door; he heard quick, heavy footsteps along the passage—heard them ascend the stairs—heard them on the uncarpeted floor of the chamber immediately overhead.

Saylor promptly drew his pistol, and groping his way up the stairs entered the chamber, dimly lighted from the street. No one was there. He heard footsteps in an adjoining room and entered that. It was dark and silent. He struck his foot against some object on the floor, knelt by it, passed his hand over it. It was a human head—that of a woman. Lifting it by the hair this iron-nerved man returned to the half-lighted room below, carried it near the window and attentively examined it. While so engaged he was half conscious of the rapid opening and closing of the outer door, of footfalls sounding all about him. He raised his eyes from the ghastly object of his attention and saw himself the centre of a crowd of men and women dimly seen; the room was thronged with them. He thought the people had broken in.

"Ladies and gentlemen," he said, coolly, "you see me under suspicious circumstances, but—" his voice was drowned in peals of laughter—such laughter as is heard in asylums for the insane. The persons about him pointed at the object in his hand and their merriment increased as he dropped it and it went rolling among their feet. They danced about it with gestures grotesque and attitudes obscene and indescribable. They struck it with their feet, urging it about the room from wall to wall; pushed and overthrew one another in their struggles to kick it; cursed and screamed and sang snatches of ribald songs as the battered head bounded about the room as if in terror and trying to escape. At last it shot out of the door into the hall, followed by all, with tumultuous haste. That moment the door closed with a sharp concussion. Saylor was alone, in dead silence.

Carefully putting away his pistol, which all the time he had held in his hand, he went to a window and looked out. The street was deserted and silent; the lamps were extinguished; the roofs and chimneys of the houses were sharply outlined against the dawn-light in the east. He left the house, the door yielding easily to his hand, and walked to the *Commercial* office. The city editor was still in his office—asleep. Saylor waked him and said: "I have been at the haunted house."

The editor stared blankly as if not wholly awake. "Good God!" he cried, "are you Saylor?"

"Yes—why not?"

The editor made no answer, but continued staring.

"I passed the night there—it seems," said Saylor.

"They say that things were uncommonly quiet out there," the editor said, trifling with a paper-weight upon which he had dropped his eyes, "did anything occur?"

"Nothing whatever."

THE SPOOK HOUSE

n the road leading north from Manchester, in eastern Kentucky, to Booneville, twenty miles away, stood, in 1862, a wooden plantation house of a somewhat better quality than most of the dwellings in that region. The house was destroyed by fire in the year following—probably by some stragglers from the retreating column of General George W. Morgan, when he was driven from Cumberland Gap to the Ohio river by General Kirby Smith. At the time of its destruction, it had for four or five years been vacant. The fields about it were overgrown with brambles, the fences gone, even the few n———o quarters, and outhouses generally, fallen partly into ruin by neglect and pillage; for the n———oes and poor whites of the vicinity found in the building and fences an abundant supply of fuel, of which they availed themselves without hesitation, openly and by daylight. By daylight alone; after nightfall no human being except passing strangers ever went near the place.

It was known as the "Spook House." That it was tenanted by evil spirits, visible, audible and active, no one in all that region doubted any more than he doubted what he was told of Sundays by the travelling preacher. Its owner's opinion of the matter was unknown; he and his family had disappeared one night and no trace of them had ever been found. They left everything—household goods, clothing, provisions, the horses in the stable, the cows in the field, the n——oes in the quarters—all as it stood; nothing was missing—except a man, a woman, three girls, a boy and a babe! It was not altogether surprising that a plantation where seven human beings could be simultaneously effaced and nobody the wiser should be under some suspicion.

One night in June, 1859, two citizens of Frankfort, Col. J. C. McArdle, a lawyer, and Judge Myron Veigh, of the State Militia, were driving from Booneville to Manchester. Their business was so important that they decided to push on, despite the darkness and the mutterings of an approaching storm, which eventually broke upon them just as they arrived opposite the "Spook House." The lightning was so incessant that they easily found their way through the gateway and into a shed, where they hitched and unharnessed their team. They then went to the house, through the rain, and knocked at all the doors without getting any response. Attributing this to the continuous uproar of the thunder they pushed at one of the doors, which yielded. They entered without further ceremony and closed the door. That instant they were in darkness and silence. Not a gleam of the lightning's unceasing blaze penetrated the windows or crevices; not a whisper of the awful tumult without reached them there. It was as if they had suddenly been stricken blind and deaf, and McArdle afterward said that for a moment he believed himself to have been killed by a stroke of lightning as he crossed the threshold. The rest of this adventure can as well be related in his own words, from the Frankfort *Advocate* of August 6, 1876:

"When I had somewhat recovered from the dazing effect of the transition from uproar to silence, my first impulse was to reopen the door which I had closed, and from the knob of which I was not conscious of having removed my hand; I felt it distinctly, still in the clasp of my fingers. My notion was to ascertain by stepping again into the storm whether I had been deprived of sight and hearing. I turned the door-knob and pulled open the door. It led into another room!

"This apartment was suffused with a faint greenish light, the source of which I could not determine, making everything distinctly visible, though nothing was sharply defined. Everything, I say, but in truth the only objects within the blank stone walls of that room were human corpses. In number they were perhaps eight or ten—it may well be understood that I did not truly count them. They were of different ages, or rather sizes, from infancy up, and of both sexes. All were prostrate on the floor, excepting one, apparently a young woman, who sat up, her back supported by an angle of the wall. A babe was clasped in the arms of another and older woman. A half-grown lad lay face downward across the legs of a full-bearded man. One or two were nearly naked, and the hand of a young girl held the fragment of a gown which she had torn open at the breast. The bodies were in various stages of decay, all greatly shrunken in face and figure. Some were but little more than skeletons.

"While I stood stupefied with horror by this ghastly spectacle and still holding open the door, by some unaccountable perversity my attention was diverted from the shocking scene and concerned itself with trifles and details. Perhaps my mind, with an instinct of self-preservation, sought relief in matters which would relax its dangerous tension. Among other things, I observed that the door that I was holding open was of heavy iron plates, riveted. Equidistant from one another and from the top and bottom, three strong bolts protruded from the bevelled edge. I turned the knob and they were retracted flush with the edge; released it, and they shot out. It was a spring lock. On the inside there was no knob, nor any kind of projection—a smooth surface of iron.

"While noting these things with an interest and attention which it now astonishes me to recall I felt myself thrust aside, and Judge Veigh, whom in the intensity and vicissitudes of my feelings I had altogether forgotten, pushed by me into the room. 'For God's sake,' I cried, 'do not go in there! Let us get out of this dreadful place!'

"He gave no heed to my entreaties, but (as fearless a gentleman as lived in all the South) walked quickly to the centre of the room, knelt beside one of the bodies for a closer examination and tenderly raised its blackened and shrivelled head in his hands. A strong disagreeable odour came through the doorway, completely overpowering me. My senses reeled; I felt myself falling, and in clutching at the edge of the door for support pushed it shut with a sharp click!

"I remember no more: six weeks later I recovered my reason in a hotel at Manchester, whither I had been taken by strangers the next day. For all these weeks I had suffered from a nervous fever, attended with constant delirium. I had been found lying in the road several miles away from the house; but how I had escaped from it to get there I never knew. On recovery, or as soon as my physicians permitted me to talk, I inquired the fate of Judge Veigh, whom (to quiet me, as I now know) they represented as well and at home.

"No one believed a word of my story, and who can wonder? And who can imagine my grief when, arriving at my home in Frankfort two months later, I learned that Judge Veigh had never been heard of since that night? I then regretted bitterly the pride which since the first few days after the recovery of my reason had forbidden me to repeat my discredited story and insist upon its truth.

"With all that afterward occurred—the examination of the house; the failure to find any room corresponding to that which I have described; the attempt to have me adjudged insane, and my triumph over my accusers—the readers of the *Advocate* are familiar. After all these years I am still confident that excavations which I have neither the legal right to undertake nor the wealth to make would disclose the secret of the disappearance of my unhappy friend, and possibly of the former occupants and owners of the deserted and now destroyed house. I do not despair of yet bringing about such a search, and it is a source of deep grief to me that it has been delayed by the undeserved hostility and unwise incredulity of the family and friends of the late Judge Veigh."

Colonel McArdle died in Frankfort on the thirteenth day of December, in the year 1879.

THE THING AT NOLAN

o the south of where the road between Leesville and Hardy, in the State of Missouri, crosses the east fork of May Creek stands an abandoned house. Nobody has lived in it since the summer of 1879, and it is fast going to pieces. For some three years before the date mentioned above, it was occupied by the family of Charles May, from one of whose ancestors the creek near which it stands took its name. Mr. May's family consisted of a wife, an adult son and two young girls. The son's name was John—the names of the daughters are unknown to the writer of this sketch.

John May was of a morose and surly disposition, not easily moved to anger, but having an uncommon gift of sullen, implacable hate. His father was quite otherwise; of a sunny, jovial disposition, but with a quick temper like a sudden flame kindled in a wisp of straw, which consumes it in a flash and is no more. He cherished no resentments, and his anger gone, was quick to make overtures for reconciliation. He had a brother living near by who was unlike him in respect of all this, and it was a current witticism in the neighbourhood that John had inherited his disposition from his uncle.

One day a misunderstanding arose between father and son, harsh words ensued, and the father struck the son full in the face with his fist. John quietly wiped away the blood that followed the blow, fixed his eyes upon the already penitent offender and said with cold composure, "You will die for that."

The words were overheard by two brothers named Jackson, who were approaching the men at the moment; but seeing them engaged in a quarrel they retired, apparently unobserved. Charles May afterward related the unfortunate occurrence to his wife and explained that he had apologized to the son for the hasty blow, but without avail; the young man not only rejected his overtures, but refused to withdraw his terrible threat. Nevertheless, there was no open rupture of relations: John continued living with the family, and things went on very much as before.

One Sunday morning in June, 1879, about two weeks after what has been related, May senior left the house immediately after breakfast, taking a spade. He said he was going to make an excavation at a certain spring in a wood about a mile away, so that the cattle could obtain water. John remained in the house for some hours, variously occupied in shaving himself, writing letters and reading a newspaper. His manner was very nearly what it usually was; perhaps he was a trifle more sullen and surly.

At two o'clock he left the house. At five, he returned. For some reason not connected with any interest in his movements, and which is not now recalled, the time of his departure and that of his return were noted by his mother and sisters, as was attested at his trial for murder. It was observed that his clothing was wet in spots, as if (so the prosecution afterward pointed out) he had been removing blood-stains from it. His manner was strange, his look wild. He complained of illness, and going to his room took to his bed.

May senior did not return. Later that evening the nearest neighbours were aroused, and during that night and the following day a search was prosecuted through the wood where the spring was. It resulted in little but the discovery of both men's footprints in the clay about the spring. John May in the meantime had grown rapidly worse with what the local physician called brain fever, and in his delirium raved of murder, but did not say whom he conceived to have been murdered, nor whom he imagined to have done the deed. But his threat was recalled by the brothers Jackson and he was arrested on suspicion and a deputy sheriff put in charge of him at his home. Public opinion ran strongly against him and but for his illness he would probably have been hanged by a mob. As it was, a meeting of the neighbours was held on Tuesday and a committee appointed to watch the case and take such action at any time as circumstances might seem to warrant.

On Wednesday all was changed. From the town of Nolan, eight miles away, came a story which put a quite different light on the matter. Nolan consisted of a school house, a blacksmith's shop, a "store" and a half-dozen dwellings. The store was kept by one Henry Odell, a cousin of the elder May. On the afternoon of the Sunday of May's disappearance Mr. Odell and four of his neighbours, men of credibility, were sitting in the store smoking and talking. It was a warm day; and both the front and the back door were open. At about three o'clock Charles May, who was well known to three of them, entered at the front door and passed out at the rear. He was without hat or coat. He did not look at them, nor return their greeting, a circumstance which did not surprise, for he was evidently seriously hurt. Above the left eyebrow was a wound—a deep gash from which the blood flowed, covering the whole left side of the face and neck and saturating his light-grey shirt. Oddly enough, the thought uppermost in the minds of all was that he had been fighting and was going to the brook directly at the back of the store, to wash himself.

Perhaps there was a feeling of delicacy—a backwoods etiquette which restrained them from following him to offer assistance; the court records, from which, mainly, this narrative is drawn, are silent as to anything but the fact. They waited for him to return, but he did not return.

Bordering the brook behind the store is a forest extending for six miles back to the Medicine Lodge Hills. As soon as it became known in the neighbourhood of the missing man's dwelling that he had been seen in Nolan there was a marked alteration in public sentiment and feeling. The vigilance committee went out of existence without the formality of a resolution. Search along the wooded bottom lands of May Creek was stopped and nearly the entire male population of the region took to beating the bush about Nolan and in the Medicine Lodge Hills. But of the missing man no trace was found.

One of the strangest circumstances of this strange case is the formal indictment and trial of a man for murder of one whose body no human being professed to have seen—one not known to be dead. We are all more or less familiar with the vagaries and eccentricities of frontier law, but this instance, it is thought, is unique. However that may be, it is of record that on recovering from his illness John May was indicted for the murder of his missing father. Counsel for the defence appears not to have demurred and the case was tried on its merits. The prosecution was spiritless and perfunctory; the defence easily established—with regard to the deceased—an *alibi*. If during the time in which John May must have killed Charles May, if he killed him at all, Charles May was miles away from where John May must have been, it is plain that the deceased must have come to his death at the hands of someone else.

John May was acquitted, immediately left the country, and has never been heard of from that day. Shortly afterward his mother and sisters removed to St. Louis. The farm having passed into the possession of a man who owns the land adjoining, and has a dwelling of his own, the May house has ever since been vacant, and has the sombre reputation of being haunted.

One day after the May family had left the country, some boys, playing in the woods along May Creek, found concealed under a mass of dead leaves, but partly exposed by the rooting of hogs, a spade, nearly new and bright, except for a spot on one edge, which was rusted and stained with blood. The implement had the initials C. M. cut into the handle.

This discovery renewed, in some degree, the public excitement of a few months before. The earth near the spot where the spade was found was carefully examined, and the result was the finding of the dead body of a man. It had been buried under two or three feet of soil and the spot covered with a layer of dead leaves and twigs. There was but little decomposition, a fact attributed to some preservative property in the mineral-bearing soil.

Above the left eyebrow was a wound—a deep gash from which blood had flowed, covering the whole left side of the face and neck and saturating the light-grey shirt. The skull had been cut through by the blow. The body was that of Charles May.

But what was it that passed through Mr. Odell's store at Nolan?

AT OLD MAN ECKERT'S

hilip Eckert lived for many years in an old, weather-stained wooden house about three miles from the little town of Marion, in Vermont. There must be quite a number of persons living who remember him, not unkindly, I trust, and know something of the story that I am about to tell.

"Old Man Eckert," as he was always called, was not of a sociable disposition and lived alone. As he was never known to speak of his own affairs nobody thereabout knew anything of his past, nor of his relatives if he had any. Without being particularly ungracious or repellent in manner or speech, he managed somehow to be immune to impertinent curiosity, yet exempt from the evil repute with which it commonly revenges itself when baffled; so far as I know, Mr. Eckert's renown as a reformed assassin or a retired pirate of the Spanish Main had not reached any ear in Marion. He got his living cultivating a small and not very fertile farm.

One day he disappeared and a prolonged search by his neighbours failed to turn him up or throw any light upon his whereabouts or whyabouts. Nothing indicated preparation to leave: all was as he might have left it to go to the spring for a bucket of water. For a few weeks little else was talked of in that region; then "old man Eckert" became a village tale for the ear of the stranger. I do not know what was done regarding his property—the correct legal thing, doubtless. The house was standing, still vacant and conspicuously unfit, when I last heard of it, some twenty years afterward.

Of course it came to be considered "haunted," and the customary tales were told of moving lights, dolorous sounds and startling apparitions. At one time, about five years after the disappearance, these stories of the supernatural became so rife, or through some attesting circumstances seemed so important, that some of Marion's most serious citizens deemed it well to investigate, and to that end arranged for a night session on the premises. The parties to this undertaking were John Holcomb, an apothecary; Wilson Merle, a lawyer, and Andrus C. Palmer, the teacher of the public school, all men of consequence and repute. They were to meet at Holcomb's house at eight o'clock in the evening of the appointed day and go together to the scene of their vigil, where certain arrangements for their comfort, a provision of fuel and the like, for the season was winter, had been already made.

Palmer did not keep the engagement, and after waiting a half-hour for him the others went to the Eckert house without him. They established themselves in the principal room, before a glowing fire, and without other light than it gave, awaited events. It had been agreed to speak as little as possible: they did not even renew the exchange of views regarding the defection of Palmer, which had occupied their minds on the way.

Probably an hour had passed without incident when they heard (not without emotion, doubtless) the sound of an opening door in the rear of the house, followed by footfalls in the room adjoining that in which they sat. The watchers rose to their feet, but stood firm, prepared for whatever might ensue. A long silence followed—how long neither would afterward undertake to say. Then the door between the two rooms opened and a man entered.

It was Palmer. He was pale, as if from excitement—as pale as the others felt themselves to be. His manner, too, was singularly distrait: he neither responded to their salutations nor so much as looked at them, but walked slowly across the room in the light of the failing fire and opening the front door passed out into the darkness.

It seems to have been the first thought of both men that Palmer was suffering from fright—that something seen, heard or imagined in the back room had deprived him of his senses. Acting on the same friendly impulse both ran after him through the open door. But neither they nor anyone ever again saw or heard of Andrus Palmer!

This much was ascertained the next morning. During the session of Messrs. Holcomb and Merle at the "haunted house" a new snow had fallen to a depth of several inches upon the old. In this snow Palmer's trail from his lodging in the village to the back door of the Eckert house was conspicuous. But there it ended: from the front door nothing led away but the tracks of the two men who swore that he preceded them. Palmer's disappearance was as complete as that of "old man Eckert" himself—whom, indeed, the editor of the local paper somewhat graphically accused of having "reached out and pulled him in."

A VINE ON A HOUSE

bout three miles from the little town of Norton, in Missouri, on the road leading to Maysville, stands an old house that was last occupied by a family named Harding. Since 1886 no one has lived in it, nor is anyone likely to live in it again. Time and the disfavour of persons dwelling thereabout are converting it into a rather picturesque ruin. An observer unacquainted with its history would hardly put it into the category of "haunted houses," yet in all the region round such is its evil reputation. Its windows are without glass, its doorways without doors; there are wide breaches in the shingle roof, and for lack of paint the weatherboarding is a dun grey. But these unfailing signs of the supernatural are partly concealed and greatly softened by the abundant foliage of a large vine over-running the entire structure. This vine—of a species which no botanist has ever been able to name—has an important part in the story of the house.

The Harding family consisted of Robert Harding, his wife Matilda, Miss Julia Went, who was her sister, and two young children. Robert Harding was a silent, cold-mannered man who made no friends in the neighbourhood and apparently cared to make none. He was about forty years old, frugal and industrious, and made a living from the little farm which is now overgrown with brush and brambles. He and his sister-in-law were rather tabooed by their neighbours, who seemed to think that they were seen too frequently together—not entirely their fault, for at these times they evidently did not challenge observation. The moral code of rural Missouri is stern and exacting.

Mrs. Harding was a gentle, sad-eyed woman, lacking a left foot.

At some time in 1884 it became known that she had gone to visit her mother in Iowa. That was what her husband said in reply to inquiries, and his manner of saying it did not encourage further questioning. She never came back, and two years later, without selling his farm or anything that was his, or appointing an agent to look after his interests, or removing his household goods, Harding, with the rest of the family, left the country. Nobody knew whither he went; nobody at that time cared. Naturally, whatever was movable about the place soon disappeared and the deserted house became "haunted" in the manner of its kind.

One summer evening, four or five years later, the Rev. J. Gruber, of Norton, and a Maysville attorney named Hyatt met on horseback in front of the Harding place. Having business matters to discuss, they hitched their animals and going to the house sat on the porch to talk. Some humorous reference to the sombre reputation of the place was made and forgotten as soon as uttered, and they talked of their business affairs until it grew almost dark. The evening was oppressively warm, the air stagnant.

Presently both men started from their seats in surprise: a long vine that covered half the front of the house and dangled its branches from the edge of the porch above them was visibly and audibly agitated, shaking violently in every stem and leaf.

"We shall have a storm," Hyatt exclaimed.

Gruber said nothing, but silently directed the other's attention to the foliage of adjacent trees, which showed no movement; even the delicate tips of the boughs silhouetted against the clear sky were motionless. They hastily passed down the steps to what had been a lawn and looked upward at the vine, whose entire length was now visible. It continued in violent agitation, yet they could discern no disturbing cause.

"Let us leave," said the minister.

And leave they did. Forgetting that they had been travelling in opposite directions, they rode away together. They went to Norton, where they related their strange experience to several discreet friends. The next evening, at about the same hour, accompanied by two others whose names are not recalled, they were again on the porch of the Harding house, and again the mysterious phenomenon occurred: the vine was violently agitated while under the closest scrutiny from root to tip, nor did their combined strength applied to the trunk serve to still it. After an hour's observation they retreated, no less wise, it is thought, than when they had come.

No great time was required for these singular facts to rouse the curiosity of the entire neighbourhood. By day and by night crowds of persons assembled at the Harding house "seeking a sign." It does not appear that any found it, yet so credible were the witnesses mentioned that none doubted the reality of the "manifestations" to which they testified.

By either a happy inspiration or some destructive design, it was one day proposed—nobody appeared to know from whom the suggestion came—to dig up the vine, and after a good deal of debate this was done. Nothing was found but the root, yet nothing could have been more strange!

For five or six feet from the trunk, which had at the surface of the ground a diameter of several inches, it ran downward, single and straight, into a loose, friable earth; then it divided and subdivided into rootlets, fibres and filaments, most curiously interwoven. When carefully freed from soil they showed a singular formation. In their ramifications and doublings back upon themselves they made a compact network, having in size and shape an amazing resemblance to the human figure. Head, trunk and limbs were there; even the fingers and toes were distinctly defined; and many professed to see in the distribution and arrangement of the fibres in the globular mass representing the head a grotesque suggestion of a face. The figure was horizontal; the smaller roots had begun to unite at the breast.

In point of resemblance to the human form this image was imperfect. At about ten inches from one of the knees, the *cilia* forming that leg had abruptly doubled backward and inward upon their course of growth. The figure lacked the left foot.

There was but one inference—the obvious one; but in the ensuing excitement as many courses of action were proposed as there were incapable counsellors. The matter was settled by the sheriff of the county, who as the lawful custodian of the abandoned estate ordered the root replaced and the excavation filled with the earth that had been removed.

Later inquiry brought out only one fact of relevancy and significance: Mrs. Harding had never visited her relatives in Iowa, nor did they know that she was supposed to have done so.

Of Robert Harding and the rest of his family nothing is known. The house retains its evil reputation, but the replanted vine is as orderly and well-behaved a vegetable as a nervous person could wish to sit under of a pleasant night, when the katydids grate out their immemorial revelation and the distant whippoorwill signifies his notion of what ought to be done about it.

THE OTHER LODGERS

n order to take that train," said Colonel Levering, sitting in the Waldorf-Astoria hotel, "you will have to remain nearly all night in Atlanta. That is a fine city, but I advise you not to put up at the Breathitt House, one of the principal hotels. It is an old wooden building in urgent need of repairs. There are breaches in the walls that you could throw a cat through. The bedrooms have no locks on the doors, no furniture but a single chair in each, and a bedstead without bedding—just a mattress. Even these meagre accommodations you cannot be sure that you will have in monopoly; you must take your chance of being stowed in with a lot of others. Sir, it is a most abominable hotel.

"The night that I passed in it was an uncomfortable night. I got in late and was shown to my room on the ground floor by an apologetic night-clerk with a tallow candle, which he considerately left with me. I was worn out by two days and a night of hard railway travel and had not entirely recovered from a gunshot wound in the head, received in an altercation. Rather than look for better quarters I lay down on the mattress without removing my clothing and fell asleep.

"Along toward morning I awoke. The moon had risen and was shining in at the uncurtained window, illuminating the room with a soft, bluish light which seemed, somehow, a bit spooky, though I dare say it had no uncommon quality; all moonlight is

that way if you will observe it. Imagine my surprise and indignation when I saw the floor occupied by at least a dozen other
lodgers! I sat up, earnestly damning the management of that
unthinkable hotel, and was about to spring from the bed to go
and make trouble for the night-clerk—him of the apologetic
manner and the tallow candle—when something in the situation
affected me with a strange indisposition to move. I suppose I
was what a story-writer might call 'frozen with terror.' For those
men were obviously all dead!

"They lay on their backs, disposed orderly along three sides
of the room, their feet to the walls—against the other wall, farthest from the door, stood my bed and the chair. All the faces
were covered, but under their white cloths the features of the
two bodies that lay in the square patch of moonlight near the
window showed in sharp profile as to nose and chin.

"I thought this a bad dream and tried to cry out, as one
does in a nightmare, but could make no sound. At last, with
a desperate effort I threw my feet to the floor and passing
between the two rows of clouted faces and the two bodies
that lay nearest the door, I escaped from the infernal place and
ran to the office. The night-clerk was there, behind the desk,
sitting in the dim light of another tallow candle—just sitting
and staring. He did not rise: my abrupt entrance produced
no effect upon him, though I must have looked a veritable
corpse myself. It occurred to me then that I had not before
really observed the fellow. He was a little chap, with a colour-
less face and the whitest, blankest eyes I ever saw. He had no
more expression than the back of my hand. His clothing was
a dirty grey.

"'Damn you!' I said; 'what do you mean?'

"Just the same, I was shaking like a leaf in the wind and did not recognize my own voice.

"The night-clerk rose, bowed (apologetically) and—well, he was no longer there, and at that moment I felt a hand laid upon my shoulder from behind. Just fancy that if you can! Unspeakably frightened, I turned and saw a portly, kind-faced gentleman, who asked:

"'What is the matter, my friend?'

"I was not long in telling him, but before I made an end of it he went pale himself. 'See here,' he said, 'are you telling the truth?'

"I had now got myself in hand and terror had given place to indignation. 'If you dare to doubt it,' I said, 'I'll hammer the life out of you!'

"'No,' he replied, 'don't do that; just sit down till I tell you. This is not a hotel. It used to be; afterward it was a hospital. Now it is unoccupied, awaiting a tenant. The room that you mention was the dead-room—there were always plenty of dead. The fellow that you call the night-clerk used to be that, but later he booked the patients as they were brought in. I don't understand his being here. He has been dead a few weeks.'

"'And who are you?' I blurted out.

"'Oh, I look after the premises. I happened to be passing just now, and seeing a light in here came in to investigate. Let us have a look into that room,' he added, lifting the sputtering candle from the desk.

"'I'll see you at the devil first!' said I, bolting out of the door into the street.

"Sir, that Breathitt House, in Atlanta, is a beastly place! Don't you stop there."

"God forbid! Your account of it certainly does not suggest comfort. By the way, Colonel, when did all that occur?"

"In September, 1864—shortly after the siege."

THE WAYS
OF GHOSTS

My peculiar relation to the writer of the following narratives is such that I must ask the reader to overlook the absence of explanation as to how they came into my possession. Withal, my knowledge of him is so meagre that I should rather not undertake to say if he were himself persuaded of the truth of what he relates; certainly such inquiries as I have thought it worth while to set about have not in every instance tended to confirmation of the statements made. Yet his style, for the most part devoid alike of artifice and art, almost baldly simple and direct, seems hardly compatible with the disingenuousness of a merely literary intention; one would call it the manner of one more concerned for the fruits of research than for the flowers of expression. In transcribing his notes and fortifying their claim to attention by giving them something of an orderly arrangement, I have conscientiously refrained from embellishing them with such small ornaments of diction as I may have felt myself able to bestow, which would not only have been impertinent, even if pleasing, but would have given me a somewhat closer relation to the work than I should care to have and to avow.

—A. B.

PRESENT AT A HANGING

n old man named Daniel Baker, living near Lebanon, Iowa, was suspected by his neighbours of having murdered a peddler who had obtained permission to pass the night at his house. This was in 1853, when peddling was more common in the western country than it is now, and was attended with considerable danger. The peddler with his pack traversed the country by all manner of lonely roads, and was compelled to rely upon the country people for hospitality. This brought him into relation with queer characters, some of whom were not altogether scrupulous in their methods of making a living, murder being an acceptable means to that end. It occasionally occurred that a peddler with diminished pack and swollen purse would be traced to the lonely dwelling of some rough character and never could be traced beyond. This was so in the case of "old man Baker," as he was always called. (Such names are given in the western "settlements" only to elderly persons who are not esteemed; to the general disrepute of social unworth is affixed the special reproach of age.) A peddler came to his house and none went away—that is all that anybody knew.

Seven years later the Rev. Mr. Cummings, a Baptist minister well known in that part of the country, was driving by Baker's farm one night. It was not very dark: there was a bit of moon somewhere above the light veil of mist that lay along the earth. Mr. Cummings, who was at all times a cheerful person, was whistling a tune, which he would occasionally interrupt to speak a word of friendly encouragement to his horse. As he came to a little bridge across a dry ravine he saw the figure of a man standing upon it, clearly outlined against the grey background of a misty forest. The man had something strapped on his back and carried a heavy stick—obviously an itinerant peddler. His attitude had in it a suggestion of abstraction, like that of a sleep-walker. Mr. Cummings reined in his horse when he arrived in front of him, gave him a pleasant salutation and invited him to a seat in the vehicle—"if you are going my way," he added. The man raised his head, looked him full in the face, but neither answered nor made any further movement. The minister, with good-natured persistence, repeated his invitation. At this the man threw his right hand forward from his side and pointed downward as he stood on the extreme edge of the bridge. Mr. Cummings looked past him, over into the ravine, saw nothing unusual and withdrew his eyes to address the man again. He had disappeared. The horse, which all this time had been uncommonly restless, gave at the same moment a snort of terror and started to run away. Before he had regained control of the animal the minister was at the crest of the hill a hundred yards along. He looked back and saw the figure again, at the same place and in the same attitude as when he had first observed it. Then for the first time he was conscious of a sense of the supernatural and drove home as rapidly as his willing horse would go.

On arriving at home he related his adventure to his family, and early the next morning, accompanied by two neighbours, John White Corwell and Abner Raiser, returned to the spot. They found the body of old man Baker hanging by the neck from one of the beams of the bridge, immediately beneath the spot where the apparition had stood. A thick coating of dust, slightly dampened by the mist, covered the floor of the bridge, but the only footprints were those of Mr. Cummings' horse.

In taking down the body the men disturbed the loose, friable earth of the slope below it, disclosing human bones already nearly uncovered by the action of water and frost. They were identified as those of the lost peddler. At the double inquest the coroner's jury found that Daniel Baker died by his own hand while suffering from temporary insanity, and that Samuel Morritz was murdered by some person or persons to the jury unknown.

A COLD GREETING

his is a story told by the late Benson Foley of San Francisco:

"In the summer of 1881 I met a man named James H. Conway, a resident of Franklin, Tennessee. He was visiting San Francisco for his health, deluded man, and brought me a note of introduction from Mr. Lawrence Barting. I had known Barting as a captain in the Federal army during the civil war. At its close he had settled in Franklin, and in time became, I had reason to think, somewhat prominent as a lawyer. Barting had always seemed to me an honourable and truthful man, and the warm friendship which he expressed in his note for Mr. Conway was to me sufficient evidence that the latter was in every way worthy of my confidence and esteem. At dinner one day Conway told me that it had been solemnly agreed between him and Barting that the one who died first should, if possible, communicate with the other from beyond the grave, in some unmistakable way—just how, they had left (wisely, it seemed to me) to be decided by the deceased, according to the opportunities that his altered circumstances might present.

"A few weeks after the conversation in which Mr. Conway spoke of this agreement, I met him one day, walking slowly down Montgomery Street, apparently, from his abstracted air, in deep thought. He greeted me coldly with merely a movement of the head and passed on, leaving me standing on the walk, with half-proffered hand, surprised and naturally somewhat piqued. The next day I met him again in the office of the Palace Hotel, and seeing him about to repeat the disagreeable performance of the day before, intercepted him in a doorway, with a friendly salutation, and bluntly requested an explanation of his altered manner. He hesitated a moment; then, looking me frankly in the eyes, said:

"'I do not think, Mr. Foley, that I have any longer a claim to your friendship, since Mr. Barting appears to have withdrawn his own from me—for what reason, I protest I do not know. If he has not already informed you he probably will do so.'

"'But,' I replied, 'I have not heard from Mr. Barting.'

"'Heard from him!' he repeated, with apparent surprise. 'Why, he is here. I met him yesterday ten minutes before meeting you. I gave you exactly the same greeting that he gave me. I met him again not a quarter of an hour ago, and his manner was precisely the same: he merely bowed and passed on. I shall not soon forget your civility to me. Good morning, or—as it may please you—farewell.'

"All this seemed to me singularly considerate and delicate behaviour on the part of Mr. Conway.

"As dramatic situations and literary effects are foreign to my purpose I will explain at once that Mr. Barting was dead. He had died in Nashville four days before this conversation. Calling on Mr. Conway, I apprised him of our friend's death, showing him the letters announcing it. He was visibly affected in a way that forbade me to entertain a doubt of his sincerity.

"'It seems incredible,' he said, after a period of reflection. 'I suppose I must have mistaken another man for Barting, and that man's cold greeting was merely a stranger's civil acknowledg-ment of my own. I remember, indeed, that he lacked Barting's moustache.'

"'Doubtless it was another man,' I assented; and the subject was never afterward mentioned between us. But I had in my pocket a photograph of Barting, which had been inclosed in the letter from his widow. It had been taken a week before his death, and was without a moustache."

A WIRELESS MESSAGE

I n the summer of 1896 Mr. William Holt, a wealthy manufacturer of Chicago, was living temporarily in a little town of central New York, the name of which the writer's memory has not retained. Mr. Holt had had "trouble with his wife," from whom he had parted a year before. Whether the trouble was anything more serious than "incompatibility of temper," he is probably the only living person that knows: he is not addicted to the vice of confidences. Yet he has related the incident herein set down to at least one person without exacting a pledge of secrecy. He is now living in Europe.

One evening he had left the house of a brother whom he was visiting, for a stroll in the country. It may be assumed—whatever the value of the assumption in connection with what is said to have occurred—that his mind was occupied with reflections on his domestic infelicities and the distressing changes that they had wrought in his life. Whatever may have been his thoughts, they so possessed him that he observed neither the lapse of time nor whither his feet were carrying him; he knew only that he had passed far beyond the town limits and was traversing a lonely region by a road that bore no resemblance to the one by which he had left the village. In brief, he was "lost."

Realizing his mischance, he smiled; central New York is not a region of perils, nor does one long remain lost in it. He turned about and went back the way that he had come. Before he had gone far he observed that the landscape was growing more distinct—was brightening. Everything was suffused with a soft, red glow in which he saw his shadow projected in the road before him. "The moon is rising," he said to himself. Then he remembered that it was about the time of the new moon, and if that tricksy orb was in one of its stages of visibility it had set long before. He stopped and faced about, seeking the source of the rapidly broadening light. As he did so, his shadow turned and lay along the road in front of him as before. The light still came from behind him. That was surprising; he could not understand. Again he turned, and again, facing successively to every point of the horizon. Always the shadow was before—always the light behind, "a still and awful red."

Holt was astonished—"dumbfounded" is the word that he used in telling it—yet seems to have retained a certain intelligent curiosity. To test the intensity of the light whose nature and cause he could not determine, he took out his watch to see if he could make out the figures on the dial. They were plainly visible, and the hands indicated the hour of eleven o'clock and twenty-five minutes. At that moment the mysterious illumination suddenly flared to an intense, an almost blinding splendour, flushing the entire sky, extinguishing the stars and throwing the monstrous shadow of himself athwart the landscape. In that unearthly illumination he saw near him, but apparently in the air at a considerable elevation, the figure of his wife, clad in her night-clothing and holding to her breast the figure of his child. Her eyes were fixed upon his with an expression which he afterward professed himself unable to name or describe, further than that it was "not of this life."

The flare was momentary, followed by black darkness, in which, however, the apparition still showed white and motionless; then by insensible degrees it faded and vanished, like a bright image on the retina after the closing of the eyes. A peculiarity of the apparition, hardly noted at the time, but afterward recalled, was that it showed only the upper half of the woman's figure: nothing was seen below the waist.

The sudden darkness was comparative, not absolute, for gradually all objects of his environment became again visible.

In the dawn of the morning Holt found himself entering the village at a point opposite to that at which he had left it. He soon arrived at the house of his brother, who hardly knew him. He was wild-eyed, haggard, and grey as a rat. Almost incoherently, he related his night's experience.

"Go to bed, my poor fellow," said his brother, "and—wait. We shall hear more of this."

An hour later came the predestined telegram. Holt's dwelling in one of the suburbs of Chicago had been destroyed by fire. Her escape cut off by the flames, his wife had appeared at an upper window, her child in her arms. There she had stood, motionless, apparently dazed. Just as the firemen had arrived with a ladder, the floor had given way, and she was seen no more.

The moment of this culminating horror was eleven o'clock and twenty-five minutes, standard time.

AN ARREST

Having murdered his brother-in-law, Orrin Brower of Kentucky was a fugitive from justice. From the county jail where he had been confined to await his trial he had escaped by knocking down his jailer with an iron bar, robbing him of his keys and, opening the outer door, walking out into the night. The jailer being unarmed, Brower got no weapon with which to defend his recovered liberty. As soon as he was out of the town he had the folly to enter a forest; this was many years ago, when that region was wilder than it is now.

The night was pretty dark, with neither moon nor stars visible, and as Brower had never dwelt thereabout, and knew nothing of the lay of the land, he was, naturally, not long in losing himself. He could not have said if he were getting farther away from the town or going back to it—a most important matter to Orrin Brower. He knew that in either case a posse of citizens with a pack of bloodhounds would soon be on his track and his chance of escape was very slender; but he did not wish to assist in his own pursuit. Even an added hour of freedom was worth having.

Suddenly he emerged from the forest into an old road, and there before him saw, indistinctly, the figure of a man, motionless in the gloom. It was too late to retreat: the fugitive felt that at the first movement back toward the wood he would be, as he afterward explained, "filled with buckshot." So the two stood there like trees, Brower nearly suffocated by the activity of his own heart; the other—the emotions of the other are not recorded.

A moment later—it may have been an hour—the moon sailed into a patch of unclouded sky and the hunted man saw that visible embodiment of Law lift an arm and point significantly toward and beyond him. He understood. Turning his back to his captor, he walked submissively away in the direction indicated, looking to neither the right nor the left; hardly daring to breathe, his head and back actually aching with a prophecy of buckshot.

Brower was as courageous a criminal as ever lived to be hanged; that was shown by the conditions of awful personal peril in which he had coolly killed his brother-in-law. It is needless to relate them here; they came out at his trial, and the revelation of his calmness in confronting them came near to saving his neck. But what would you have?—when a brave man is beaten, he submits.

So they pursued their journey jailward along the old road through the woods. Only once did Brower venture a turn of the head: just once, when he was in deep shadow and he knew that the other was in moonlight, he looked backward. His captor was Burton Duff, the jailer, as white as death and bearing upon his brow the livid mark of the iron bar. Orrin Brower had no further curiosity.

Eventually they entered the town, which was all alight, but deserted; only the women and children remained, and they were off the streets. Straight toward the jail the criminal held his way. Straight up to the main entrance he walked, laid his hand upon the knob of the heavy iron door, pushed it open without command, entered and found himself in the presence of a half-dozen armed men. Then he turned. Nobody else entered.

On a table in the corridor lay the dead body of Burton Duff.

MYSTERIOUS DISAPPEARANCES

THE DIFFICULTY OF CROSSING A FIELD

ne morning in July, 1854, a planter named Williamson, living six miles from Selma, Alabama, was sitting with his wife and a child on the veranda of his dwelling. Immediately in front of the house was a lawn, perhaps fifty yards in extent between the house and public road, or, as it was called, the "pike." Beyond this road lay a close-cropped pasture of some ten acres, level and without a tree, rock, or any natural or artificial object on its surface. At the time there was not even a domestic animal in the field. In another field, beyond the pasture, a dozen slaves were at work under an overseer.

Throwing away the stump of a cigar, the planter rose, saying: "I forgot to tell Andrew about those horses." Andrew was the overseer.

Williamson strolled leisurely down the gravel walk, plucking a flower as he went, passed across the road and into the pasture, pausing a moment as he closed the gate leading into it, to greet a passing neighbour, Armour Wren, who lived on an adjoining plantation. Mr. Wren was in an open carriage with his son James, a lad of thirteen. When he had driven some two hundred yards from the point of meeting, Mr. Wren said to his son: "I forgot to tell Mr. Williamson about those horses."

Mr. Wren had sold to Mr. Williamson some horses, which were to have been sent for that day, but for some reason not now remembered it would be inconvenient to deliver them until the morrow. The coachman was directed to drive back, and as the vehicle turned Williamson was seen by all three, walking leisurely across the pasture. At that moment one of the coach horses stumbled and came near falling. It had no more than fairly recovered itself when James Wren cried: "Why, father, what has become of Mr. Williamson?"

It is not the purpose of this narrative to answer that question.

Mr. Wren's strange account of the matter, given under oath in the course of legal proceedings relating to the Williamson estate, here follows:

"My son's exclamation caused me to look toward the spot where I had seen the deceased [*sic*] an instant before, but he was not there, nor was he anywhere visible. I cannot say that at the moment I was greatly startled, or realized the gravity of the occurrence, though I thought it singular. My son, however, was greatly astonished and kept repeating his question in different forms until we arrived at the gate. My black boy Sam was similarly affected, even in a greater degree, but I reckon more by my son's manner than by anything he had himself observed. [This sentence in the testimony was stricken out.] As we got out of the carriage at the gate of the field, and while Sam was hanging [*sic*] the team to the fence, Mrs. Williamson, with her child in her arms and followed by several servants, came running down the walk in great excitement, crying: 'He is gone, he is gone! O God! what an awful thing!' and many other such exclamations, which I do not distinctly recollect. I got from them the impression that they related to something more than the mere disappearance of her husband, even if that had occurred before her eyes. Her manner was wild, but not more so, I think, than was natural under the circumstances. I have no reason to think she had at that time lost her mind. I have never since seen nor heard of Mr. Williamson."

This testimony, as might have been expected, was corroborated in almost every particular by the only other eye-witness (if that is a proper term)—the lad James. Mrs. Williamson had lost her reason and the servants were, of course, not competent to testify. The boy James Wren had declared at first that he *saw* the disappearance, but there is nothing of this in his testimony given in court. None of the field hands working in the field to which Williamson was going had seen him at all, and the most rigorous search of the entire plantation and adjoining country failed to supply a clew. The most monstrous and grotesque fictions, originating with the blacks, were current in that part of the State for many years, and probably are to this day; but what has been here related is all that is certainly known of the matter. The courts decided that Williamson was dead, and his estate was distributed according to law.

AN UNFINISHED RACE

ames Burne Worson was a shoemaker who lived in Leamington, Warwickshire, England. He had a little shop in one of the by-ways leading off the road to Warwick. In his humble sphere he was esteemed an honest man, although like many of his class in English towns he was somewhat addicted to drink. When in liquor he would make foolish wagers. On one of these too frequent occasions he was boasting of his prowess as a pedestrian and athlete, and the outcome was a match against nature. For a stake of one sovereign he undertook to run all the way to Coventry and back, a distance of something more than forty miles. This was on the 3d day of September in 1873. He set out at once, the man with whom he had made the bet—whose name is not remembered—accompanied by Barham Wise, a linen draper, and Hamerson Burns, a photographer, I think, following in a light cart or wagon.

For several miles Worson went on very well, at an easy gait, without apparent fatigue, for he had really great powers of endurance and was not sufficiently intoxicated to enfeeble them. The three men in the wagon kept a short distance in the rear, giving him occasional friendly "chaff" or encouragement, as the spirit moved them. Suddenly—in the very middle of the roadway, not a dozen yards from them, and with their eyes full upon him—the man seemed to stumble, pitched headlong forward, uttered a terrible cry and vanished! He did not fall to the earth—he vanished before touching it. No trace of him was ever discovered.

After remaining at and about the spot for some time, with aimless irresolution, the three men returned to Leamington, told their astonishing story and were afterward taken into custody. But they were of good standing, had always been considered truthful, were sober at the time of the occurrence, and nothing ever transpired to discredit their sworn account of their extraordinary adventure, concerning the truth of which, nevertheless, public opinion was divided, throughout the United Kingdom. If they had something to conceal, their choice of means is certainly one of the most amazing ever made by sane human beings.

CHARLES ASHMORE'S TRAIL

he family of Christian Ashmore consisted of his wife, his mother, two grown daughters, and a son of sixteen years. They lived in Troy, New York, were well-to-do, respectable persons, and had many friends, some of whom, reading these lines, will doubtless learn for the first time the extraordinary fate of the young man. From Troy the Ashmores moved in 1871 or 1872 to Richmond, Indiana, and a year or two later to the vicinity of Quincy, Illinois, where Mr. Ashmore bought a farm and lived on it. At some little distance from the farmhouse was a spring with a constant flow of clear, cold water, whence the family derived its supply for domestic use at all seasons.

On the evening of the 9th of November in 1878, at about nine o'clock, young Charles Ashmore left the family circle about the hearth, took a tin bucket and started toward the spring. As he did not return, the family became uneasy, and going to the door by which he had left the house, his father called without receiving an answer. He then lighted a lantern and with the eldest daughter, Martha, who insisted on accompanying him, went in search. A light snow had fallen, obliterating the path, but making the young man's trail conspicuous; each footprint was plainly defined. After going a little more than half-way— perhaps seventy-five yards—the father, who was in advance, halted, and elevating his lantern stood peering intently into the darkness ahead.

"What is the matter, father?" the girl asked.

This was the matter: the trail of the young man had abruptly ended, and all beyond was smooth, unbroken snow. The last footprints were as conspicuous as any in the line; the very nail-marks were distinctly visible. Mr. Ashmore looked upward, shading his eyes with his hat held between them and the lantern. The stars were shining; there was not a cloud in the sky; he was denied the explanation which had suggested itself, doubtful as it would have been—a new snowfall with a limit so plainly defined. Taking a wide circuit round the ultimate tracks, so as to leave them undisturbed for further examination, the man proceeded to the spring, the girl following, weak and terrified. Neither had spoken a word of what both had observed. The spring was covered with ice, hours old.

Returning to the house they noted the appearance of the snow on both sides of the trail its entire length. No tracks led away from it.

The morning light showed nothing more. Smooth, spotless, unbroken, the shallow snow lay everywhere.

Four days later the grief-stricken mother herself went to the spring for water. She came back and related that in passing the spot where the footprints had ended she had heard the voice of her son and had been eagerly calling to him, wandering about the place, as she had fancied the voice to be now in one direction, now in another, until she was exhausted with fatigue and emotion. Questioned as to what the voice had said, she was unable to tell, yet averred that the words were perfectly distinct.

In a moment the entire family was at the place, but nothing was heard, and the voice was believed to be an hallucination caused by the mother's great anxiety and her disordered nerves. But for months afterward, at irregular intervals of a few days, the voice was heard by the several members of the family, and by others. All declared it unmistakably the voice of Charles Ashmore; all agreed that it seemed to come from a great distance, faintly, yet with entire distinctness of articulation; yet none could determine its direction, nor repeat its words. The intervals of silence grew longer and longer, the voice fainter and farther, and by midsummer it was heard no more.

If anybody knows the fate of Charles Ashmore it is probably his mother. She is dead.

SCIENCE TO THE FRONT

In connection with this subject of "mysterious disappearance"—of which every memory is stored with abundant example—it is pertinent to note the belief of Dr. Hern, of Leipsic; not by way of explanation, unless the reader may choose to take it so, but because of its intrinsic interest as a singular speculation. This distinguished scientist has expounded his views in a book entitled "Verschwinden und Seine Theorie," which has attracted some attention, "particularly," says one writer, "among the followers of Hegel, and mathematicians who hold to the actual existence of a so-called non-Euclidean space—that is to say, of space which has more dimensions than length, breadth, and thickness—space in which it would be possible to tie a knot in an endless cord and to turn a rubber ball inside out without 'a solution of its continuity,' or in other words, without breaking or cracking it."

Dr. Hern believes that in the visible world there are void places—*vacua*, and something more—holes, as it were, through which animate and inanimate objects may fall into the invisible world and be seen and heard no more. The theory is something like this: Space is pervaded by luminiferous ether, which is a material thing—as much a substance as air or water, though almost infinitely more attenuated. All force, all forms of energy must be propagated in this; every process must take place in it which takes place at all. But let us suppose that cavities exist in this otherwise universal medium, as caverns exist in the earth, or cells in a Swiss cheese. In such a cavity there would be absolutely nothing. It would be such a vacuum as cannot be artificially produced; for if we pump the air from a receiver there remains the luminiferous ether. Through one of these cavities light could not pass, for there would be nothing to bear it. Sound could not come from it; nothing could be felt in it. It would not have a single one of the conditions necessary to the action of any of our senses. In such a void, in short, nothing whatever could occur. Now, in the words of the writer before quoted—the learned doctor himself nowhere puts it so concisely: "A man inclosed in such a closet could neither see nor be seen; neither hear nor be heard; neither feel nor be felt; neither live nor die, for both life and death are processes which can take place only where there is force, and in empty space no force could exist." Are these the awful conditions (some will ask) under which the friends of the lost are to think of them as existing, and doomed forever to exist?

Baldly and imperfectly as here stated, Dr. Hern's theory, in so far as it professes to be an adequate explanation of "mysterious disappearances," is open to many obvious objections; to fewer as he states it himself in the "spacious volubility" of his book. But even as expounded by its author it does not explain, and in truth is incompatible with some incidents of, the occurrences related in these memoranda: for example, the sound of Charles Ashmore's voice. It is not my duty to indue facts and theories with affinity.

A. B.

AFTERWORD

The Fate of Ambrose Bierce

How could someone as well known and as famous as Ambrose Bierce just vanish?

That question has been asked by many for over a century and there have been countless proposals, some more sensible than others, but no firm evidence to prove any of them.

As we have seen, Bierce was fascinated by mysterious disappearances, and it was not beyond the realms of possibility that he would enjoy the fame of creating his own. But by 1913, when he was seventy-one, he was tired, dejected and increasingly disappointed with life. He had lost too many friends, as well as his wife and two sons. He had walked away from his employment with William Randolph Hearst and had little interest in further journalism. He had seen the destruction of San Francisco in the great earthquake and felt it had taken away his world of memories. What was left?

To escape... To have one last adventure and see what fate might bring.

It was evident during his final days in America that Bierce was settling his affairs. In January 1913 he had already transferred to his daughter Helen the ownership of a cemetery plot in St. Helena, north of San Francisco. His note to her added, rather cryptically, "I do not wish to lie there. That matter is all arranged and you will not be bothered about the mortal part of Your Daddy." One questions; had he already arranged a burial site elsewhere (in which case you'd think he'd say) or did he have other plans?

One of Bierce's closest friends, who served as his unpaid personal secretary, was a Washington school-teacher, Carrie Christiansen. Walter Neale claimed that they were married, which was untrue, but there was probably no one else closer to Bierce at the end. In September 1913 he assigned to her all his rights and royalties. Bierce requested that she destroy all his letters to her. She also kept a detailed log of his movements at this time. You might think that if anyone knew what Bierce planned to do it would be her, and yet after his disappearance she was as baffled as anyone as to what had happened.

Bierce planted thoughts in the minds of others in his final letters. Another close friend was an old widow, Mrs. Josephine McCrackin, or "Joe", whose ranch in California was a place of refuge for Bierce. He wrote to her on 10 September 1913 saying, in part:

> ...I am going away and have no notion when I shall return. I expect to go to, perhaps across, South America possibly via Mexico, if I can get through without being stood up against a wall and shot as a Gringo. But that is better than dying in bed, is it not?

He said something similar in a letter to his favourite niece, Lora, on 1 October 1913:

Good-bye. If you hear of my being stood up against a
Mexican stone wall and shot to rags please know that I
think that a pretty good way to depart this life. It beats
old age, disease, or falling down the cellar stairs. To be
a Gringo in Mexico ah, that is euthanasia!

A last letter to Lora dated 6 November 1913 ends like a final
farewell.

I shall not be here long enough to hear from you, and
don't know where I shall be next. Guess it doesn't
matter much.

Several other letters had the same sentiment. He was heading
to South America, via Mexico, and did not expect to return.

Prior to that last letter Bierce had revisited several Civil War
battlefields, remembering old friends and painful moments.
By mid-October he had reached the site of that most terrible
of battles, Shiloh, where he spent four days—twice as long as
intended—and apparently on one day he just sat on a rock and
stared at the battlefield. A sudden snowstorm brought an end
to his tour and he hastened south to New Orleans where he
was interviewed by a local journalist who reported that he was
heading for Mexico. He quoted him as saying, "I like the fighting. I want to see it." It seems an unlikely sentiment for Bierce,
because he loathed war. One of the reasons he had fallen out
with Hearst was because of Hearst's desire to encourage a war
between the United States and Spain over Cuba. The newspaper, though, did give one final image of Bierce that is always

remembered. Six feet tall, dressed entirely in black, with a shock of unkempt white hair and those piercing blue eyes that made him so handsome.

The Mexican Revolution had erupted at the end of 1910 as the decades long dictatorship of President Díaz came to an end. Díaz expected to be the sole candidate in the 1910 election but he was challenged by Francisco Madero who was imprisoned. That led to an uprising which the Federal Army could not control, and Díaz went into exile. Madero became President but faced an uprising led by Emiliano Zapata in the south. In February 1913 Díaz's former generals staged a coup in which Madero was killed by orders of Victoriano Huerta who became the new President. This led to further hostilities with the formation of a Constitutionalist army under Venustiano Carranza. Huerta's presidency ended in July 1914, defeated by the army of the North under Pancho Villa and there was now fighting between the individual rebel armies led by Villa, Carranza and Zapata. It was into this cauldron that Bierce was prepared to go.

His last letter to Lora, dated 6 November 1913, was sent from Laredo, Texas where he had come from San Antonio. He was right on the border with Mexico, just across the Rio Grande. Seven weeks later Bierce sent a letter to Carrie Christiansen dated 26 December, posted from Chihuahua. It's not impossible for Bierce to have travelled the 400 or so miles from Laredo to Chihuahua in seven weeks—or about eight miles a day—but he was an old man, journeying through a war-stricken country. What's more, there was no direct road or railway between the towns—it's almost entirely desert. And if Bierce intended to head to South America you would think he'd travel south from

Laredo, not due west. In order to travel by train he would have needed to return to San Antonio, get the train to El Paso, and then a further train to Chihuahua. He had plenty of money on him, so that would not be a problem—in fact it was a concern that he would attract too much attention and be robbed—but it does suggest that initially he had intended to cross into Mexico from Laredo, and something must have stopped him. Indeed, it was not easy to cross the border. The Mexican side, the town of Nuevo Laredo, was in the hands of the Huertistas, supporters of President Huerta. They were anti-American journalists. Perhaps realizing this, Bierce did take the train to El Paso.

That Bierce had been in El Paso seems to be supported by journalist George F. Weeks. He had met another journalist, William A. Willis, in 1918 who recalled meeting Bierce there, just before he crossed the border to Mexico. The crossing here was marginally safer than at Laredo, though only just. The revolutionary leader, Pancho Villa, had recently taken control of the town of Juárez, across the border from El Paso, and now effectively controlled the towns to the south, including Chihuahua.

If Willis's recollection is true then it's likely that Bierce did make it to Chihuahua, as implied by his letter to Christiansen. However, the American consul in Chihuahua had no record of Bierce visiting the town. During the civil unrest the consulate staff kept detailed records of Americans arriving in the state of Chihuahua. Bierce was well known to both government officials and newspaper reporters who thronged the town and it seems almost beyond belief that Bierce could have arrived there without at least someone noticing. Well, somebody did, but I'll come to that a little later.

There are those who believe that Bierce never made it into Mexico at all, and that through his letters he was deliberately obfuscating his route, creating a smokescreen to hide his true destination.

That is certainly what was believed by Bierce's friend and publisher Walter Neale. When Bierce had visited California the previous year, and met Jack London, he made it clear to friends that he would not be returning to the state. On his way back to Washington he apparently stopped at the Grand Canyon and took several photographs of isolated spots. He told Neale that he had found the ideal place where he could end his life in peace and his bones would never be found. It's a long journey from El Paso to anywhere along the Grand Canyon, but the route he took from California to Washington would overlap with such a journey somewhere north of Flagstaff, Arizona. Indeed the Atchison, Topeka and Santa Fe railway heads north from El Paso and connects with the track Bierce would have taken back to Washington the previous year. Having told everyone he was going to Mexico, no one would be looking for him heading into Arizona. If he had planned to commit suicide, this was certainly a way to do it and not be found.

Bierce had had a morbid fascination for suicide for much of his life. He had written a column about it in the *San Francisco News Letter* as far back as April 1870 when he considered the various methods and their effectiveness. In *The Argonaut* in 1877 he commented that San Francisco offered many advantages for the potential suicide as well as providing a motive. Suicide appears in several of his stories such as "A Tough Tussle" reprinted here. Bierce knew many who committed suicide, not least his son Day. The question, though, is whether by the end of his life, Bierce had the temperament or courage to kill himself. There was no denying his courage in the Civil War and his moral courage in his exhortations against corrupt officials. He was also a rather solitary guy who had found it difficult to sustain long-held relationships. Whilst one can imagine that in his old age, still troubled by asthma and the headaches from his war wound, and now having to walk with a cane, Bierce might not want to linger and become a burden to others, but he did have a genuine affection for his nephew Carlton and his nephew's wife Lora, as well as for his daughter Helen, and his friends Carrie Christiansen and Josephine McCrackin. Would he have wanted to leave them so dramatically, not knowing what had happened?

Suicide is an interesting theory, but not one easy to prove, whilst the weight of evidence, such that it is, does come down on the side of Bierce's final days in Mexico. But just where and when and how is another matter.

Bierce's one-time collaborator, Gustav Danziger, knew well of Bierce's interest in suicide but was certain it was something he would never do. Danziger maintained that Bierce would rather walk a thousand miles and die of exhaustion than be shot. Danziger was also of the view that Bierce did not intend to "disappear". He believed that Bierce was an idealist and wanted to share his knowledge of warfare with the authorities. While living in Washington D.C., Bierce belonged to the Army and Navy Club where he would have joined in much discussion about the revolution in Mexico. Bierce may indeed have developed an interest in witnessing first hand the battle tactics being employed, especially by Pancho Villa who had become something of a hero in the eyes of many Americans. Villa had taken control of a formidable army, known as the División del Norte. Despite his antipathy to war, could Bierce have been tempted to see how this army operated? Might he even have had a more covert project? When he wrote to Josephine McCrackin on 10 September 1913 he said, in part, "Yes, I shall go into Mexico with a pretty definite purpose which, however, is not at present disclosable." What purpose was this?

Was it, perhaps, to meet Villa and learn about the army. Danziger, who rather overstated his friendship with Bierce in *Portrait of Ambrose Bierce*, determined to find out and went into Mexico himself, though because of the War and the subsequent political sensitivities he found he could not do so until 1923. To pave the way, he wrote to Pancho Villa, who by then had retired to his hacienda near Chihuahua following an amnesty with the President. Villa's response was that he could not help, but Danziger decided to go anyway and turned up at Villa's home much to the General's surprise and annoyance. Danziger took the approach that he disliked Bierce intensely and this seemed to appeal to Villa. According to Danziger, Villa said that he had known Bierce but that "he had passed" and would no longer be a problem. He confirmed that Bierce had wanted to meet General Carranza, who had fallen out with Villa. Apparently Bierce drank too much tequila and spoke unwisely about Villa. At that point Villa's brother Hipólito, let out a stream of abuse about Bierce and Danziger realized he was looking at the men who had killed him either directly or via their soldiers.

Neither Pancho Villa nor his brother admitted to the fate of Bierce. It was Danziger's interpretation. Villa had always maintained that he had never met Bierce. Danziger left Villa's home soon after, firm in his belief of what had happened. His timing was, perhaps, fortunate, because only a couple of months later, in July 1923, Pancho Villa was assassinated.

In his last letter to Christiansen, Bierce had said that he planned to leave Chihuahua the next day (27 December) and head for Ojinaga where Huerta's forces had retreated. Bierce had, apparently, been accepted by the revolutionaries and it was agreed he would accompany the army—which may have been how he planned to rendezvous with Villa. Villa's forces took the town of Ojinaga on 11 January 1914 and Bierce might have witnessed the siege. Some contend that during the siege, Bierce was killed and his body burned with all the other dead—burned rather than buried because of the fear of typhus. However, there is not a single report that Bierce was there. Had he been killed it is likely that the reporters who were covering the battle for the American press would have known, as would the American military authorities who were monitoring events. Ojinaga was just across the border from the United States.

It is unlikely that Bierce met Villa at Ojinaga, and indeed unlikely that Bierce was ever there. There is a first-hand account of Bierce's movements at this time, admittedly not recorded for another nineteen years, but it is the *only* first-hand account. It is by Edward ("Tex") O'Reilly, an American soldier-for-hire who was allied to Villa's forces. He was known for exaggerating his own abilities—he would later create the Pecos Bill series of tall tales which began in *Century Magazine* in 1917—so he was good at spinning a yarn. But his account of a near-miss encounter with Bierce does not sound exaggerated and has the ring of truth.

O'Reilly had congratulated Villa on his success at Juárez and had, so O'Reilly says, been granted the commission of Major. He accompanied Villa at the siege of Ojinaga and afterwards returned to Chihuahua. Over the next few weeks he was organizing supplies and made the occasional trip to El Paso. On one trip he revealed that while in El Paso he received a note from Bierce who had heard O'Reilly was with Villa and wanted to discuss events. O'Reilly tried to arrange a meeting but they missed each other by an hour or two and O'Reilly then returned to Chihuahua. While there he received another note from Bierce, who seemingly had followed O'Reilly, but once again they failed to meet.

O'Reilly does not date these events and his memory may have tricked him, but he suggests that Bierce was in El Paso *after* the battle of Ojinaga, which would be later in January 1914. Perhaps Bierce had returned to El Paso after the battle, or maybe after he left Chihuahua at the end of December 1913. In any event, O'Reilly definitely placed Bierce in Chihuahua in January 1914, most likely at the end of the month. O'Reilly then makes an important statement about Bierce and Villa.

> It is a pity he did not talk with anyone in Chihuahua City. Villa was there at the time and I would have been glad to introduce Bierce to him. It is always printed that Villa killed him, but Villa never even heard of him till after he was dead. Bierce did not go near any of Villa's officers or talk to any of the Americans there. Evidently

he wandered around quite alone. He could not speak
Spanish.

Soon after the abortive meeting, O'Reilly went south with
Villa's army, pursuing the Federal forces as far as Escalon. At
that point they learned there was a number of Federalists just
north of Escalon at the one-time mining town of Sierra Mojada.
General Ortega sent a force to the town and the Federalists left.
While there O'Reilly heard that an American had been killed.
O'Reilly managed to find a Mexican who had witnessed the
event and though his English was poor, O'Reilly learned the
story. Here's what he remembered in full.

> They said he was an old man who had come riding in
> there on horseback, alone. He spoke only a little broken
> Spanish and did not explain who he was or what he
> wanted, and they were suspicious of him. He stayed
> there several days, in the midst of the Federals, but
> apparently he did not know they were Federals. It is wild,
> mountainous country all around there, deserted mining
> country with very few ranches. He asked questions about
> the trails and made notes and maps, and they thought he
> was a spy. When the Federals heard that he was asking
> how to reach Villa's army they decided to kill him.
>
> One afternoon he was drinking in a cantina with
> three Federal volunteers, and they decided to kill
> him then. They borrowed his pistol, and when he left
> they walked out with him to the edge of town. I talked
> with two eye-witnesses who had seen the whole thing.

Apparently he suspected nothing until the three men turned on him and began shooting.

The first shot must have struck him in the leg or belly, because he dropped down, squatting on his heels. And the two Mexicans were impressed by the strange way in which he died. He squatted there in the dust of the road and began to laugh heartily. The three men kept shooting him, hitting him, but they could not kill him, and he did not stop laughing. He sat there and laughed till finally they shot him in the heart. The Mexicans were amazed because he was laughing as though it were a tremendous joke that he was being killed.

They took me to the house where he had stayed with an old Mexican. I asked if he had left any personal possessions, anything that would identify him, and the old Mexican said, "No, the three Federals came and took his things. He had only saddlebags and a blanket roll."

"You have nothing that belonged to him? No article of clothing? Not a scrap of paper?"

The old fellow reached up behind a rafter on the wall and brought out two old empty envelopes left by the Americano, and they were both addressed to Ambrose Bierce.

That was my first knowledge that the old man was Bierce. How he had wandered down there ahead of us I don't know. We never found anyone he had met after he left El Paso. He said in Sierra Mojada that he was looking for Villa's army, when as a matter of fact he had left us behind him in Chihuahua City. But he was drinking heavily all the time, and he did not speak Spanish. Some Mexican may have told him where we were going, and he may have understood that we had already gone. Nobody knows why he acted as he did.

The Mexicans in Sierra Mojada described Bierce exactly. He was then an old man, past seventy, but he looked younger than that and was vigorous and very strong for his age. They said he was a dictatorial old fellow who wanted to be left alone and who insulted everybody who bothered him. He had been buried a week or ten days before I arrived.

They showed me where he had been buried beside the adobe wall of the little cemetery. The envelopes and their descriptions convinced me he was Ambrose Bierce, and I burned his name into a board with a hot iron and set up this wooden headboard at the grave.

(Edward S. O'Reilly, *Born to Raise Hell*, Garden City: Doubleday, Doran, 1936)

Does that ring true to you? Despite O'Reilly's delight in tall tales, this sounds convincing. And why do you think Bierce laughed as he died? I wonder if it's because his death was exactly as he had predicted in his letters to Lora and Joe. And, if we believe his account, Bierce's death can be dated to within a week or two. O'Reilly's tale continues with him accompanying Villa's army to Torreón where another battle occurred with the Federalists. This began on 21 March 1914. It would have taken Villa's men less than a week to reach Torreón and O'Reilly was told that Bierce had been killed a week to ten days before

O'Reilly reached Sierra Mojada, so at most Bierce's death happened two to three weeks before 21 March.

But what proof is there? If the grave could be found it would answer everything.

Back in 1989 or so a retired local priest, Father James Lienert, who had been interested in Bierce's disappearance since 1967, encountered an old man, Don Chuy, who remembered, when he was a boy witnessing the death by firing squad of an old "gringo", believed to be a spy, who was shot and buried in the local cemetery. The man showed Father Lienert the spot and five years later Lienert erected a headstone there. In 2010 the investigative reporter Geoffrey Gray took a team of engineers to the spot and used ground penetrating radar to see whether there were any remains under the headstone. It detected some bones—not too surprising in a graveyard—but nothing that would suggest bullets or any metal that might have been in Bierce's clothes or pockets. Proof still awaits.

Strangely, there is a different account of Bierce being shot by a firing squad though not in Sierra Mojada but at Icamole, over 200 miles away to the south-east, near Monterey. Significantly, Icamole is due south of Laredo, so if Bierce had been heading through Mexico to South America from Laredo, he would pass near Icamole. However, the account sounds somewhat unlikely. For a start the incident is supposed to have happened in the summer of 1915 which means that somehow Bierce had survived in Mexico for eighteen months without anyone reporting his presence. The story was revealed by the Texas journalist, George F. Weeks, though not until 1919. He had heard from his associate editor, Edmond Melero, that Bierce had been captured along with a peasant when both were transporting a machine gun and ammunition by mule-train intended for the government forces of Carranza. Both were questioned and as Bierce could not speak Spanish he could offer no defence. The two were promptly shot by the forces of General Tomás Urbina. Urbina was himself executed soon after by his fellow general, Rodolfo Fierro, both serving Pancho Villa.

A reporter from the San Francisco *Bulletin*, James H. Wilkins, was sent to Mexico City to verify the story. He reported back to the *Bulletin* for 24 March 1920 which bore the headline NOTED S. F. AUTHOR'S FATE DISCLOSED BY VILLA CAPTIVE, with the sub-heading "Mysterious Death of Ambrose Bierce Cleared." The report, which was rapidly reprinted by almost all US newspapers, did no such thing. It seems that Wilkins had encountered a soldier who had served with Urbina and had witnessed the execution. This soldier had found a photograph of Bierce on the victim's body but Wilkins neither identified the soldier nor produced the picture. Weeks did subsequently publish the photograph in his own account of Bierce's death and although the photo claims to be of Bierce, it bears only a passing resemblance.* Gustav Danziger was convinced it was a photograph of General Viljoen who had fought with the Mexican Revolutionary army at the Battle of Juárez.

Both these accounts suggest that Bierce was shot by soldiers, either as a spy or a collaborator, and it could indeed have happened that way though, of course, they could not both be true. And if one "gringo" could be mistaken for Bierce, why not two?

---

* See the Washington *Evening Star*, 27 December 1925.

It's also beyond belief that Bierce would have spent eighteen months in Mexico with no one else having seen him and with Bierce not having written to friends or family.

It does though give some support to the recollection of the Californian writer Gertrude Atherton. Although she had no great liking for Bierce after he had tried to seduce her many years before, they had maintained a friendly correspondence for years and she regarded him as America's greatest writer. She believed that Bierce had ventured into Mexico as an agent for President Woodrow Wilson to deliver a message to President Huerta but was intercepted and shot as a spy.

There were still many other theories.

In July 1918 Gertrude Atherton overheard various rumours that Bierce had been undertaking work for the British General Staff, or that he had become special military advisor to the Mikado of Japan, or that he had been killed at Gallipoli in 1916. Others claimed he had emigrated to Paris to share his knowledge of warfare with the French government. Perhaps the most preposterous was that he wanted to explore the ruins of the old Mayan civilization in the hope of finding one of the legendary crystal skulls.

One thing is for sure. If Bierce had vanished in order to ensure his literary immortality, it worked, because here we are still talking about him, as many have over the years and will continue to do so.

My belief is that Tex O'Reilly came closest and that Bierce probably was shot at Sierra Mojada, as that does have two eye-witness reports, albeit one told second hand by a writer of tall tales and the other remembered by an old man recollecting events seventy years before. We can't rule out that he committed suicide, though despite his age there is nothing to suggest he had reached that level of desperation, despite his fascination with the act of self-destruction. It's most unlikely that he was killed at Ojinaga because no one saw him, and Bierce was not someone who would be overlooked. It leaves the enticing matter of the nature of the "definite purpose" for which he was entering Mexico and which he mentioned to Josephine McCrackin. Perhaps he really was serving as a spy.

Bierce's fate was kept alive by another form of literary immortality, because his disappearance provoked a number of stories and novels. This was prompted by the collector of weird phenomena, Charles Fort. He became aware of the disappearance of theatre magnate Ambrose Small in 1919 and in his book *Wild Talents* (1933) Fort linked this to the disappearance of Bierce and asked the question "Was someone collecting Ambroses?"

It was a delightful idea, just the type that would intrigue fantasists. In 1971 Los Angeles science-fiction fan, Arthur Jean Cox, wrote "A Collector of Ambroses" in which book hunters stumble upon an ancient mage who was acquiring all those called Ambrose. Bierce's disappearance had already found its way into other stories. Robert A. Heinlein, for instance, included Bierce as a character in his 1941 novella "Lost Legacy" where Bierce had developed psychic powers, like the Force in *Star Wars*, and used them to help heal the world. Bierce now lives in Mount Shasta with other writers and artists, and helps three university friends who have been studying these psychic forces. In "The Oxoxoco Bottle" (1957) by Gerald Kersh, the narrator discovers a strange bottle inside of which is the last written record by Bierce himself which describes how he found his way to a remote Mexican hideaway and became the latest victim of a cannibal—that would certainly explain why his body was never found!

Other novels include *The Old Gringo* (1985) by Carlos Fuentos which attempts to describe the historical fate of Bierce. It was filmed as *Old Gringo* in 1989 with Gregory Peck as Bierce. More recently Forrest Gander's *The Trace* (2014) has a couple trying to rebuild their lives after a personal disaster and who travel through Mexico tracing what they believe to be Bierce's final journey. Bierce has even become a detective in a series of five novels by Oakley Hall, starting with *Ambrose Bierce and the Queen of Spades* (1998).

There is little doubt that not only because of the brilliance of his best work but the mystery of his disappearance, people will continue to talk about and read Bierce for many, many years. We have all become collectors of Ambrose's!

MIKE ASHLEY

REFERENCE SOURCES

If you'd like to know more about Ambrose Bierce and what happened to him I would recommend the following items. In particular, the Ambrose Bierce website run by Don Swaim at http://donswaim.com/index.html which includes the survey of Bierce's disappearance undertaken by Leon Day, "My Hunt for Ambrose Bierce". Many of the following books can also be found online either at Project Gutenberg or the Internet Archive.

Danziger, Gustav Adolphe, *Portrait of Ambrose Bierce*, New York: Century, 1929.

Gale, Robert L., *An Ambrose Bierce Companion*, Westport, CT: Greenwood Press, 2001.

Gray, Geoffrey, "Finding the Bones of Ambrose Bierce (or not)", Alta Online, 21 July 2021.

——"——, "An Occurrence at Sierra Mojada", *Alta Journal*, Summer 2021.

McWilliams, Carey, *Ambrose Bierce: A Biography*, New York: A. & C. Boni, 1929.

——"——, "The Mystery of Ambrose Bierce", *American Mercury*, March 1931.

Mahoney, Tom, "The End of Ambrose Bierce", *Esquire*, February 1936.

Mencken, H. L., "The Ambrose Bierce Mystery", *American Mercury*, September 1929.

Morris, Jr., Roy, *Ambrose Bierce: Alone in Bad Company*, New York: Oxford University Press, 1998.

Neale, Walter, *Life of Ambrose Bierce*, New York: Neale, 1929.

O'Connor, Richard, *Ambrose Bierce: A Biography*, Boston: Little, Brown, 1967.

Pope, Bertha Clark (ed), *The Letters of Ambrose Bierce*, San Francisco: Book Club of California, 1922, which includes "A Memoir of Ambrose Bierce" by George Sterling.

Thomas, Lowell & O'Reilly, Edward S., *Born to Raise Hell*, Garden City: Doubleday, Doran, 1936.

STORY SOURCES

All of the stories collected here are in the public domain. The following lists the original publication date in the order in which they first appeared and which of Bierce's volumes in which it was first collected.

"Mrs. Dennison's Head" first published in *Fun*, 12 July 1873 and collected in *Cobwebs From an Empty Skull* (as by 'Dod Grile'), London: Routledge, 1874.

"An Inhabitant of Carcosa" first published in *San Francisco News Letter*, 25 December 1886 and collected in *Tales of Soldiers and Civilians*, San Francisco: Steele, 1891 [1892].

"One of the Missing" first published in *The San Francisco Examiner*, 11 March 1888 and collected in *Tales of Soldiers and Civilians*, San Francisco: Steele, 1891 [1892].

"Bodies of the Dead" first published in *The San Francisco Examiner*, 22 April 1888 and collected in *Can Such Things Be?*, New York: Cassell, 1893.

"The Isle of Pines" first published in *The San Francisco Examiner*, 26 August 1888 and collected in *Can Such Things Be?*, New York: Cassell, 1893.

"A Cold Greeting" first published in *The San Francisco Examiner*, 26 August 1888 and collected in *Can Such Things Be?*, volume III of *The Collected Works*, New York: Neale, 1910.

"A Tough Tussle" first published in *The San Francisco Examiner*, 30 September 1888 and collected in *Tales of Soldiers and Civilians*, San Francisco: Steele, 1891 [1892].

"Charles Ashmore's Trail", "The Difficulty of Crossing a Field" and "An Unfinished Race" first published in *The San Francisco Examiner*, 14 October 1888 and collected in *Can Such Things Be?*, New York: Cassell, 1893.

"A Horseman in the Sky" first published in *The San Francisco Examiner*, 14 April 1889 and collected in *Tales of Soldiers and Civilians*, San Francisco: Steele, 1891 [1892].

"Present at a Hanging" first published in *Current Literature*, June 1889 and collected in *Can Such Things Be?*, volume III of *The Collected Works*, New York: Neale, 1910.

"A Fruitless Assignment" first published in *Current Literature*, July 1889 [as "An Assignment"] and collected in *Can Such Things Be?*, New York: Cassell, 1893.

"The Spook House" first published in *The San Francisco Examiner*, 7 July 1889 and collected in *Can Such Things Be?*, volume III of *The Collected Works*, New York: Neale, 1910.

"A Watcher by the Dead" first published in *The San Francisco Examiner*, 29 December 1889 and collected in *Tales of Soldiers and Civilians*, San Francisco: Steele, 1891 [1892].

"An Occurrence at Owl Creek Bridge" first published in *The San Francisco Examiner*, 13 July 1890 and collected in *Tales of Soldiers and Civilians*, San Francisco: Steele, 1891 [1892].

"The Middle Toe of the Right Foot" first published in *The San Francisco Examiner*, 7 August 1890 and collected in *Tales of Soldiers and Civilians*, San Francisco: Steele, 1891 [1892].

"The Boarded Window" first published in *The San Francisco Examiner*, 12 April 1891 and collected in *Tales of Soldiers and Civilians*, San Francisco: Steele, 1891 [1892].

"The Secret of Macarger's Gulch" first published in *The San Francisco Examiner*, 25 April 1891 and collected in *Can Such Things Be?*, New York: Cassell, 1893.

"The Thing at Nolan" first published in *The San Francisco Examiner*, 2 August 1891 and collected in *Can Such Things Be?*, New York: Cassell, 1893.

"The Death of Halpin Frayser" first published in *Wasp*, 19 December 1891 and collected in *Can Such Things Be?*, New York: Cassell, 1893.

"John Bartine's Watch" first published in *The San Francisco Examiner*, 22 January 1893 and collected in *Can Such Things Be?*, New York: Cassell, 1893.

"A Jug of Sirup" first published in *San Francisco Examiner*, 17 December 1893 and collected in *Can Such Things Be?*, New York: Cassell, 1893.

"The Damned Thing" first published in *Town Topics*, 7 December 1893 and collected in *In the Midst of Life*, New York: Putnam's, 1898.

"The Eyes of the Panther" first published in *The San Francisco Examiner*, 17 October 1897 and collected in *In the Midst of Life*, New York: Putnam's, 1898.

"At Old Man Eckert's" first published in *The San Francisco Examiner*, 17 November 1901 and collected in *Can Such Things Be?*, volume III of *The Collected Works*, New York: Neale, 1910.

"A Vine on a House", "A Wireless Message" and "An Arrest" all first published in *Cosmopolitan*, October 1905 [as part of

"Some Uncanny Tales"] and collected in *Can Such Things Be?*, volume III of *The Collected Works*, New York: Neale, 1910.

"Staley Fleming's Hallucination" first published in *Cosmopolitan*, March 1906 and collected in *Can Such Things Be?*, volume III of *The Collected Works*, New York: Neale, 1910.

"The Moonlit Road" first published in *Cosmopolitan*, January 1907 and collected in *Can Such Things Be?*, volume III of *The Collected Works*, New York: Neale, 1910.

"The Other Lodgers" first published in *Cosmopolitan*, August 1907 and collected in *Can Such Things Be?*, volume III of *The Collected Works*, New York: Neale, 1910.

"Beyond the Wall" first published in *Cosmopolitan*, December 1907 and collected in *Can Such Things Be?*, volume III of *The Collected Works*, New York: Neale, 1910.

"A Resumed Identity" first published in *Cosmopolitan*, September 1908 and collected in *Can Such Things Be?*, volume III of *The Collected Works*, New York: Neale, 1910.

For more Tales of the Weird titles
visit the British Library Shop (shop.bl.uk)

We welcome any suggestions, corrections or feedback you may have, and will
aim to respond to all items addressed to the following:

The Editor (Tales of the Weird), British Library Publishing,
The British Library, 96 Euston Road, London NW1 2DB

We also welcome enquiries through our Twitter account, @BL_Publishing.